Feeding the Wolf

Jennifer Leigh

BEACON
PUBLISHING GROUP

For information, or to order additional copies, please contact:

Beacon Publishing Group
P.O. Box 41573 Charleston, S.C. 29423
800.817.8480| beaconpublishinggroup.com

Publisher's catalog available by request.

ISBN-13: 978-1-949472-67-7

ISBN-10: 1-949472-67-1

Published in 2019. New York, NY 10001.

First Edition. Printed in the USA.

Invictus

Out of the night that covers me,
    Black as the Pit from pole to pole,
I thank whatever gods may be
    For my unconquerable soul.

In the fell clutch of circumstance
    I have not winced nor cried aloud.
Under the bludgeonings of chance
    My head is bloody, but unbowed.

Beyond this place of wrath and tears
    Looms but the Horror of the shade,
And yet the menace of the years
    Finds, and shall find, me unafraid.

It matters not how strait the gate,
    How charged with punishments the scroll,
I am the master of my fate:
    I am the captain of my soul.

—William Ernest Henley, *Book of Verses*

~ Chapter One ~

Bodies everywhere. We'd long since removed our dead, which numbered less than fifty. Thank the gods. But the others, all disillusioned men who had fallen for their doomed cause still littered the ground. A chill wind blew across the land, carrying away most of the remaining smoke. And stench.

From the crest of a hill overlooking the battlefield's charred remains, I tried yet failed to celebrate our hollow victory. The enemy had fought with minimal effort, as if they'd known the outcome and had accepted the inevitable. We'd won, but only by default or disqualification. If I hadn't seen it with my own eyes, I never would have believed it.

A cadet still in his teen years hiked up the hill to stand beside me. The ragged gash at his temple dripped blood. His vacant stare turned my stomach. "What is it, soldier?"

"Captain Ellsbree, sir. The men are ready to move out on your command." He waited with respect, swaying with exhaustion. Like the rest of us.

I tore my gaze from the scene below, and he fell in step behind me as we trudged down the muddy hill. The men stood in formation alongside the loaded wagons, waiting for me to lead them. I peered at the line of haggard faces, the blood-soaked uniforms. Wounded, yet willing to walk. To march home.

A lieutenant brought my horse forward, and I took the reins with a curt nod. I mounted, every muscle straining in protest, and nudged the horse into a fast walk. I reached the front of the line and stopped. All eyes rested on me, and I met them in turn. "Move out."

Night fell, and still the company trekked onward. Loath to push them beyond endurance, I debated setting up camp near the woods. Though likely more than eager for a hot meal and a warm bed, the men would collapse if they continued much longer without rest. I gave the order and a collective sigh traveled through the ranks. Murmured conversations floated in the frosty air while the men erected tents up and down the tree line.

"Paxton," I barked.

He jogged over from the wagon he'd been unloading. "Sir."

"Make sure the men have everything they need for a solid night's rest. They've earned it."

"Yes, sir." He saluted then rushed back to the wagon. He'd survived, along with most of the company, yet several of our wagons carried the less fortunate. As captain, I'd have to notify their kin. Their tragic deaths weighed heavily on my conscience and guilt gnawed at my insides. I'd sworn to protect them, to see them home. Safe. A promise I'd broken again and again.

A commanding officer should not suffer an emotional crisis in front of his men, so I headed into the forest, seeking solace among the trees. The full moon barely lit my path, and I stumbled along. Rocks tripped me, and branches grabbed at my cloak, but I pushed deeper until I reached a clearing. A million stars shone overhead, glittering on the surface of a small pond. I sat on a boulder at the water's edge and finally cried. Tears of anger, frustration, despair streaked down my face as I railed against fate, cursing the gods for the senseless loss of so many lives. Such needless waste. I wiped my eyes, calmed my shuddering breaths. Alone but for the smiling moon, the peaceful quiet settled around me.

❊

The sky lightened as the sun rose to begin another day. I hadn't slept much and exited my tent with a heavy sigh. Soldiers scurried about their work, packing and gathering supplies, all without a word from me. Well-trained and loyal, to the last.

Paxton approached with a hesitant smile. "Good morning, Captain."

"Paxton."

"Can I help with your tent, sir?"

"Not necessary, but thank you."

"Are you sure, sir? It's no trouble–"

I clapped him on the shoulder and smiled. "I'm sure."

"Sir." He ambled off toward the fire where breakfast cooked, its pleasant aroma wafting through the air. I followed slowly, nodding to the men, then sat down to eat. I glanced at their grim faces, and my heart twisted. Some of these boys would never recover, their spirits broken, their souls irrevocably damaged by the brutality of war. The melancholy mood kept the conversations short, and we finished the meal in somber quiet. I gave the order. The men launched into action, and we set out within the hour.

We couldn't haul the wagons through the woods, which meant taking the long way around. And with stopping often to change bandages and check the wounded, it would take another hard day's march before we reached the city gates. Soldiers through and through, the company traveled without complaint, even though many of them limped. I marveled at the sheer stubbornness of will, the utter refusal to give in to the grief.

At last, we sighted the stone walls of Evanston looming on the horizon. Our energy renewed, we picked up the pace, arriving as dusk fell. In pairs and groups of three or four, the company dispersed into the shadows of the barracks. My chest ached with pride, a frequent experience during the months I'd spent as their commanding officer. They'd fought well, unmatched in bravery and honor. Now, the decisive battle won, we could rest. The war had finally come to an end.

Hooves clomped on stone as the wagons lumbered through the gates, carrying our fallen comrades. With a heavy sigh and an even heavier heart, I welcomed them home.

~ Chapter Two ~

I bolted upright, chest heaving. Hand over my heart, I panted in the semi-darkness, eyes darting around the room as I oriented myself. *Home. Safe.*

In my room, my bed. No longer in a tent or on the battlefield. I took a deep breath to calm my racing pulse and raked a hand through my hair. A bad dream? A strange noise? Whatever had woken me, I wouldn't be able to sleep now. I swung my legs over the side of the bed, debating whether to get up. What would I even do? Exhaustion still plagued me, pulling me under like a boulder chained to my ankle. I could feel the bags under my eyes, yet I forced my feet to the floor.

I crossed to the window and pulled back the curtain. Moonlight shone on the peaceful garden, the water in the fountain sparkling with milky light. Sentries meandered back and forth below despite our recent, well-earned peace. Captain or no, I still stood to inherit the throne and security shadowed me even behind castle walls. Precautions, protection against all threats to the royal family.

I padded to the sitting room and glanced at the books strewn across my desk. None of them the least bit interesting, not anymore. Not even the billiards table appealed to me. I'd suffered a loss too great to ignore and needed time. A chance to deal with what I'd seen and done. The soldiers I'd killed.

Images of blood and gore and death rose in my mind. I gripped an imaginary weapon, shoulder still aching from swinging my sword over and over, hacking into flesh and bone. A shudder ran down my spine and I clenched my jaw hard enough to crack a tooth. I would not, could not allow recent events to cripple me. My men needed their captain to weather the storm and emerge still intact. Lead by example, my father always said. The only surefire way to earn a soldier's respect and trust, yet my heart ached, raw as any wound.

Overwhelmed by the intense pain, I collapsed onto the nearest chair. Stillness covered me like a shroud, my mind comfortably numb for the first time in weeks, if not months. I saw nothing, felt nothing, until at dawn, a soft knock broke the trance. "Come in."

Maxwell breezed in. "Good morning, your highness." He placed a silver tray laden with enough food to satisfy a giant on the table. But the mere idea of eating soured my stomach.

"Morning."

"How are you feeling? Did you sleep well?" He studied my haggard features and arched a gray brow. "Or at all?" I shook my head, and he sighed. "Taryn, you need to rest. It will help."

"I know, but I can't shut off my mind. Everything is too … raw."

Maxwell clucked with sympathy as he pulled back the curtains. He turned toward me, a warm smile on his weathered face. "I can't imagine what you've been through these past months. Perhaps if you talked to someone …"

"I … don't think I can."

"You should, Taryn."

"Fine." I crossed my arms and tried to not look like a chastised child. "Send someone after lunch."

"What about after breakfast?"

My frown turned into a scowl. "No."

"After lunch then," he said softly. "Now eat before you waste away." His leveled stare suggested I not argue, yet my food remained untouched in favor of a bath. Afterwards I lay on my bed, staring at the canopy. A minute or an hour passed, and another light knock sounded from the sitting room. "Come in." From my prone position, I couldn't drag myself up or even glance at the door.

"Prince Taryn?" a hesitant female voice called. "Are you here?"

I sat up so quickly my head spun. I should've eaten. "Yes, I'm here." I climbed out of bed and headed to the sitting room where a young woman, the rarest of beauties waited. Stunned, I almost tripped over my feet.

"Your highness." She dropped into a low curtsy. "Maxwell asked me to come see you."

I swallowed hard and willed my legs to propel me forward. "Yes. Thank you."

She angled her head, golden curls cascading over her shoulders. "How can I help?"

"What …" I cleared my throat. "What is your name?"

"Grace, your highness. Grace Dupont."

I'd never heard the name, nor seen her face. I would have certainly remembered those emerald-green eyes. Striking, even from a distance. I managed to stop staring and gestured to the couch. "Would you like to sit down?"

She nodded and brushed past me, smelling of spring. I fought the urge to breathe her in as she perched on the edge of a cushion. I fidgeted, suddenly nervous and shy. Yet I'd been with plenty of beautiful girls. *Women.*

But Grace's beauty surpassed them all. Ethereal, like a goddess come to life. She studied me boldly, and I somehow didn't squirm under her assessing gaze. "Would you like something to drink?"

"No thank you, your highness."

"Please. It's Taryn."

She inclined her head and smiled with mischievous humor. Intrigued, I sat on the opposite end of the couch, feigning a casualness I certainly didn't feel with her so close. "What now? I'm … new to this sort of thing."

She lifted a slim shoulder. "It's entirely up to you, your high … Taryn. We can talk about anything you'd like. The weather, if it pleases you."

"Then I'd like to talk about you." She opened her mouth, likely to protest but then pressed her lips together in a thin line. Had I upset her? "I apologize if I overstepped."

"No, of course not. I rarely talk about myself. I'm usually listening to others."

"Do you mind it? The listening?"

She shook her head. "Not if it helps someone work through their issues, recover from a traumatic experience."

"Heal them, you mean."

"In a way, I suppose."

I arched a brow. What did Maxwell expect this young woman to do for me, other than distract me from my current misery? Indeed, all thoughts of recent events had flown from my head the minute I laid eyes on her. And though she may have been an excellent listener, I did not want her pity. "Where are you from?"

"A small town west of here. You've likely never heard of it."

"I doubt that. I've memorized every square mile of Nogardia."

"Of course you have. Forgive me. I'm from Montclair."

I bit my cheek to hide a smirk. "I know of it. What brought you to Evanston?"

She shifted in her seat. "It's … a long story."

"I have time."

"I'm sure, but I'd like to hear about you."

My story made less than interesting conversation, and she likely knew everything already. Royal life did not lend itself to privacy or seclusion, no matter how hard I tried. Gossip flowed from the castle in a river of rumors and speculation, rife with false impressions and conjecture. I'd learned from an early age to simply ignore the whispers and endure the stares. "There's not much to tell, I'm afraid." She pierced me with a stare of her own. Offensive from anyone else. But not her. "I'm a prince," I said with a shrug.

"I'm well aware," she said in a tone reserved for exasperated mothers. "What else?"

"Soldier."

"Go on."

"Brother, son, heir to the throne." The conversation took an uncomfortable turn. Admitting my feelings, bearing my soul, did not come naturally. Hoping to develop such a skill would only lead to disappointment. For both of us.

"Taryn," she chided. "You have to talk to me if you want to move past whatever is upsetting you."

A dark chuckle rumbled out of me, and she blanched as if suddenly realizing what she'd said and to whom. "Who said I wanted to move past it?"

She swallowed, her slender throat bobbing. "Your highness, I meant no disrespect. Please forgive me, I didn't … I shouldn't have …"

Her adorable stammering cooled any heat behind my words. "It's fine. I'm actually pleased you feel comfortable enough to speak your mind. Quite refreshing I assure you, especially from someone so beautiful."

Color stained her cheeks, sharpening her features. "Well, then I suppose we should continue."

"I agree. But not here."

"Excuse me?"

"Dinner. Tonight."

"I couldn't possibly accept such an invitation."

"Are you defying your prince?" I grinned broadly, enjoying the slight widening of her eyes and the sharp intake of breath.

"No, of course not. I–"

"Relax, Grace. If you're otherwise engaged, I'll completely understand."

"It's only …"

"What? Am I not handsome enough? Charming enough?" I hated resorting to such manipulation, but the way she spoke to me, as if I didn't have a royal title, made me want to spend every minute listening to her voice. I couldn't imagine occupying my considerable amount of free time with anyone else.

She bit her lip. "Are you sure you want to dine with me?"

I nodded. *Say yes. Please.*

She dipped her chin. "I'd be honored."

The tightness in my chest eased and I almost slumped in relief. "I'll send a coach for you … Where, exactly?"

"There's no need. What time should I return?"

"Eight. Ask for Maxwell. He'll escort you to the dining hall."

"The dining hall?"

I arched a brow. "It is where I dine."

"But, the king … the queen …"

"They will be there, of course, along with my sister. Will it be a problem for you?" She shook her head and I stood. "Dinner it is." I held out my hand, which she took after an awkward beat of silence. I pressed my lips to her knuckles. "Until tonight," I said with a bow.

She pulled away and bobbed another curtsy. "Your highness." Her skirts swirled around her ankles as she hurried from the room without a backwards glance. An idiotic grin stretched across my face. Dinner with a beautiful young woman would cure anyone's heartache, even my own.

~ Chapter Three ~

Grace hurried from the castle as fast as her feet would carry her, hurtling through the gates and into the street. In her haste, she tripped on a loose cobblestone but managed to stay upright then practically ran the rest of the way home. She burst inside, and her father jolted in his seat as the door crashed open. She slammed it closed, leaning on it in blessed relief.

"What in the name of–"

"I'm sorry, Father," she gasped, chest heaving.

"Are you all right?" His narrowed gaze raked over her.

"Yes, I'm fine." She waved away his paternal concern.

"If you say so. Did you have a good day?"

She headed to the kitchen, glancing over her shoulder. "I suppose."

He arched a brow. "You suppose? Come now, Grace. Surely your day at the castle involved more excitement. Tell me."

She leaned on the sink, staring at the dirty dishes piled high. "It …" Well, she didn't exactly know how to describe her day. Interesting? Terrifying? And so much more. Prince

Taryn. *Holy gods*. He'd invited her to dinner. Tonight. She whirled around, flashing a dimpled grin. "I had the most amazing day!" She rushed to sit beside him and took his hand. "I met the prince."

His eyes widened. "What? How?"

She grinned. "I know. It's quite incredible. He apparently needed someone to talk to, about what he's been through with the war."

"But why you? Your healing skills don't cater to emotional injuries."

"Cara had to attend a difficult birth so I answered the summons. In the right place at the right time, I suppose."

"And did you help him?"

"I tried, but he refused to talk about himself, insisted we talk about me instead. He's a strange man, Father. Not at all what I expected."

"But?"

"But what?"

"Grace, you haven't stopped smiling since you started talking about him."

"I haven't?"

He laughed softly, shaking his head. "Oh, my dear daughter. He's the prince."

"Meaning?" She stood, hands on her hips, a stance she'd learned from her mother. He tried to stand, muscles straining as he pushed against the arms of his chair. She stopped him before he could hurt himself. "Don't, Father."

He sank onto the chair, the breath whooshing out of him. "I just mean he's the prince. You cannot under any circumstances expect anything from him."

She sighed and resumed her seat. "I know."

He gripped her chin and lifted her gaze to his. "There is someone out there for you, Grace. Have patience. And faith."

She smiled weakly. Suitors had been few and far between. Most young men she met wanted only to get under her skirts.

No lifelong commitments, no declarations of undying love. She hadn't given them what they asked of her though, choosing to save herself. Much good it did her. "What would you like for dinner?"

He returned her smile, his brown eyes warm. "Whatever you make will be fine."

She set about preparing the evening meal, a task she'd done a thousand times and would likely do a thousand more. She did it gladly, taking pride in her work both at home and as a healer. Her mother had taught her well, alternating lessons between the healing arts and how to efficiently run a household. She'd taught her everything she knew before she'd left this world, and Grace would be forever grateful.

Meal prepared, she set a plate on the table next to her father's chair. He laid aside the book he'd been reading and smiled up at her. She sank onto the couch with her own plate, picking at her food.

"Grace? What is it?"

"I … The prince invited me to dinner tonight at the castle with the king and queen and princess." She exhaled a shaky breath.

He set down his fork with an incredulous look. "Then what are you doing here? With me?"

"I want to go, but I'm worried I'm not …"

"Don't you dare say it, Grace. You are more than good enough for any man, even a prince. And he invited you. He must like you." His eyes twinkled merrily, and she couldn't help but smile at his fatherly reassurance.

"Thank you, Father. But still. I don't know what to wear. Or what to say. Or even which fork to use. I'll likely end up embarrassing myself horribly and never be invited back."

"I highly doubt it. You're a beautiful young woman. And you can buy a new dress."

She snorted. "With what money?"

"Don't you worry. Just find something you love, and I'll take care of it."

Tears clouded her vision, and she wrapped her arms around his neck. They truly couldn't afford such an extravagance, but the fact he'd offered meant the world to her. She leaned back, and he brushed a stray tear from her cheek.

"You look so much like your mother."

She smiled at the familiar compliment, missing her mother now more than ever. She'd surely know what advice to give. Without her guidance, Grace worried the night would end in disaster. But she could hardly pass up an opportunity to dine with the prince. At the castle. Even if she made a fool of herself.

~ Chapter Four ~

I had an hour left before Grace returned for dinner, time I planned to use rehearsing clever things to say, witty banter and charming anecdotes to make her laugh. Surely a sound not unlike a choir of angels. Someone knocked, shattering any hope of perfecting my performance. "Come in."

Maxwell strode into the room, a concerned look on his face. "Your highness."

"What is it, Maxwell?"

"I'm so sorry, Taryn, but one of your men … is dead."

"What?" If I hadn't been sitting, I would've fallen. "When?"

"A stable hand found him just minutes ago."

"What happened?"

Maxwell swallowed then took a deep breath. "He drowned in the river."

My strength fled, leaving me weak and sick to my stomach. "I don't understand. Did he … fall off the bridge?"

Maxwell wrung his hands and my heart thumped once, twice. Unshed tears glistened in his eyes. "He jumped."

A dark well of anguish opened underneath me, black as death. This could not be happening. I'd brought them home, safe and sound, and had tried so hard for so long to keep them all alive, often against insurmountable odds. One of them couldn't have taken his life. Not possible, not after everything we'd endured. My hands shook with a violent jerk, up my arms, through my spine, down my legs until my entire body trembled. "Who?" I croaked.

"Paxton Whitmore."

No. I squeezed my eyes shut as the image of Paxton's earnest face swam in my vision. Such a young man, with a long and happy life ahead of him. Why?

With rising fury, I opened my eyes to find Maxwell staring at me with a mixture of pity and shock. I had to act against this invisible enemy. Legs shaking, I rose to my feet, using the rage to focus my energy. "Where is he now?"

"With his family. General Creston is on his way."

I clenched my jaw. Of course they had contacted my uncle. Now I'd have to deal with him. Unavoidable, yet necessary. The soldier in me balked at our upcoming conversation. He knew I took the responsibility of command seriously, yet he still delighted in reminding me of my inferiority and inexperience. He'd want to know every detail of Paxton's time under my command in the hopes he'd find something he could pin on me, a reason to blame me for the young man's death. "And my father?"

"They have notified the king but he will leave the details to the general." He paused, a shadow crossing his face. "Is there anything I can do for you?"

I squared my shoulders and willed steel into my voice. "No, Maxwell. Thank you."

He bowed then fled, leaving me alone once again. With the general taking control of the situation, I had little choice but to wait for a summons. Only after I'd explained the circumstances would he allow me to pay my respects to

Paxton's family. I pushed the pain into a dark corner where I hoped it would wither and die. My heart could only take so much.

The sun set, shadows increasing until darkness nearly enveloped me. I glanced out the window at the night sky. Grace would be here in a matter of minutes, yet I'd stood staring at the walls. Like an idiot. I rushed to the dressing room and pawed through silk vests and velvet jackets, none worthy of the occasion. I settled for a silver and black combination then raked a hand through my hair. Longer than usual, but I had no time for further grooming and barreled out the door.

Servants gawked as I raced past, but my steps didn't slow. I reached the courtyard just as a hired coach pulled to a stop. A servant rushed forward to open the door. A gloved hand reached out followed by Grace's lithe body. She glanced around as if unsure what to do next. Our eyes met, and I begged my heart to not explode. Normally, I would have waited for Maxwell, but her radiant smile drew me like a moth to a flame, yet I still hadn't moved. She descended the coach steps while I remained rooted to the spot, staring. She thanked the servant and the coach clattered off, leaving us beaming smiles at each other. Finally, I remembered how to walk and stepped toward her. She dipped a low curtsy, her gorgeous eyes even more so as I took her hand.

"Your highness." Her voice sent a shiver racing up my spine.

"Grace. Welcome back."

"Thank you."

She took my offered arm then fell in step beside me as I led her across the courtyard and into the castle. I couldn't tear my gaze from her exquisite features. Pure poetry. Eyes like a spring meadow, lips like a newborn rose, hair like a golden wave. Not to mention her dress. What it revealed and what it left to the imagination drove me to madness. I'd completely lost my head over this girl, and I didn't care.

... Nothing more than a distraction.

We reached the dining hall, its heavy oak doors flung wide in welcome. The evening meal often took place here, and we strode toward the royal table on the dais. Grace's steps faltered, and she tugged on my arm. I turned to face her. "What is it?"

"We're not sitting … with them? Are we?"

I followed her gaze to the table, where my parents and sister sat in their usual places. "Of course. Why?"

"But they're …"

I squeezed her hand, still tucked tightly in the crook of my arm. "They're just my parents, Grace. Come. I want you to meet them." Like a reluctant child, she let me tow her forward and stood rigid at my side as I introduced her. "This is Grace Dupont, the healer I told you about."

"Your majesties. Your highness," Grace whispered as she dropped into a curtsy.

My father dipped his chin. "Welcome. Please join us."

"Yes, do sit down Taryn," my mother cooed, beaming a smile. "We've been waiting."

Gracious hosts to a fault. I grinned at my mother, whose eyes sparkled with mischief. Grace's head swiveled as she noticed the guests seated nearby, noblemen and their wives along with other friends of my parents. All well-known faces I'd dined with most of my life. I pulled her around the table and held out a chair. "Grace," I whispered at her ear. "They're harmless, I swear it. And I'll be right beside you."

She turned toward me, the gold ring around her enlarged pupils glowing softly. "All right."

I released a shaky breath and took a seat beside her. She seemed anxious based on the scared rabbit look on her face, something I'd have to remedy, quickly. A drink, perhaps. I poured a healthy amount of wine into a crystal goblet and handed it to her. She didn't hesitate before chugging it down.

I stared, open-mouthed, watching her slim throat bob as she swallowed.

"Thank you." She placed the empty goblet on the table. "Just what I needed."

I barked a laugh and poured my own drink, more than ready to enjoy the night.

~ Chapter Five ~

Grace could not keep her pure astonishment from showing. Jewels glittered everywhere, blazing like miniature suns in the flickering candlelight. And the faces. So many beautiful, smiling faces. Her head ached just looking at them. Taryn's face captivated her more than any other. She'd been fully aware of his rugged handsomeness before meeting him. But since then he'd grown even more good-looking, devastatingly so tonight. Not to mention fit. Serving in the military had done wonders for his physique.

Conversation floated in the air, but court gossip had never interested her, and she lost herself in the mindless hum. She'd much rather meet someone, get to know them, and then form an opinion. Exactly as she'd done with Taryn. He'd seemed larger than life, always going off to battle. A stalwart captain astride a war horse as he led his men to victory. But now she knew him, and the young man at her side replaced the previous image. Eager to please and quick to laugh, as well as kind, generous, and playful.

He could never be hers, yet he had captured her in his orbit like a wayward moon seeking direction in the vastness of space. The strong force of his pull tugged her toward him, but she kept her heart carefully closed. As the crown prince, he had obligations to the throne and Nogardia, like marrying a princess or at least a lady of noble birth. She did not qualify on either count. Any relationship she developed with him would stop at friendship. She couldn't afford to hope for anything more. But she could look. She sighed wistfully then turned to admire him once more. He stared back at her, a crooked smile on his perfect face. Heat crept up her neck, and she ducked her head before it reached her cheeks. She blushed far too easily and far too often, especially in his presence.

Not once in her wildest dreams had she ever imagined even working at the castle let alone dining in this glorious room. It seemed more fantastic than factual, yet here she sat, brushing elbows and thighs with the crown prince. As his invited guest. She didn't know nor care what it meant. Even if she never set foot in this grand hall again.

A plate of decadent chocolate cake appeared on the table in front of her. Dessert, served at long last. A bittersweet ending to a surreal night. As much as she hated the idea of leaving him, she didn't belong here, with these people. With *him*.

King Merrick rose from his seat and the room quieted. "Good evening." His rich voice carried the words to every ear. "I know we've all enjoyed ourselves tonight, which is always my hope. Now I'd like to recognize my son for his efforts in ending this war. Taryn."

Taryn seemed pleased at the admiration as if they had heaped it on him his entire life. But his smile looked forced. Pained. He bowed to the king before resuming his seat then turned to her. Regret and sorrow lurked in his eyes and her breath caught. His mask had slipped but before she knew it, he righted it, disappearing behind a false version of himself.

The king had remained standing and addressed the room again. "On a more somber note, I ask you all to observe a moment of silence in honor of the fallen, those men who did not survive."

Grace bowed her head, stealing a sidelong glance at Taryn. He'd hung his head and closed his eyes, as if upset by the mere thought of those men. He had a right to be. She certainly would have been, had the situation been reversed. She could see how deeply he card, with his whole heart. No wonder he needed someone to talk with, to guide him through the guilt and grief. Her task, then. Not gazing at him with longing or fawning over him like some lovesick maiden. No. She'd help him, in any and every way she could to heal, and bring him back from the brink of despair.

The king lifted his head. "Thank you. I implore you to respect those men by living your lives, enjoying the peace they fought so hard to protect. Do not waste their sacrifice." He raised his goblet then took a sip of wine. The guests followed suit, and the atmosphere regained its earlier jovial air. Taryn, however, remained in a funk, a frown etched onto his face. "Your highness?" She placed a tentative hand on his arm. "Are you unwell?"

He shook his head, a muscle twitching in his jaw. How could she help him navigate the emotional storm raging within him? She bit her lip and considered her limited options. She had to get him out of this room, out of this place. Away from the constant reminder of everything he'd endured. "Taryn," she urged softly. "Taryn."

He raised his head and the suffering behind his eyes broke her heart. "Yes, Grace? What is it?"

"Will you come with me?"

He blinked then nodded. "Of course."

She held out her hand. He stared at it for a heartbeat then slowly stood.

"Taryn," the queen said. "Where are you going?"

He glanced at her over his shoulder. "Out." He turned back to Grace and smiled weakly. "Hurry, before she demands I stay."

She towed him from the room with hurried steps, yet her half-formed plan left her with no idea where to go. She only knew they had to leave, immediately. When they burst out into the moon-washed courtyard, her sense of urgency doubled, though she couldn't say why.

"Grace." Taryn's voice rasped behind her. "Where are we going?"

"I actually don't know. I just thought it wise to get you out of there. Before … " He arched a brow and she huffed out a breath. "Before something happened."

"Like what?"

"You tell me." She searched his face, looking for a way past his defenses. But the wall he'd erected to keep unwanted visitors out loomed there instead, barring her entrance. If he didn't let her in, she wouldn't be able to help him.

"Taryn!" They both jerked as the princess's voice rang against the stone walls. "Where are you?"

He threw a tortured glance at the door then grabbed Grace's hand and took off running. She followed, keeping pace with him as they zig-zagged through the maze of hedges bordering the garden. Soon even the moonlight failed to light their way and he slowed to a stop, chest heaving. Her own breath came fast and ragged, tearing at her lungs. "What's … wrong?" she gasped.

He shook his head, turning to peer into the shadows beyond the hedge. "Nothing."

"Then why are we here?"

She strained to see him as he raked a hand through his hair, tousling it into disarray. Somehow it made him seem more common. Quite unlike the prince she knew.

"I don't know! I can't …"

He paced in front of her, his figure a dark shape floating like smoke. Perhaps she could use this sense of anonymity to her advantage. "Taryn."

He stopped. "Yes?"

"Would you like to talk about it?"

"No." A lengthy pause. "Yes."

She laughed under her breath. "Which is it? I'm here either way."

Another, lengthier pause. "I suppose we can talk here, if you don't mind."

The night had cooled, but her long sleeves should keep her warm enough. "I don't mind at all."

"Where do I start? I don't know how to–"

"The beginning is always the best place. Don't you think?"

He huffed a breath. "I feel … sad."

"And?"

"Depressed?"

"Are you asking me or telling me?"

Gravel crunched under his boots as he resumed pacing. "I don't know. I've never done this before."

"And what is this?"

"Do you always ask so many questions?"

"Well, yes. It's my job."

"It's infuriating."

"I can stop, if you'd prefer."

"Please."

She'd found the cover of darkness helpful but now she only wished to see his face, to read his expression for any insight as to his true feelings. Most people didn't realize how much a simple look could convey. She'd practiced and studied and honed her skills for this very task. She felt him step forward and fought the urge to back away even as his body heat wrapped around her.

"Grace," he said so close to her ear she almost jumped.

"Yes, your highness?" She could barely speak past the lump in her throat, could barely hear over the pounding of her heart. And now his scent bombarded her, earthy and utterly masculine. She bit her lip, waiting.

"I'm sorry."

"For what?"

"I'm sorry I dragged you out here. This behavior is so unlike me. I'm not quite myself, I'm afraid. Forgive me."

She reached out blindly and managed to latch onto his hand. "There is nothing to forgive. You have every right to be upset, to feel everything you're feeling. I only want to help, I swear it. But you must let me in. Please, Taryn."

"I know." He sighed, his warm breath tickling the side of her neck. "But we need to get back. I don't want anyone to think we'd come here to …"

"To what?"

"Never mind." He tightened his grip on her hand and tugged her back through the maze, into the courtyard. He turned to her with a weary sigh. "I think we should say good night."

She tried to keep the disappointment from her voice. "Oh. All right. But we should talk again. Soon."

He nodded then pressed his lips to her hand. "Wait here. I'll send someone to escort you out." He strode away, leaving her achingly alone.

~ Chapter Six ~

Battle images flashed again and again in my mind, making it impossible to keep my eyes closed for more than a minute. I tried replacing those gruesome scenes with images of Grace, but they persisted. I eventually gave up and eased into the corridor outside my room then walked in a daze, unable to sleep for fear of dreaming. I needed to process my feelings, but couldn't brave such a daunting task, not with the painful wounds still fresh. Time. It would take time for me to come to terms with what had happened.

I reached the end of the hall and turned around, heading back toward my room. My thoughts drifted to Grace. Perhaps I'd send for her tomorrow, though it didn't seem soon enough. I rubbed at my chest, trying to soothe the ache. It felt like an arrow had pierced right through my heart. She'd captivated me like no woman ever had. If only I could reveal myself to her the way she'd asked, but every time I opened my mouth to divulge a secret, express a feeling, nothing happened. Something held me back, as if my mind refused to let me say the words.

❡

Daylight gilded the room. I squinted and sat up, rubbing sleep from my eyes. Morning had come and gone it seemed, by the high position of the sun. Thank the gods Maxwell hadn't woken me. I felt better, or at least not as tired.

An hour later, I found Maxwell in his usual midday haunt. He claimed he preferred the peaceful quiet of the lower kitchen, but I knew better. The head baker used the space to make bread every day, and every day Maxwell loitered there. To watch her knead dough. I shook my head as I stepped into the warm room, grinning at his back. He glanced over his shoulder at the sound of my footsteps, clearly not expecting me, yet jumping to his feet just the same.

"Tar … your highness," he stammered, red-faced.

"Your highness," the baker echoed with a curtsy.

"Please, don't let me interrupt." She nodded and returned to her task, arching a brow at Maxwell.

He cleared his throat. "What can I do for you?"

"I need to see Grace."

His eyes twinkled. "I'm so pleased she helped you."

My conversation with Grace replayed in my head. Had I found it helpful? Perhaps. But more than anything, I wanted to hear her voice, see her face. "Will you please send word to her?"

"Of course." He scurried from the room, leaving me alone with the baker. She simply smiled and turned to place a loaf of bread in the oven.

❡

My nerves tightened with every turn around my sitting room as I paced, waiting for word of Grace's arrival. The minutes ticked by, each one stretching to infinity. Finally, a knock sounded. "Come in." The door opened and there she stood. My gaze traveled the length of her body. Beautiful, despite the simple homespun dress she wore. Maxwell cleared his throat and I snapped my head toward him.

"Your highness," he drawled. "Grace Dupont."

"Thank you, Maxwell. You may go."

His stern expression warned me to behave, then he disappeared out the door. Grace waited at the threshold, shifting as if I made her nervous.

"Please come in." I motioned her inside.

She dipped a curtsy then breezed past me. She sat in a chair, hands folded in her lap.

"Would you like something to eat? Or drink?"

She shook her head, and I sat across from her on the couch. She held herself differently today, a subtle change in demeanor. More formal, professional. All business, then.

"Are you prepared to talk?" The question dropped into the silence from nowhere.

I blinked. "Yes."

"Fine. Whenever you're ready."

"Grace, did I–"

"Please, your highness. We have only a few hours. I need to be home by sundown. My father is expecting me."

Of course she had a home, a family. Friends. A male friend? *No.* Why hadn't I considered her life apart from the time she spent with me?

"Your highness?"

"What? Oh, yes. I … can't sleep. I keep thinking about the battles, the violence. The death." I shuddered. "My men trusted me to keep them safe, yet I lost so many on the battlefield." My voice hitched, and I took a deep breath. "And Paxton …" I briefly closed my eyes against the struggle to keep the pain at bay. His death would haunt me forever, another brutal scar on my soul. Grace moved to sit beside me and placed her hand on my arm.

She smiled warmly. "Go on, Taryn. I'm here."

And then the floodgates opened. I sobbed and raged through my feelings, extracting them one by one until I had nothing left to give. Grace cradled my head against her shoulder as the last of my tears dried. I leaned back and wiped my face, mortified and emasculated. Men didn't cry, especially in the company of beautiful young women. I hung my head as heat seared my cheeks but her cool fingers gripped my chin and forced my gaze to meet hers. Nothing but compassion filled her eyes. No pity, no mockery. I took a shuddering breath.

"What a wonderful start."

"Excuse me?"

"Absolutely wonderful." A smile lit up her face, though I couldn't imagine why. Unless gloating over my childish display of emotion somehow brought her joy. "Tomorrow we can talk more about why you're feeling this way."

I gaped at her, mouth hanging open like a fish on dry land. She couldn't be serious. I'd bared myself to her, offered up my very soul. I'd cried for gods' sake. And she wanted me to do it again? "Are you mad?"

Her smile faltered. "What do you mean? Of course not. I'm so pleased we were able to–"

I jerked to my feet. "No, Grace. I've done enough, trust me."

She crossed her arms and held her ground. "Taryn ..."

"Are you not convinced? I feel much better."

She nodded. "I'm sure you think so, but your recovery is just beginning. Healing is a process, often a long and difficult one. We really should work on this. You're hurt. You're ..." She seemed to fumble for a polite way to speak her mind.

"Broken?"

"Well, yes."

"Not every broken thing needs fixing." Voice tight with emotion, I fought to maintain my composure.

"I didn't mean ..."

I shoved my hands into my pockets and shrugged. "It doesn't matter. We're done."

"But I–"

"Goodbye, Grace."

She frowned then stood. I turned away, refusing to watch her leave, even though I'd ordered her to go. The door closed behind her with a soft click. Only then did my shoulders slump, my posture slip. How she'd seen right through me both impressed and annoyed me. I'd tried so hard to hide, but she cared more than anyone else. My parents hadn't shown an ounce of concern for my mental well-being. And Maxwell, who knew me better than most, thought a conversation or two with her would solve my problems. Yet if anyone could do it, she could. She had braved the brutal landscape of my mind, pushing past my anger and self-doubt with admirable courage. Unafraid and undaunted, she'd reached out to me, even in the darkness I called home.

~ Chapter Seven ~

Grace stared at Taryn's closed door for an embarrassing amount of time. She'd only tried to help. Yet he'd gone on the defensive, attacking her as if she were an enemy combatant. Perplexing and hurtful behavior. But she'd change his mind. How hard could it be?

Harder than hard, as it turned out. Not only did Grace fail to convince Taryn to continue their conversations, she didn't even see him in the days following their heated exchange. She waited for a summons, yet it never came. And she knew better than to pester him. He obviously needed time to deal with his emotions. Now if she could only deal with hers, life would return to normal.

She frowned at her reflection as she braided her hair. Foolish girl. What had she been thinking, voicing her opinions to the prince? She should have kept her mouth shut and simply listened, as her training had taught her. But no. Once again, her compulsive need to solve everyone's problems had gotten the better of her. Taryn would not benefit from a quick fix or an immediate solution. Only steady guidance and kind words would bring him back to himself. If he even wanted to come back. His behavior certainly hadn't suggested a desire to heal. He'd done nothing but push her away, except for the breakdown in his room, which had surprised her. She hadn't expected such an intense display from him.

If she could just meet with him again, engage in a civil conversation, he might show his vulnerable side one more time. Then she would show him the way to happiness. Or at least acceptance. She could almost see the darkness in his soul, eating away at him. If he didn't take measures now, it would eventually consume him, and he'd be lost, perhaps forever. She refused to let him, or anyone suffer such a fate. Prince or not, enough coddling.

❧

The castle gates swung wide at her approach. She nodded to the sentries then continued through to the courtyard. No one stopped her or even asked what business she had, and she strolled down the corridors as if she belonged.

Taryn's door stood partway open and she raised her fist. Did one simply knock on a prince's door? Unsure of the proper protocol, she hesitated. Voices floated out to where she stood. Eavesdropping on a royal conversation surely broke at least one rule. Before she could decide to go or stay, the door swung open and Maxwell's startled face appeared in front of her.

He closed the door behind him. "Miss Dupont. I don't recall the prince having an appointment with you today."

Or ever again. She backed up several steps as he walked toward her. "He doesn't. But he's been avoiding me, so I took matters into my own hands."

He arched a brow. "Defying your prince? A bold move."

She grinned at his wink. "Can I see him now? Is he busy?"

He glanced over his shoulder at the still closed door. "He is indisposed. Perhaps another time."

Indisposed? "Perhaps. Please let him know I stopped by, and I look forward to seeing him soon."

He gave a small bow. "Of course."

She accepted her dismissal, more determined than ever to mend the tear in the prince's heart. But how? His insistence they disregard his royal status did not grant permission to disrespect his wishes. There had to be a way she could see him without causing a scene. Or committing treason.

Bright sunshine bounced off the water in the fountain and she squinted against the glare, crashing into someone right in front of her. Staggering back, she shielded her eyes and opened her mouth to apologize. The words stuck in her throat as she stared down at Princess Natalie sprawled on the grass, looking none too happy about it.

"You could at least help me up, instead of just standing there, gawking."

Grace snapped to attention and reached out a hand then hauled the princess to her feet. "Your highness. I'm so - "

"Sorry?" she offered with a sly grin. "Don't be. It happens. Well, not to me, but I've seen it several times. In fact," she whispered, leaning forward like a co-conspirator, "a few years ago, Taryn broke his arm after he ran smack into a sentry." She covered her mouth to stifle a giggle. "Hilarious."

Despite her still reddened cheeks, Grace smiled, all too easily picturing a young Taryn cradling his arm while he pouted. Her smile faded as she realized she'd yet to apologize—to the princess—and dipped into a low curtsy. "Forgive me, your highness."

"Consider yourself forgiven. And please call me Natalie."

"Thank you," she said as she straightened.

"You were with Taryn at dinner the other night. Are your talks going well?"

"They were. We haven't been doing much lately."

"Well, I'm sure he's just being stubborn. And please don't worry about bumping into me. I'm only glad I didn't have a cake in my hands. I would hate to ruin this dress." She smoothed the front of her beaded skirt.

"A terrible shame for sure. It's beautiful." A stab of jealousy pierced through Grace's heart.

Natalie's smile rivaled the sun as she twirled. "It is, isn't it? Father did not understand when I told him I had to have a new dress for the party. Luckily, Mother convinced him otherwise."

"Party? What's the occasion?"

Natalie blinked, apparently surprised she didn't already know. "Taryn's welcome home party tonight. Surely he mentioned it?"

Her heart sank. No, he hadn't mentioned it. Why would he? They'd barely spoken and could hardly be considered friends. "He didn't say anything about it to me."

Natalie scoffed. "My brother can be so pig-headed. You have to attend."

Grace almost fainted from shock. Dinner she could handle. But a party? "Thank you, but I couldn't possibly."

"You must, as my guest"

"But I have nothing suitable to wear."

"Nonsense. I insist." Grace opened her mouth to protest but Natalie looped her arm through hers and towed her back into the castle. "Now. Let's find you something to wear."

❧

Grace stared at her reflection, pinching her arm. This had to be a dream. No reality existed where she'd be here, in this dress, Invited to a royal party. For the prince, no less.

"You look beautiful," Natalie breathed behind her. "Truly."

"Thank you. And thank you for the dress." She twisted her hips, and the skirt swished around her ankles.

"It suits you. Taryn will regret not inviting you himself." Her blue eyes sparkled with sibling rivalry, a feeling completely foreign to Grace.

Her smile faltered. "I don't want to upset him, not on his special night."

Natalie waved a hand. "He's a big boy. He'll be fine."

Grace remained skeptical of Taryn's ability to be fine, especially given recent events. But she kept her opinion to herself and trailed behind Natalie out the door.

Dukes and duchesses, lords and ladies glittered like a thousand stars in the crowded ballroom. Grace couldn't help but gawk at the bejeweled guests, all people she would never ordinarily meet, let alone socialize with. Panic stalked the room, circling her like a predator sizing up its prey. She kept a wary eye on it even as she scanned the area looking for Taryn. "Where is the guest of honor? I don't see him anywhere."

Natalie stood on her toes, her head on a swivel as she searched the crowd. "Neither do I. He's likely still preening. My brother is vain to a fault. But worry not, dear Grace. The prince will make his grand entrance soon enough." Spoken like a true little sister.

"And what of your parents? Will they be here?"

"Eventually. In the meantime, let's get a drink." She took Grace's hand and towed her toward a roving servant. She grabbed two glasses of sparkling wine and thrust one at Grace. "Cheers."

She beamed a smile then took a dainty sip. She'd never tasted anything so delicious, surely a special vintage for Taryn. Natalie gulped hers down as if to quench a thirst. Grace stared, shaking her head, unable to imagine having an excess of something so priceless.

A ripple of energy surged through the room, followed by a cascading hush. Had Taryn arrived at long last? Or the king and queen? Grace couldn't see over the many taller heads but plainly heard the king's booming voice.

"Welcome, friends. Thank you for joining us tonight to celebrate my son's return. Please be seated."

She turned to Natalie, unsure what to do. They hadn't discussed where Grace would sit. Panic winked from the shadows, setting loose a swarm of butterflies in her stomach. Natalie's hand once again gripped hers and they wove through the throng toward the front of the room. And the royal table.

Her steps faltered, and she almost tripped on her dress as Natalie pulled her to a stop. "Father. Mother."

She couldn't help but smile and dipped into a curtsy. "Your majesties."

"Welcome back, my dear," the queen chirped. "Please join us."

"Over here." Natalie gestured toward the far-right side of the table. Two empty chairs waited there, and Natalie plopped down onto the one closest to the queen, leaving the one on the end for Grace. She sat carefully, not wanting to crush or wrinkle the dress any more than necessary and clenched her shaking hands in her lap. Heart thundering, she took in the view from her lofty position. The room appeared far lovelier from up here. Now she just had to eat and drink without dropping food down her bodice or knocking her glass onto the floor.

A door opened across the room and Taryn strode in, his golden crown gleaming in the candlelight. The guests rose to their feet and he beamed a regal smile, nodding to some as he passed. He stood in front of the table, bowing slightly to his parents then ambled off to sit at the other end. She held her breath, waiting for the dreaded moment when he'd notice her. She'd considered the consequences of crashing his party and hoped he'd be flattered and not offended. But he didn't even glance in her direction. Rude. And not very prince-like. Perhaps he hadn't recognized her. This dress certainly did wonders for her figure and Natalie had styled her hair into a complicated coiffure. Still, she looked more like herself than not. He could have at least pretended to have seen her. She swallowed hard. She really shouldn't have come.

The king stood, lifting his glass. "Thank you all for coming. I realize we are still grieving but I encourage you to enjoy yourselves tonight as we celebrate and officially welcome Taryn home. Please enjoy."

The king lowered himself onto his chair and the guests all sat. Grace took a long swallow of wine, willing it to go straight to her head. The night would be so much more pleasant if she were little drunk. Or a lot.

Servants entered carrying huge silver trays overflowing with delicacies Grace had only ever heard about. Now she had the chance to taste them all. And she did. Plate piled high with a bit of everything, she grinned at Natalie then filled her belly. Conversations flowed around her as she ate. She listened but nothing interested her enough to participate and she soon tuned it all out until Natalie elbowed her side.

"Are you ever going to stop eating?"

"Oh. Yes." Grace finally relinquished her fork. "I've just never had such delicious food."

Natalie arched a brow. "Really? Well, you'll have to dine with us more often, then."

Grace almost choked on her wine. "What?"

"We are friends now, aren't we?"

Grace dipped her chin to hide her smile. "I'd like to be. But I'm just a–"

"I don't care," Natalie assured her. "I want to be your friend. And I always get what I want. I am a princess, after all." She tossed her auburn hair over her shoulder.

Grace giggled, marveling at her astounding luck. If she hadn't insisted on visiting Taryn today, she wouldn't have bumped into Natalie, nor attended this lavish party or worn this exquisite dress. Even if Taryn refused to say another word to her, she'd made a friend. A treasure worth more than just about anything.

~ Chapter Eight ~

*H*oly gods.

Grace had come to my party and sat mere feet away. So close and yet too far. My heart hadn't stopped racing since the moment I noticed her sitting so casually at the royal table as if she'd always been here. Natalie leaned toward her and whispered something in her ear, something she found hilarious. She threw her head back and laughed. Actually laughed. I couldn't remember the last time I'd truly found joy in anything, let alone laughed about it. But thinking such thoughts led to a bad place, a place I'd vowed to forget even existed.

I focused instead on the sound of Grace's voice as she and my sister conspired. No doubt scheming, planning some way to torment me. And on such an important night, no less. A skill Natalie had perfected, much to my dismay. She delighted in pushing as many buttons as she could before I exploded. She needed a husband. Soon. And what of Grace? Did she have someone waiting for her, warming her bed? I'd never asked. Hadn't truly cared until this moment, in fact. And why should

I? We couldn't be together, not in any official capacity at least. So, it didn't matter. Did it?

What in the hell had happened to me? I'd lost my edge. She'd gotten under my skin, past my defenses. Breached the crumbling walls. But should I let her in? If I did, she'd see me, all of me, stripped down to my very core where only pain and guilt remained. But first, I needed to know I could trust her. And feel safe with my fragile soul in her hands.

Strength and courage on the battlefield, weakness and fear in my heart. Two sides of the same tarnished coin, yet a tiny crack had formed in the bottomless pit of despair I'd thrown myself into. A light shone through, like a beacon of hope beckoning to me from deep, deep down. If the light didn't go out, I'd be fine. *Completely fine.*

And in the meantime, dessert and dancing. The party had raged while I brooded, music and laughter chasing each other around the room. Never one to shy away from a good time, I shoved the negativity into its box and slammed the lid closed. Enough for now.

Grace and Natalie continued their gossip session, likely sharing secrets. I fought the urge to roll my eyes as I headed toward them. They ignored me, and I had to clear my throat twice before they deigned to notice me. Natalie smirked but Grace, to her credit, looked mortified.

"Ladies," I said with a slight bow. "Enjoying yourselves?"

"Taryn." Natalie's leveled gaze warned I'd better have a damn good reason for the interruption.

Grace swallowed, her throat bobbing. "Your highness."

"You look lovely. Both of you." I flashed her a smile and a pretty blush painted her cheeks. My heart jerked in response as if tethered to her.

… Dangerous ... Very dangerous.

Natalie would have stuck her tongue out if a hundred pairs of eyes hadn't been watching. She settled for a feral grin instead. "And you, Prince Taryn. What a dashing young man you are." She batted her eyelashes yet failed to get a rise out of me. Not tonight. Ignoring her, I turned to Grace. "Would you like to dance?"

Her blush deepened from pink to crimson as she stammered a reply. "I would be honored."

I offered my hand, which she held tightly in hers, and led her to the center of the room. As tradition dictated, the royal family had exclusive use of the dance floor. I intended to use it and nodded to the musicians, who immediately started playing one of my favorite songs. I glanced down at Grace, so light and precious in my arms, and took a step. And then another until we were dancing, floating, sailing around the room. Everyone and everything else ceased to exist. Only she remained.

Her feet steady underneath her, she kept up with me while the music soared, ending in a final bittersweet note, echoing in my bones. Breathless with delight and eyes sparkling, she beamed a smile.

"Thank you for the amazing dance. I didn't know you were so graceful."

"It's the training. Fighting with a sword is a lot like dancing. Moves and countermoves. Would you like to sit down? Are you tired? Or thirsty?"

She laughed under her breath. "Whatever you'd like is fine with me."

"Then let's go out on the balcony." I tucked her hand into the crook of my elbow and led her outside just as the next song began to play. The doors closed behind us, muffling the music to a soft hum. A night-chilled breeze ruffled the hair at my collar and I shivered. Grace must be freezing. I laid my jacket across her shoulders, and she briefly closed her eyes with a soft sigh. I rested my elbows on the railing, marveling at the vastness of the velvet sky patterned with a million points of light.

She turned toward me and smiled, moonlight reflecting in her eyes.. "What a beautiful view."

"Indeed it is."

"Taryn?"

"Yes?"

"You're staring."

"Am I?" She dipped her head as if she wanted to hide. I took her chin and forced her gaze to meet mine. "What's wrong?"

She swallowed. "Nothing."

I took her hand. "Please tell me."

"I can't …"

"Of course you can. Please, Grace. Tell me."

She took a deep breath. "I'm afraid of my feelings for you."

My heart boomed like a cannon. "What kind of feelings?"

She pulled her hand from mine and shook her head. "Feelings I can't feel, shouldn't feel for you. You're the prince. And I …"

"What about *my* feelings?"

Her eyes widened as if she thought I didn't have the capacity to feel anything other than sadness and despair. And anger. She may have been right. I sighed heavily and stared into the darkened garden. The shadows seemed to ebb and flow, their promise of nothingness calling to me. Too dark.

I turned toward the light, toward her. "Grace. I have feelings for you, too. And I know you think because I'm the prince, I'm not an option. But I could be. If you'll trust me."

She took a step, closing the distance between us to practically nothing. Heat poured off her despite the chill in the air. I held my breath and she angled her head, staring intently as if trying to memorize my face. I couldn't look away, captured by the force of her gaze. Everything but her emerald eyes faded from view. *Kiss her.*

The balcony doors opened behind us and we jumped apart. Two rowdy courtiers stumbled out. A deep growl rumbled in my chest as I glared at the offenders. "Leave us." Their smiles disappeared, quickly replaced by shock. And fear. They turned and fled, crashing into each other in their haste. I scowled at their backs as the doors banged closed with a boom like cannon fire. The sound ricocheted in my skull. Tormented cries of the dying rang out across the battlefield. Piles of dead soldiers littered the ground at my feet. *Bodies everywhere.* So many. And blood. Dripping, flowing, running in crimson rivers. I squeezed my eyes shut to block out the horror.

Not real. I shook my head trying to clear it. Darkness stalked the edge of my vision, a ravenous wolf.

"Taryn?"

I whirled around, chest heaving, muscles tense. Ready to fight. My mind stumbled at the look on her face.

Real. I gulped down air and took a deep breath then another. My tight muscles uncoiled, and the adrenaline slowly wore off, leaving me light-headed and shaking.

"Are you all right?" Her voice sounded far, far away.

The shadows called my name, a moaning, keening wail. I covered my ears, but the sound vibrated in my head. Terror like I'd never known arced through me and my knees cracked on the stone floor. The pain didn't compare to the agony in my heart, the darkness in my soul yanking, clenching, crushing me in its vise-like grip. My death, at last.

"Taryn."

A gentle voice caressed my ear and I opened my eyes. "Mother?"

Her hands fluttered near my face, holding a glass to my mouth. "Drink this."

"What is it?" I rasped.

"It will help."

I raised my head from the sweat-soaked pillow and sipped. The foul brew slid down my throat, making my eyes water. "What happened?"

Light bloomed as she lit a lamp. Shadows retreated to the corner, waiting. "I don't know what happened, Taryn. Perhaps you could tell me."

I cleared my throat and studied her pale skin, the lines around her mouth. "I don't … remember."

"Anything? The healer said even the smallest detail could help."

Brow furrowed, I concentrated, straining to bring forth a memory, any memory other than the look on Grace's face right before I … what? Had I kissed her? If I had, I likely would remember it. But something must have stopped me. We'd been interrupted. On the balcony. But everything since then remained hidden, shrouded in darkness. I briefly closed my eyes and rubbed my temples. My mother's concerned face hovered nearby. "I'm sorry, Mother. Perhaps once I rest."

Her face paled further, nearly translucent. "Taryn. You've been asleep for two days."

Impossible, yet it took several swallows to unstick my tongue from the roof of my mouth. And I obviously hadn't bathed recently. Panic rushed in like the tide. *What is wrong with me?*

… Nothing.

"I'll send for the healer." She stood, concern marring her features. "She asked to know when you'd woken."

"Mother, I–"

She smiled and smoothed the damp hair from my brow. "It's going to be all right, my sweet boy. Don't worry."

I nodded mutely, and she bent down to kiss my cheek. Eager shadows pooled around me as soon as she left the room. Overwhelmed and overburdened, my mind began to shut down. I stared with blank indifference at the flickering lamplight dancing on the walls, with no thought, no worry. Just pure emptiness. A quiet lack of awareness. In the absence of reality, I felt no pain. The persistent, paralyzing grief didn't exist here in the darkness. I basked in the blissful relief flowing through me as it took over my mind, my heart. My soul. Disconnected from caring, from feeling, despair no longer consumed me. I had found peace.

… *Freedom.*

The constant misery and heartache suddenly vanished as if it had never existed. My breathing eased, my heartbeat slowed, and a smile crept across my face.

… *Stay here.*

A knock echoed in the sitting room and my gaze slid to the door. "Who is it?"

"It's Grace. Can I come in?"

"Yes."

The thick rug muffled her footsteps as she made her way toward the bedroom. She pushed the door all the way open, gaze darting around nervously until she noticed me on the bed. Shadows hid her face, but her breath hitched, likely from the shock of seeing me incapacitated. And weak. So weak I could barely lift my head from the pillow as she sat beside me. I managed to prop myself up enough to sit level with her. She studied me, her eyes twin pools of liquid emerald. I breathed in. Out. Enduring her assessment, knowing full well what she'd find. My soul. Shattered.

"Taryn," she whispered. "What happened?"

I lifted a shoulder. "Nothing."

Her mouth fell open. "Nothing? How can you say such a thing? We were star-gazing on the balcony, and then you started raving like a lunatic about a field full of dead bodies. The guards had to drag you away."

The star-gazing I remembered with startling clarity. But the raving like a lunatic episode had been obliterated from my memory. Too painful to recall, perhaps. A blessing in disguise and far better than the alternative. "I'm sorry if I frightened you, Grace. Truly."

"You didn't frighten me, Taryn. But you did worry me."

"There is nothing to worry about." I flashed a bright smile. "I am perfectly fine." Her eyes narrowed with suspicion, but she held her tongue. "I'm actually quite tired. Can we talk later?"

Her face paled slightly. "Oh, yes. Of course. I'm so sorry. I'll just … be going, then. Good night."

She hurried from the room as if she couldn't get away fast enough. Had I said something to upset her? Or did I look as if I'd risen from the dead? Likely the latter, in which case I couldn't blame her for running.

~ Chapter Nine ~

Apparently, I'd had enough rest. Sunlight streamed through the windows opposite my bed as Natalie barged into my room, chirping like a deranged bird. "Good morning, sleepyhead."

I sighed and turned my back to her. She grabbed my shoulder and rolled me over. Her glower would have been unattractive on anyone else. "Taryn," she chided, hands on her hips. "You need to get up."

"Why?"

"Because Mother said so."

Ah, playing the mother-guilt card. "All right." I'd rather pretend than pick a fight. "I'll get up." She crossed her arms, glaring suspiciously. "I promise, Natalie."

"Good. And don't forget to bathe. I'll wait in the sitting room."

She stomped out and I slowly sat up, no longer groggy. In fact, my head felt clearer than it had in weeks. Whatever my mother had given me worked wonders.

I let Natalie drag me outside into a pleasant fall afternoon fit for a picnic. She towed me through the garden, around the fountain, along the forest. We finally stopped at the stables. "What are we doing here?"

"I thought you might like to go for a ride." She smiled brightly, as if I were a small child.

Cajoling, needling, pressuring me to do something I'd rather not. But I could hardly argue, and a ride might be fun. A concept I'd almost forgotten while drowning in melancholy. And since I wanted to be left alone, for everyone to stop treating me like a murderer about to start a killing spree, I'd have to act accordingly. Like a normal person. As if my mind hadn't betrayed me. But I could do it. I would do it, if it helped keep the pain at bay. A solid plan.

We rode for miles under a cloudless, blue sky. Natalie maintains the steady stream of conversation, to which I contributed very little. She didn't seem to notice or mind and finished the ride with color high on her cheeks. I climbed from the saddle and handed the reins to the stable boy. "Now what, dear sister? I assume you've been tasked with entertaining me, lest I do something dangerous."

She blanched. "Taryn, I–"

"It's fine. Truly." I grinned to emphasize the fineness of the situation. Convincingly, it seemed.

"Wonderful." Her easy smile returned, and she looped her arm through mine. "Are you hungry? Shall we get something to eat?"

On any other day, I would have balked at her placating tone but I enjoyed the attention. A wicked spark flared in my blood. Perhaps I knew the meaning of fun after all.

❈

At dinner I behaved as expected. Fine, fixed, fully restored. I played my part, smiling, laughing, eating. Every inch the young prince and heir to the throne. I dined and danced until exhaustion demanded I at least sit, if not collapse in a heap.

My mother beamed a smile, clearly pleased to see me up and about.

Easy. All too easy to fool her, fool them. I could pretend all I wanted but I couldn't escape the darkness seeping through the cracks in my shattered soul. A poisonous secret.

"Your highness." Maxwell came to a breathless stop at my side. "The general has arrived."

I arched a brow. "Has he?"

He nodded, glancing around furtively as if the general would materialize out of thin air. His fondness for barking obscene orders to torture our staff knew no bounds. I'd suffered at his hands long enough to know the feeling intimately.

"Relax, Maxwell. I can handle my uncle." He bowed then turned on his heel, fleeing through the door.

I almost followed him. I'd seen battle, blood. Death. Yet I'd shrink in my uncle's commanding presence, tremble under his steely gaze. For once in my life I wanted to stand up to him. Perhaps I should. The shadows whispered encouragement and I smiled. Let the general come. I could handle him.

~ Chapter Ten ~

I strolled toward the council chamber, hands deep into my pockets as if I didn't have a care in the world. Completely true. In fact, I looked forward to the upcoming chat with my uncle. Whatever the general said, the questions he asked, I would not break or fold under the pressure.

The doors swung open, and I nodded to the sentries then strode inside, brimming with confidence. My uncle's withering stare tracked my progress as I crossed the marble floor to stand at the table where he sat next to my father. I bowed graciously. "Father. Uncle."

"Taryn," my father said. "Thank you for joining us. Please sit."

My uncle sneered, a rebel among kings. I pulled out a chair and sank onto it. Shadows curled at my feet like a faithful pet.

"You know what this is about." My father's sympathetic tone made my teeth ache. "And I'm sorry to put you through it, but it is necessary."

"Protocol," my uncle clarified as if my simple mind couldn't grasp the concept.

I glanced at him. "Understood." His face lit up, but I smiled and leaned back in my chair. An endless minute ticked by.

"Captain Ellsbree," he barked. "One of your men took his own life while under your command. Explain."

I held my breath, expecting to feel the sting of loss, the bite of regret, but only an echo remained. *Scarred.*

"There is nothing to explain. We all were distraught. He didn't see a way past it, so he jumped."

My father's mouth fell open as his gaze flicked from me to the general. "Taryn–"

"No." My uncle held up a hand. "Let the boy speak. Go on, Captain."

I shrugged. "I don't know what else you expect me to say. The fault is his and his alone."

A wicked gleam flashed behind his eyes. "Failure without fear is not bravery. Or courage."

"I never claimed to be brave or courageous."

He slowly rose and leaned on the table to snarl in my face. "Watch your tone, boy. I do not believe you are faultless."

"Regardless of your opinion, Uncle, Paxton chose his path. He escaped the darkness forever, which is more than I can say for most of us."

A different look crossed his face then, as if he could see through my mask of normalcy. "Indeed."

"Are we done here?"

A curt nod and then he sat. "Dismissed."

... *Escape.*

❧

I lounged in my room, alternating between billiards and books until Maxwell reminded me to dress for dinner. I changed clothes and joined my family at the royal table as required, more crowded with my uncle's domineering presence. How much longer would he be here? Hadn't he gotten whatever he needed from me? Surely he had better things to do than torment me. My poor aunt. Father had done a terrible job protecting his sister-in-law from her husband.

Several mind-numbing hours passed, blending together into a perfect remedy for madness. Another night, another meal. But then Grace arrived. Charming and more beautiful than ever, her alluring smile jolted my dormant senses. Her musical laugh bounced off the walls, lighting a path through the darkness. I turned, drawn by the familiar pull.

"Captain," my uncle called from the other end of the table. "A word."

I jerked at his sharp tone then followed him from the room, not as easily intimidated by his heavy footfalls this time. Apparently, I'd grown a backbone in the five years I'd spent at war and his usual tactics were not having the desired effect.

We entered his rooms, ornately furnished and fit for a king. For someone used to sleeping on a cot under a canvas roof, he seemed quite comfortable as he sat behind his massive desk. I stood at attention in front of it, wary and watchful.

"You may sit."

I sat and remained quiet. What could he want now? He'd already had his fun berating me. Without my father present, he had no reason to hold back. Fear coiled in a dark corner of my mind, ready to strike at the first hint of weakness, yet I refused to show anything other than stalwart strength.

"I've spoken with your father about reassigning you."

"I hadn't realized I needed reassignment. Sir."

"You are idle here, your talents wasted. I have use for you in the north."

"The garrison?" I arched a brow. The northern garrison offered nothing but freezing winds and blinding snowstorms. A dismal, remote place only suited for training new recruits. "For what purpose, sir?"

"You will accompany me when I leave tomorrow. Dismissed."

I bristled at his tone, but old habits died hard. "Understood."

My mind whirled with every step I took down the corridor. What possible use would I be at the northern garrison? I'd served for so long, fought so hard and deserved a respite. And I still hadn't fully processed my grief. Or guilt. I slowed my pace. I hadn't even had a chance to visit Paxton's family. And now I had to leave. Tomorrow.

~ Chapter Eleven ~

Dawn broke over the castle walls, throwing sunbeams into my room. I'd been up for hours, packing and pacing while curiosity ate me alive. But I wouldn't dare ask the general. He'd given an order and I'd obey it. Besides, I'd find out soon enough. A brisk knock sounded. "Come in."

Maxwell stepped in. "A letter, your highness." He handed me an envelope. The wax seal bore no insignia. Brow furrowed, I cracked it open then read the single page of flowing script.

Prince Taryn,

I heard of your departure and wanted to wish you well. I know we had differences of opinion on certain matters, but I still want nothing but happiness for you. I hope you find true peace.

Yours,
Grace

Differences of opinion? An understatement of epic proportions. I crumpled the note and tossed it into the fireplace.

Maxwell eyed the burning paper. "Not good news, I take it?"

I glanced at him and sighed. "From Grace. I just don't understand what happened between us. I tried, Maxwell, truly. And I thought …"

"What?"

I raked a hand through my hair. "Nothing. It doesn't matter. Has my uncle sent word?"

"Yes. You are to meet him at the stables in two hours."

Two hours. Plenty of time to see Paxton's family. We left the room together then parted ways at the end of the hall.

"Your highness." He dipped his chin. "Safe travels. And good luck."

"Thank you, Maxwell."

❦

Paxton's family lived at the south end of the city. I'd met his parents before we'd left for the war, but his siblings had been too young to see him off. Two brothers and a sister, if memory served. How devastated they all must be. I held Paxton in high regard as one of the finest men I'd ever known, soldier or not. The world would be a darker place without him.

My steps slowed as Paxton's house came into view. I suddenly had no idea what to say. A simple apology seemed wholly inadequate. Perhaps I could offer to extend his benefit.

I approached the door and straightened my jacket then raised my fist to knock. The door swung open before I got the chance. A small girl stood on the other side, regarding me with open curiosity. Her cornflower blue eyes widened in recognition and her mouth fell open. I bowed with a friendly smile. "Milady."

She giggled as only a young child could and curtsied. "Your highness." She lisped horribly through the large gap in her front teeth.

My smile broadened. "Is your father at home? Or your mother?"

"Please wait here." Her brown curls bounced on her shoulders as she disappeared into the house, leaving me standing on the step.

She returned moments later, towing a reluctant young man behind her. "See, Alec. He's here."

"I told you, Maddie. I don't believe the prince–"

"Good morning." I forced brightness into my voice.

"Your … highness," Alec stammered, cheeks red as he stared at me. Maddie tugged on his hand and he jerked into a bow then straightened. "What … who …?"

I laughed under my breath. "I'm here to see your parents. Are they available?"

He shook his head, biting his lip as if in some kind of trouble.

"They went to visit our aunt," Maddie supplied. "They'll be back tomorrow."

"You have an older brother, yes?"

"He's in Iredale, your highness." Alec's somber tone said more than those five words ever could.

Knowing Paxton, I should've guessed or at least suspected his younger brother would join the king's army. I swallowed hard. "When?"

"Just last week, your highness. After …"

My heart twisted, knowing full well what had happened. "I see. Well, please tell them I stopped by. To offer my condolences."

Maddie's eyes filled with tears, but the young man stood even straighter, clearly proud of both his older brothers. "Thank you."

I handed him a pouch of coins, which he took with a solemn expression. Too overwhelmed to say more, I bowed and left them gaping after me. I'd write to Paxton's parents once we settled in Iredale to let them know I'd do everything in my power to keep their son safe. *Broken promises.*

After a brief goodbye to my family, I headed to the stables to wait. The horses calmed me, as they always did, and I wandered among the stalls, telling them my secrets. Their mournful eyes regarded me with quiet sympathy while shadows trailed me, a welcome presence.

The general arrived, and the stable hands all rushed to do his bidding, saddling horses and loading bags. I pitied them, though I could easily sympathize. When the general said jump, a smart man jumped and didn't stop until he gave the order. His shrewd gaze missed nothing as he supervised the activity.

"Sir."

"Captain."

Two words, the entire extent of our conversation. I hadn't expected or wanted anything more. My general first, my uncle tenth. Or eleventh. In truth, I barely knew him, at least on a familial level. He'd never bounced me on his knee or patted me on the head. But he had taught me battle strategy and leadership, along with a myriad of other skills I would forever be grateful for.

The horses saddled, the general swung up, followed by his men. I took my time, gazing out over the vast castle grounds. Would I ever see it again? Anxious dread curled in my gut. Whatever my uncle had in store for me, it wouldn't be good. I shook my head. Nothing to be done, except bear it.

~ Chapter Twelve ~

Four days later, our large party arrived in Iredale, the small village nestled at the base of the northern garrison. The garrison itself didn't have a name. The civilians simply referred to it as Iredale. More creative and clever names had been suggested based on the forbidding black stone walls, desolate wilderness, and jaw clenching cold. Hell's Rock topped my list of favorites, a term coined by a cadet in my training unit. I smiled at the memory as we clopped through the garrison's iron gates. They closed behind us with a bone-jarring clank, like a dungeon cell. Still as forlorn and soul crushing as ever. Hell's Rock, indeed.

I climbed from the saddle then turned in a slow circle as an icy wind blew past. My nose had already numbed to the cold, yet my eyes watered. I shivered as a cadet jogged to a stop at my side, saluting sharply even though my cloak covered my jacket, including the captain's badge.

"Sir." His voice cracked like a sheet of thin ice.

"Yes?"

"The general asked me to escort you to your quarters, sir."

"Lead the way."

He strode off toward the barracks, his gait awkward as if he'd only recently grown into his legs. Young, then. Probably not much past thirteen. I swallowed hard. These boys had no business serving in the army. They should be at home with their families, not having the life beaten out of them by some heavy-handed instructor. The training here hardened a soldier, prepared him for battle. But it also broke the spirit and severed the boy from the man. The boy I'd been no longer existed.

The cadet led me up a steep flight of stone stairs and down a dim corridor. He stopped at the last door and turned to me. "Sir."

"Thank you."

He nodded and flashed a crooked smile before loping off. I stepped into the spartan room and shed my cloak, a familiar sense of belonging washing over me. Despite the dungeon-like atmosphere, I'd always felt at home here, or anywhere with the army. My brothers in arms treated me as a soldier, not a spoiled, entitled prince.

Boot steps thundered down the stairs before the dinner bell had even finished pealing. I straightend my jacket and joined the fray. Food here paled in comparison to dinner at the castle, but constant training and grueling work made for hungry soldiers. I sauntered into the dining hall, jostled from behind by men eager to scarf down their meals. They formed an orderly line, however, and waited patiently for the cook to spoon tonight's selection onto their plates.

My uncle had made himself scarce, of course. He always dined in his room, presumably alone. He never bonded with the men the way I did. Perhaps because mourning a stranger came more easily than mourning a friend. The theory had merit, yet I couldn't bring myself to follow his example. Whatever my uncle had planned for me involved these men. The sooner I got to know them, the better.

I glanced around the large space now teeming with cadets, and spotted my young escort sitting with a group of nearly identical boys. All fresh-faced and grinning around mouthfuls of food. I crossed the room and stood at their table. Conversation ceased as they shot to their feet, saluting sharply.

"Sir," they droned in unison.

"Please." I motioned for them to sit.

They sat as one and stared at me, some open-mouthed, some with mild curiosity. My young escort scooted down the bench to make room for me. "You can sit here, sir."

I nodded and took my seat, meeting each pair of eyes in turn. "I'm Captain Ellsbree."

A ginger-haired cadet nodded with abundant enthusiasm. "We know who you are, Captain Ellsbree. Everyone's been talking about you. And Kieran told us he showed you to your room. Sir."

I arched a brow as my gaze slid to Kieran. "Indeed. And what has everyone been saying?"

Kieran suddenly found his food very interesting. His throat bobbed as he swallowed. "Nothing bad, sir," he stammered as he raised his head. "I swear it. It's just you're a hero and … "

I held up a hand and he snapped his mouth shut. I took no pleasure in their hero worship. If anything, it reminded me of all I'd lost. "No need to worry, cadet. I'm only teasing." His lips twitched as if he wanted to smile but thought it might break a rule. I forced a grin, hoping the gesture would slice the tension. Nervous laughter skipped around the table as I turned to Kieran. "Well met, Kieran. Where are you from?"

"Evanston, sir."

His gaze found mine and recognition jolted through me. "You look just like your brother Paxton." This young man, this boy had lost his brother. Because I hadn't kept my promise. How could I look him in the eye now? Or ever again?

Grief and guilt collided like storm-tossed waves crashing on a rocky shore, My throat tightened with emotion. I swallowed past it and faced the consequences. "I'm so sorry, Kieran. Truly."

He nodded and turned away as the dining hall door opened. Soldiers bolted to their feet, saluting as my uncle strode in. His eyes darted around the room, then his steely gaze landed on me. I stood rooted to the spot as he sauntered toward the table, his mouth set in a grim line.

"Captain Ellsbree. A word."

"Sir." I followed him from the room, glancing over my shoulder at Kieran's grief-stricken face as I walked out the door.

Night had fallen, the sky so black I couldn't tell where the garrison walls ended, and it began. Another disorienting manipulation of this place.

We entered the council chamber. I remained standing while the general sat at the head of the long table. Shadows hovered nearby, offering solace in their darkness.

"I reassigned you to this post at your father's request."

My face remained blank even as my mind whirled.

"He is concerned about your … health." He angled his head as he studied me, likely looking for a weakness to exploit. He would not find one.

"I'm fine, sir."

"Taryn," he said, using my name for the first time in my life. "Even I can see you are far from fine. And I know what you're going through. I've been a soldier since before you were born and have seen things you could not even begin to imagine. They still haunt me to this day." I clenched my jaw to keep my mouth shut. "Your father and I both feel a change of scenery will be good for you. And the post here is an easy one. Training, which I know you enjoy and excel at."

I must have been truly broken to warrant such compassion from him. Yet the idea of commanding another company turned my stomach, even if only to train them, not lead them to their deaths on the battlefield.

"Your men are expecting you at first light tomorrow, east training field."

"Understood." I pivoted on my heel and headed for the door.

"And Taryn." I glanced over my shoulder. "It does get easier."

I couldn't have agreed less and strode from the room, sucking in the frigid night air until it burned my lungs. I raked a hand through my hair and willed my heart to stop pounding, my pulse to stop racing.

Darkness spread through my body like a sickness, devouring me from the inside out. I clenched my fists and held in a scream of frustration. Would I ever be free of this nightmare? The unending, relentless pressure in my head? I just wanted it to stop, to leave me alone and let me piece myself back together. I craned my neck, beseeching the stars for the strength to fight, to slay the demons. *Save me. Please.*

I sank to my knees, ignoring the cold seeping through my pants. I begged and pleaded, silently wailing for relief, for emptiness. Anything. *Please*

… Surrender.

I hung my head, struggling and thrashing against the torment, yet my weakened soul could no longer bear it. *No. Please, no.*

… Surrender.

Defeated at last, I surrendered.

~ Chapter Thirteen ~

The deafening roar of cannon fire catapulted me from sleep. Heart thundering, I panted in the blackness of my bunk. Only a dream. I shook my head to clear the violent images, even though they were branded on my brain. I took several deep breaths and eased up onto my elbows. A brief shudder ran down my spine and I squeezed my eyes shut.

Stop. Ever so slowly, the pain receded, leaving my heart bruised and beaten, yet whole. I opened my eyes, marveling at the eerie calmness at my center, as if I'd finally managed to reassemble all my broken pieces. I tested the strength of the bonds. Not perfect but they'd hold. For now.

I leaned back on the pillow and debated whether to try to sleep. The night beyond my window loomed black as pitch. I turned onto my side and stared into the shadowed depths of my room, willing my mind to distance itself from the memories. Think of something, anything else. Horses. Wine. Women. *Grace.*

I hadn't thought much about her since arriving. Interesting how the mere memory of pain brought her to mind. If only I'd had the chance to truly get to know her outside of my affliction. But we'd met and then fought, and I'd pushed her away as if she were nothing more than an unwanted toy. A sense of longing bloomed in my heart for what might have been. But I would never know.

I lay in the dark, thinking of Grace and home and whatever I could to keep my mind occupied until dawn finally broke. The breakfast bell rang, and I couldn't get out of bed and dressed fast enough. I bolted down the stairs, into the dining hall then ate alone, quickly, before rushing out to meet my men.

The early morning sun washed the training field in pale yellow light. I stood at its edge, my breath fogging in the frigid air. This place held all the appeal of a frozen wasteland. Then again, nothing here reminded me of the recent past. Except Paxton's brother. I frowned in his direction as he and his fellow cadets strode toward the field. How could I command him every single day, knowing I had caused his brother's death? I owed it to Paxton to try.

The men halted then formed a straight line. Shivering, but at attention. Someone had given them the basics, at least. Time to find out what they didn't know. "Good morning."

"Sir."

"Today we're going to drill. Hard. I want to see what you're made of." Thirteen pairs of eyes tracked my movements as I prowled down the line. "I will test you, challenge you, and probably hurt you. But in the end, you will thank me for it. You will be soldiers, ready for any battle at any time." I scanned their faces, each one radiating only fierce determination and unwavering obedience. "Understood?"

"Sir. Yes, sir."

"Good. Now let's get started."

Icy wind tore the words from my mouth as I barked commands at my young company. In truth, more boys than men. My uncle had charged me with training the youngest of the cadets, some of them still pups, all of them full to bursting with eager innocence. Gods, had I ever been so earnest?

I strolled the length of the training field, studying each cadet's movements. Sure-footed or sloppy. Graceful or clumsy. It didn't really matter. By the time I finished training them, they'd all move the same, fight the same. *Kill the same.*

I paused to watch Kieran spar with a cadet at least a head taller. Not exactly an even match. But the boy held his own. Impressed, I nodded encouragement. A lunge, a parry, a feint. All solidly executed. His sparring partner, however, tripped on his own too-large feet and went sprawling face first into the mud. The rest of the company erupted in juvenile laughter and I barely caught myself before joining them.

I scowled a reprimand instead and the mood fell. "What did he do wrong, cadets? Can anyone tell me?" Shuffling feet and nervous glances were the only replies. I sighed heavily. "Kieran. What do you think?"

His face flushed crimson as he stammered. "I don't know, sir. Maybe he just slipped?"

"Are you asking me or telling me, cadet?"

"Telling you. Sir."

"Do you want to know what I think?" I glanced at each of them, noting with satisfaction the curiosity alight in their eyes. A hunger to learn could be just as important as the desire to win. I paced in front of him, hands clasped behind my back. "I think you are the better fighter."

His jaw dropped. "Me, sir?"

"Yes, you." I smiled at my star pupil. "Cadets. This is an excellent first lesson. Even though Kieran and his opponent were of different heights and weights, he still won. Because he turned a disadvantage into an advantage. You never know who you will face on the battlefield. You must always be prepared to fight someone bigger than you, stronger than you. And win."

"Sir. Yes, sir!"

Encourage a man and he will respect you. Punish him and he will fear you. Fear does not command men, but they will follow a respected leader anywhere.

The midday bell rang out across the field. My stomach rumbled in response. Teaching turned out to be just as arduous as learning. "Dismissed." Weapons clanged onto the sodden grass, and the men rushed past me, talking in excited bursts. I followed at a distance, not wanting to intrude or interrupt. Kieran stopped a few paces ahead then turned back. "Is something wrong, cadet?"

"Sir. No, sir."

I arched a brow. "What can I do for you?"

"I …"

I clapped him on the shoulder. "Speak up, boy."

His slim throat bobbed as he swallowed. "We'd like you to eat with us, sir. Only if you want to. You don't have to, of course. But we thought–"

"It would be an honor. Lead the way."

His eyes grew round then he beamed a smile, and we walked to the mess hall in silence. I laughed under my breath. It had taken no small amount of courage for him to talk to me at all, let alone maintain a conversation. I still found it difficult speaking to my superior officers.

The hall echoed with the sound of raised voices. I paused in the doorway, my gaze sweeping across the assembled mass. I had yet to meet anyone other than my company, including the other captains. I spotted them sitting together at a table in the corner, nothing but mean eyes and hard faces. "Go on ahead, Kieran. I'll catch up to you." He nodded and went to stand in the long line while I sauntered over to the captains' table. "Well met, gentlemen."

Three heads turned toward me. One in particular seemed to enjoy my intrusion the least and sneered. "Ellsbree. Thought I heard something about you being here."

"Spencer. Glad to see you found a comfortable spot for yourself."

His scorn nearly cracked his face. Some people never changed, Spencer being one of them. "What do you want?"

I shrugged. "Simply to say hello." The others viewed me with open hostility even though we'd never met. "Taryn Ellsbree," I bowed with a smile.

"They know who you are," Spencer growled.

What could I expect from him here? The same sort of torment he and his cronies had subjected me to during our training days? I hoped not. I'd survived those first few weeks by sheer luck. "And I'm sure we'll be fast friends. For now, I'll leave you to your conspirator's meal."

I turned on my heel and walked away, shaking my head. The situation had changed since our days as cadets. Now I held the coveted position as the most decorated captain, thanks to my recent success. My steps faltered. The victory may have catapulted me to hero status but at great cost. A price I never wanted to pay again. No amount of fame or adulation would be worth it.

~ Chapter Fourteen ~

Grace massaged the back of her neck, sore from bending over so many books. A huge stack of them laid at her elbow, yet to be read. Her continuing education into the healing arts meant more time spent in the library, poring over ancient texts, memorizing countless remedies and mentally cataloging hundreds of ailments. All so she could count herself among the best. Not just as an apprentice but as a fully trained, expertly mentored healer. With Cara's recommendation, she hoped to obtain a position of importance, perhaps even in the castle itself. The royal family seemed to always need good healers, and Grace planned to be better than most. If only she could finish all this gods' forsaken reading without falling asleep in the process.

Her jaw cracked as she yawned, again. She'd stayed up well past moonrise last night and had lurched out of bed at dawn this morning, back to the library, bleary-eyed and sleep deprived. But it would all be worth it once she earned the recognition she so greatly deserved. And yearned for. Her only shortcoming thus far had been her complete and utter failure with Taryn. When she'd first heard he'd gone to the northern garrison, she assumed she'd driven him away. Foolish, of course. If anything, he would have driven her away. Far away. Yet she couldn't help but bear some responsibility for the way he'd so eagerly picked up and left. Natalie continued to reassure her Taryn would always be Taryn. As if the simple fact explained his behavior entirely.

Grace refused to be placated so easily. As a dedicated healer, she felt heartsick at the thought of him in the frozen north, alone, in the state he'd been in. Part of her longed to find him, if only to make sure he'd arrived safely. But she needed to be here for her father. With a heavy sigh, she closed the book in front of her and reached for another. At this rate, she'd be an old crone before she finished.

The library door banged open and she jumped in her seat. Natalie strode toward her, all casual elegance and ethereal grace. If she hadn't become such an amazing friend, Grace would have hated her. But they'd bonded even more since Taryn left and Grace couldn't imagine her life without Natalie's carefree demeanor to lighten her mood. "Gods, Natalie," she breathed as the princess glided to a stop at her table. "You scared me to death."

"My apologies, dear Grace. I'm just so excited!"

Grace arched a brow. "Why, exactly?"

"Lord Preston is coming!"

"Who is Lord Preston and why do we care?" Grace stood to gather her belongings, minus the gigantic stack of books.

Natalie's mouth fell open. "You don't know who Lord Preston is?"

Grace held in her sigh. Of course she didn't. "No."

"He's only the father of the two most eligible men in Evanston, maybe even the entire kingdom."

"So, wouldn't you be more excited if *they* were coming?"

Natalie's eyes sparkled with childish delight as she looped her arm through Grace's. "But they are!"

Grace frowned. Her skin crawled uncomfortably whenever Natalie used words like 'lord' and 'eligible'. They only served as brutal reminders of her current lowly station. Natalie never seemed to notice or care. She simply towed Grace along to every dinner and party where she sat on the sidelines while her friend effortlessly flit from one handsome young man to the next. Grace wanted to see only one handsome young man. Taryn. A fantasy without even the slightest chance of happening anytime soon. Perhaps never.

They stepped out into the late afternoon sunshine. Grace cringed at the bright light, having spent so much time in the library's dim interior. "Well, I'm happy you're happy, I suppose," Grace admitted with a small sigh. "I'm sure you'll have a marvelous time."

Natalie slid a sly gaze her way. "Yes, *we* will."

Grace stopped and stared at Natalie, open-mouthed. *Not again.* "Natalie. I simply cannot attend another one of your … functions. It's exhausting."

"But I need you there." Natalie pouted, which only made her look lovelier. "And did you hear what I said? He has two sons. I cannot possibly handle them both."

Grace knew better and rolled her eyes. "Natalie …"

She held up a royal hand and pulled rank. "As your princess, I command it."

Grace's stomach turned at the thought, but she simply nodded. She couldn't do anything about it. When Natalie wanted something, she always got it. So far Grace had come out relatively unharmed after her escapades, but Natalie's devious grin worried her. She had a feeling this wouldn't be one of those times.

❇

Grace hated being right, at least when it concerned Natalie. True to form, the princess left her stranded in the dining hall while she danced with not one, but both of Lord Preston's handsome sons. Their smiles dazzled as they took turns spinning her around the dance floor, eyes alight with mischief. She could hardly blame Natalie for her exuberance over their presence here at court.

She sighed heavily, wondering not for the first time what it would feel like to be royal. If only for a minute. She pushed the thought away with a firm hand. Enough wallowing, stewing in jealousy. And what did she have to be jealous about anyway? She didn't care about eligible young lords, despite their easy grins and chiseled jaws. She couldn't.

Closing her eyes, she leaned her head against the wall. Gods, she needed rest, yet she had so much reading to do. The reminder made her groan.

"Something wrong?" a deep male voice drawled at her shoulder.

Her eyes snapped open to find Lord Preston's older son smiling down at her. She swallowed hard, acutely aware of high station. "Not at all."

"It's Grace, isn't it?"

She nodded and bit her lip. "And you're William?" Her lessons conveniently omitted how to properly speak to a young lord, especially one whose dark blue gaze sent her pulse racing. *Holy gods.*

"Yes, but please call me Will. All my friends do." He turned toward the dance floor. "The princess is a very good dancer."

"She is," Grace agreed, though it came out more squeak than speech.

His eyes found hers again. "And you, Grace? Do you dance?"

"When the occasion calls for it."

He arched a dark brow. "And does this occasion call for it?"

"It depends entirely on you. My lord."

He snorted. "I am no one's lord. I'm simply a young man asking a beautiful young woman to dance. If she'll have me."

He held out his hand and Grace stared at it, hesitating for a thousand different reasons. Taryn's face suddenly loomed in her mind, so far beyond her reach she almost laughed. He'd left her, tossed her aside and left her. But this man stood right here, not miles away in some frozen wilderness, likely having forgotten all about her. She placed her shaking hand in his steady one and followed him to the dance floor.

~ Chapter Fifteen ~

My eyes flew open as a heavy weight clamped down over my mouth. I flailed for my dagger in the darkness then stilled when a blade pressed against my windpipe.

"Move and you'll be sorry," Spencer hissed in my ear.

I almost gagged behind his hand and he lifted it away yet left the blade at my throat. A figure lurked behind him in the shadows, holding a lamp. Spencer's face shifted eerily in the low light.

"What …"

"I wouldn't talk if I were you. This blade is wicked sharp. Shame to see your pretty throat all scarred up." He chuckled under his sour breath and I blinked in response.

"Spencer, we need to hurry," a voice floated from the darkness.

"Shut up, Mason," he barked over his shoulder.

He turned to me. The look on his face sent a surge of adrenaline through my blood, followed quickly by anger. Spencer had always been a bully. And bullies only wanted to see their victims afraid. So, I simply refused to show fear. Instead, I smiled.

Clearly thrown off guard, he lowered the blade enough for me to grab his wrist without spilling my blood in the process. I applied a bone-crushing amount of pressure and the blade clattered to the floor. "Whatever you're thinking of doing, don't." I glared at Mason and he wisely fled the room, dropping the lamp.

Spencer whimpered briefly. "Ellsbree. You're going to break my wrist."

My smile turned feral, a wolfish baring of teeth. "Your comfort is not my concern," I growled. "What I do want to know, however, is how stupid are you? Truly?"

"Very stupid." He swallowed hard and licked his lips. "I meant it as a prank. You know, like we used to do."

I snorted. Spencer's previous idea of a prank often landed me in the infirmary. I slowly sat up, still gripping his wrist. He fell to his knees as I loomed over him.

Not once in my military career had I ever used my royal status to pull rank. But he'd assaulted me. In my room. An act of treason by my count. "I am your prince. I could have your head for this."

His face paled and a waxy sheen of sweat appeared on his wide forehead. "Please, Ells … your highness. I didn't mean any harm, I swear it."

I studied him a moment longer, mostly to see him squirm then released his wrist. He collapsed to the floor, cradling his arm. "Don't ever do something like this again. Understood?" He nodded vigorously. "Get out." Wasting no time, he scrambled up and bolted from the room, bumping into a startled cadet in the hallway.

"Sir?"

I raked a hand through my hair. "Come in, Kieran."

"Is everything all right? I thought I heard—"

"I'm fine. What brings you here at this hour?"

"The general, sir. He'd like a word."

"Now?"

He shrugged his narrow shoulders. "I just deliver the messages, sir."

I sighed heavily and climbed to my feet. "I'll be down shortly. You don't need to wait."

"Sir." He saluted then left me in the semi-darkness to compose myself.

Gods. What had Spencer been playing at? I'd assumed he'd outgrown such juvenile tricks but apparently not. Hopefully, I'd scared him straight.

I pulled on pants, boots and my jacket then marched through the pre-dawn stillness. A bone-deep chill had crept into the stone walls. Winter would soon arrive, with it the bleakness of continuous snowstorms. At least no battles could be waged during the crippling cold, and if no one died from exposure, all would be well. Now I only worried about my uncle's summons. In the dead of night.

A sliver of light shone under his door. I hesitated, my fist raised to knock. The last time I'd spoken to him, he'd ordered me here. There were few worse places he could send me, though I wouldn't put it past him to banish me to the outer regions, just for spite. I knocked.

"Come." He sat behind his desk, frowning at a stack of papers in his hand. He glanced up as I entered. "Ah, Taryn. Please. Have a seat."

"Sir." I sat, heart thumping like a war drum.

"Thank you for coming. I know it's late."

I nodded even as alarm bells of all shapes and sizes clanged a warning. My uncle never thanked anyone for anything. And his tone, usually so laced with contempt, sounded almost pleasant. He smiled, and I gripped the arms of my chair hard enough to crack the aged wood. Surely the axe suspended above my head would fall at any moment. I clenched my jaw to keep from adjusting my jacket collar.

"How are the cadets faring?"

"Sir?"

"The training. Are they progressing?"

"As expected, sir."

"Any issues?"

"None."

"Very good. How soon can they be ready to fight?"

A muscle twitched under my eye. "Sir?"

The pleasantness melted from his face and he sat back. "The western border has been attacked."

"Attacked? By whom?"

"General Stark."

"But … how? We just …"

He sighed wearily. "I know. And we lost too many soldiers fighting his armies at Haverton. Our numbers are low, our men spread too thin. I can't call them all back."

"Our other borders would be defenseless."

"Precisely."

"Which leaves … The cadets."

He nodded in sober resignation. "I'm afraid so."

Holy gods. These boys were nowhere near ready for battle, let alone war. But if we didn't do something immediately, war it would be. A shudder ran down my spine.

"I need them ready as soon as possible, Taryn."

Too soon. "Yes, sir."

"Dismissed."

I willed steel into my legs as I stood then walked out the door, down the hall, up the stairs. I climbed all the way to the roof. A small balcony provided a lookout point over the yawning abyss of the dark field below. I stepped around the railing, my toes hanging off the edge as I contemplated my options. The one in front of me appealed the most. A simple jump, a careless fall.

… End it all.

Shadows hovered at my shoulder, offering no advice or wisdom. On my own. As always.

~ Chapter Sixteen ~

My breath plumed in a white cloud carried with the frigid breeze blowing across the field. The company lumbered about in the frozen mud, limbs heavy with cold. We couldn't train outdoors much longer. I glanced at the lowering sky. Snow tonight. And a lot of it.

I still hadn't told my men of the impending battle, the march through the icy tundra to meet the enemy. To these boys, wars were fought by heroes, sung about in songs they'd heard since birth. They hadn't yet faced its harsh reality. I closed my eyes, clenching and unclenching my gloved hands, begging the tremors to stop. Show no fear, no weakness. I had to lead these men to victory, yet death waited. For us all.

"Captain Ellsbree, sir."

I opened my eyes at Kieran's soft voice. "Yes?"

"The midday bell rang, sir."

"Dismissed, then. Go eat."

He hesitated as if on the verge of saying more but then loped off to spread the word among his brothers. Soon the entire company had left for the hall. I stood on the field, cloak flapping behind me as I stared at their retreating backs. How could I do this to them? Some were but half my age. And Kieran. I could not be responsible for his death, yet what choice did I have? Orders were orders.

Shoulders slumped, I retreated to sulk and brood in my room, skills I'd recently honed to perfection. I opened my door and stepped on an envelope. I didn't recognize the feminine handwriting at first glance. I lit a lamp then studied it in the bright light. I tore the envelope open and pulled out a single piece of paper.

My dear Prince Taryn,

I hope this letter finds you well and warm! Natalie tells me the north is cruel this time of year and will become even more so once winter arrives. I am preparing like mad to take my final exam. I think I've read every book in the library. My studies leave me little time for anything, other than thinking of you. Though we parted on uncertain terms, I do miss you. Perhaps I'll find a way to visit. In the meantime, know you're in my thoughts and in my heart. Always.

Yours,
Grace

I swallowed the lump in my throat. We hadn't seen each other in weeks, yet she'd known just what I needed to hear. A few caring words rendered me speechless with gratitude. And an acute yearning to see her again. I sighed heavily and tucked the letter into my pocket. The chances of going home, let alone reuniting with Grace were slim to none. And even then, I'd likely be dead. Or would rather be.

The assembly bell pealed with a forlorn echo through my room. I hurried to the square where my uncle stood surrounded by the other captains. He caught my eye and motioned for me to join him. I stood at his side, waiting for the cadets to file into rank.

Once they'd lined up, he strode forward. "Cadets. The day has come for you to prove yourselves. A battle rages on the western border and our king has commanded we march to relieve our brothers fighting on the front lines." He paused, scanning the gathered men and I turned to my company. All thirteen stared straight ahead, jaws tight, backs rigid.

"I know you are young and untried. But there is no greater test than war. You have been well-trained, and I am confident you will exceed my expectations and bring honor to your fellow soldiers and your king."

A rousing speech, delivered with such passion even I felt stirred to action. The familiar itch of impending violence skittered up my spine.

"We march at dawn. You have the rest of the day to prepare."

Either frozen in fear or in shock, every man stood his ground. I turned to the general then back again. "Sir," I whispered. "What–"

"They want to hear from you, Taryn. As their prince."

I blinked at this change. My brothers in arms had never treated me as anything other than a soldier. I'd never wanted anything else yet they seemed to need something from me. A word, a gesture. A promise I couldn't make. Or keep. I cleared my throat and stepped forward. "To victory."

"To victory!" The shouted reply rang against the stone walls.

The general nodded. "Dismissed."

And then we went to war.

~ Chapter Seventeen ~

"What do you mean, *war*?" Grace struggled to accept the horrific news, even as the words echoed in her head.

Natalie sank onto the couch in her sitting room, clearly as shaken as Grace. She shook her head, twisting her hands in her lap. "It sounds impossible, yet my father assures me it's the truth. He'd hoped to thwart it at the western border. But he hasn't heard from my uncle in weeks. He fears the worst."

"And Taryn? What if he–"

"I don't know, Grace." Her eyes shone with unshed tears.

"What can we do? There must be something …"

"We're not soldiers. We cannot do anything except wait."

Grace could not, would not simply wait. There had to be a way to help. She refused to stay here while Taryn could be hurt somewhere else. "I have to go. To find him."

Natalie's eyes widened, dwarfing the rest of her features. "Are you mad?" she whispered.

"I'm a healer, Natalie. This is what I do. I've never been more sure of anything in my life."

"How will you get there? How will you find them? Grace, surely you can't–"

"Yes, I can. With your help."

She snorted. "I cannot possibly help with such an idiotic idea. I refuse to send you to your death. And what of Will?"

Grace bit her lip. She'd enjoyed Will's company the past few weeks while his brother enjoyed Natalie's. Grace had developed lukewarm feelings for him, though she sensed his feelings for her ran hotter. At least it seemed so every time they were alone, when he pressed her for more than she could give.

But she hadn't made any promises and neither had he. Deep down she knew the reason for her hesitation. Taryn. He'd held a special place in her heart since the moment they met. And with this recent news, she had no doubt what she needed to do. Despite her station and inexperience, her duty as a healer demanded she try. If she could help, she would. She just had to get there.

She sat down next to Natalie and took her hand. "Natalie, my dear friend. I beg you. Please help me do this. I cannot sit here while Taryn could be hurt. Or worse. And think of the others. They may need me as well. Please."

Natalie bit her lip. "And your studies? Your final exam?"

"It can all wait. And my father will be fine on his own for a few days. "

Natalie sucked in a breath, stared at Grace for a brief moment then let it out slowly. "What do you need me to do?"

Grace smiled. "Thank you."

"Yes, well. Don't thank me yet."

Grace's smile only widened.

❊

Two days later, Grace's horse snorted in protest as they climbed up another mound of frozen, snow-covered earth. She paused at the top and pulled out the frayed map Natalie had given her. She'd consulted it so often parts of it were illegible. But the remaining ink pointed the way to Taryn. Or at least where he'd been. She'd ridden hard, barely stopping to sleep, praying with every hoofbeat she'd reach him in time. Now she begged the gods for one more day or even an hour with him.

A few miles of riding later, Iredale's high walls loomed dark against the graying sky. Natalie had warned her about the starkness of the landscape, the brutal look and feel of the place but it still stole her breath. Evil, steeped in violence. Ravens called from bare branched trees lining the narrow streets, lending an air of foreboding to the already eerie silence. Where were the citizens? Not a soul to be seen or heard anywhere among the dilapidated structures.

A shudder ran down her spine as she continued through the ramshackle village to the garrison beyond. Its gates yawned open like the sharp-toothed maw of some mythical beast. Another shudder, this one violent enough to spook her horse. "Easy," she croaked, more to calm her own skittish heart. She slid from the saddle and eased through the gate. The courtyard beyond seemed full of ghosts as she slowly walked across. A quick glance from one side to the other, and her heart sank. The army had moved on. She'd expected this, but it still reduced her optimism to a new low.

"Miss?" Startled, she spun to find an old man approaching from around the far corner. "Are you lost?" His lined face radiated concern.

She cleared her throat. "No. I'm looking for Captain Ellsbree."

He shook his bald head, a solemn cast to his features. "They've moved on, miss. There's a war brewing, I've heard said. On the western border."

"You heard correctly. It's why I'm here."

"And how do you know Captain Ellsbree?"

"I ..." She fumbled for a plausible explanation for her connection to Taryn. The truth seemed a breach of confidentiality. A small lie, then. "I am friends with the princess."

He nodded and his lips curved into a warm smile. "Ah, young Natalie. And how is she these days?"

"Fine, sir, but I need your help. Do you know where the captain went? Where I can find him?"

"The whole garrison marched out weeks ago. They're likely halfway to the front line by now."

She didn't think her heart could sink any lower, and yet it did, all the way to the pit of her stomach where it landed with a dull thud. She'd never catch them, not without help. And though this old man had done her a kindness, he certainly couldn't guide her.

"Are you all right, miss?"

She swallowed hard and forced a smile. "Yes, I'm fine. It's just so important I find Captain Ellsbree. And I fear I'll be too late."

"Not at all." His watery eyes twinkled, giving her hope. "It's but a few days' ride to the checkpoint. You might catch them there, if you hurry."

Now her heart soared, rising from the ashes of her grief. "Truly?"

"The army would've travelled on foot through the forest, but you can take the main road. Much faster."

"And you know where the checkpoint is? I have a map. Can you show me?"

"Better yet, I'll send my grandson with you. He's been there and back several times delivering messages and supplies. And beautiful young women, it seems."

He chuckled, and she laughed along with him. "I would greatly appreciate it, sir. Thank you."

"My pleasure. Why don't you wait in the mess hall? It's not much warmer but at least it's out of this blasted wind.

Through those doors there." He pointed a crooked finger toward the far corner of the garrison wall. "I'll send Rafe in, and then you can be on your way."

She nodded mutely, not trusting herself to speak without bursting into tears. He shuffled off, his tattered cloak flapping behind him. The kindness of strangers, indeed.

She hurried to the mess hall and stepped inside, wrinkling her nose at the stale smell of too many men in an enclosed space. Still, the thick stone walls provided ample relief from the biting wind, and she sank onto the nearest bench to wait.

~ Chapter Eighteen ~

Winter arrived like a slap to the face, throwing freezing winds and biting sleet into my eyes as I led the company across the rugged territory west of Iredale. The men trudged behind me, as they'd been doing for miles upon miles through snowdrifts as tall as my shoulder, nary a whimper among them. Of course their lips were frozen, and their lungs would have been had they opened their mouths to do anything other than breathe.

We'd lost sight of my uncle and the rest of the men two days ago. They'd simply vanished into the blinding white. But we'd rendezvous soon enough when we reached the checkpoint. If we could find it. How much farther could it be? I paused to adjust the pack slung across my shoulders, cursing the lack of horses. But their bulky bodies wouldn't fit amongst the tightly packed trees of this bloody forest and we couldn't risk traveling in the open on the main road.

I called a halt to the march when the light started to fade. A collective sigh of relief rippled through the frosty air, and the men fell into the familiar rhythm of setting up camp, clearing an area wide enough for sleeping and cooking, yet small enough to corral the fire's meager warmth.

Kieran approached with an offer to help, as had become his habit. I hadn't asked, yet here he stood, loyal to a fault. I managed a small smile despite my frozen face. "Kieran," I rasped.

"Sir. Can I help with your tent?"

I shook my head. "Take care of yourself. And get something to eat, for gods' sake."

He flashed a crooked grin then bounded away. I watched him go, praying as I had each night for his safety. To keep all of them alive. Unfortunately, the gods have a wicked sense of humor.

A lone wolf howled, the mournful sound echoing in my soul. I envied him. To be alone in a world where anyone could be taken at any time. Yet my pack needed a leader. Someone to protect them. I'd die a hundred times over if it meant their safety.

❋

The first rays of dawn's light had barely penetrated the thick canopy overhead when Kieran called outside my tent.

"Captain Ellsbree?"

I groaned and scrubbed a hand over my face, rough with days' worth of stubble. "Yes, Kieran."

"The men are ready, sir."

This early? Gods. "Thank you."

His boots crunched on ice-crusted leaves as he walked away. I lurched from bed to peer outside at the world beyond. Nothing but a blank canvas, as if all color had leeched away in the night. I packed my bedroll and tent then shouldered it in the freezing chill. The men stamped their feet, blowing air into their cupped hands while they awaited my command. To move out, to march on. "To victory."

One labored step at a time, we made our way farther and farther into the wilderness. Beasts stalked us, their predator's eyes tracking our trek, yet they kept their distance while I kept my hand on the hilt of my dagger.

By midday, the faint smell of smoke wafted from the checkpoint just over the next ridge, and a weak cheer went up among the men. My pace quickened at the thought of reuniting with the rest of the garrison. There would be more food and more warmth.

We scaled the ridge, climbing higher into the endless sky. But on the other side, nothing. Or at least no men. Just scattered supplies, smoldering ashes. Deserted tents.

The group clattered to a stop behind me, Kieran at my elbow a heartbeat later. "Captain," he breathed. "Where are the others?"

"I don't know." I scanned the area as a dark sense of uneasiness washed over me. He started forward, but I grabbed his arm. "Wait here."

I shrugged my pack to the ground and drew my dagger. Chest tight with dread, I stepped toward the nearest fire. I knelt and fingered the outer ring of stones. Still warm.

... Warm as blood.

I squeezed my eyes shut. Images flashed. Battlefield. Bodies. Death. *Not this time.*

I opened my eyes and took a shuddering breath and a staggering step forward. Then another until I'd walked the camp's perimeter. Not a soul in sight, save for a curious animal watching from a nearby tree. He offered no help, so I turned back to the men. "It's empty but hasn't been for long. Spread out. Stay alert and search in pairs. Report back here in one hour."

The group dispersed yet I lingered, pawing through supplies, searching for a clue to where they might have gone or what might have happened. I found several weapons, another foreboding sign. A soldier never went without if he could help it. Which meant they'd been ambushed. Taken.

The sun arced across the sky and the shadows lengthened as I sat on my heels, twirling one of the daggers between my fingers. Thoughts ran amok through my head. Ideas and plans formed and dissolved while every muscle tensed with worry, fear, anxiety. Anger.

… Vengeance.

A branch snapped, and I launched to my feet. Kieran ducked under a bough and stepped into the clearing. He shook his head, anguish written all over his young face. A minute later the remaining men crowded around me, all reporting the same. No sign of anyone.

~ Chapter Nineteen ~

After one look at the stricken faces of my men, I gave the order to stop for the night. Soon fleeting warmth teased the edge of our camp as we huddled around the fire.

Darkness fell and still no sign of the others. I could hardly believe the enemy had breached our line, gotten close enough for an ambush. But it seemed the only logical explanation for their absence. A chill of dread slid down my spine and I clenched my jaw, refusing to let fear control me.

My uncle would never abandon his men, which meant he'd be with them. Wherever they were. We had to do something but what? Despite songs sung to the contrary, I could do very little as an army of one. And my company were barely trained enough to hold a sword, let alone swing it. I balked at having to send them into battle, yet I didn't have much choice.

An owl hooted from its lofty perch, reminding me of the late hour. I stood and stretched my stiff back. What I wouldn't give to be young and resilient. My men seemed to bounce back from everything I threw at them, on the training field and on this march. They laughed, joked, teased as only boys could do, their youthful faces flickering in the firelight. "Time to call it a night, cadets."

A few grumbled under their breath, but most simply ambled off to their respective bedrolls. I tossed a bucket of melted snow onto the fire and climbed into my tent.

Restless, I laid awake, dreading the dawn. At first light, I'd rally the troops and continue. If the rest of the garrison had fallen, then my men and I would reach the front lines and avenge them. Or die trying. Guilt soured my stomach. I'd only just escaped despair's clutches after the loss of my men at Haverton. Another would tear an irreparable hole in my heart.

There had to be a way to avoid bloodshed. A peaceful resolution to whatever grievance King Rendon now held against us. But would General Stark even talk to me, hear what I had to say? Or would he simply run a sword through my chest the moment I stepped within reach? A deadly risk but one I'd accept for the sake of my men, my kingdom. My soul.

❈

"Captain. Captain Ellsbree, sir!" An urgent voice called from outside the tent.

I shoved my feet into my boots and threw back the flaps. "What is it?"

"We heard voices, sir," Kieran rasped, wide-eyed. "A lot of them."

"And?"

"I–

"Never mind. Stay here." I grabbed my dagger and plunged into the trees, violence and bloodlust quickly replacing any fear.

The snow had stopped falling in the night but left plenty collected on tree branches. It slipped off and landed on my shoulders and head, dripping icy water down the back of my neck. I hardly noticed as I stalked through the forest, on the hunt, pausing every few yards to listen. Nothing other than the wind moaning in the treetops. Perhaps what the boys had heard, not actual voices. My skin tingled in ominous warning, however, so I pushed further into the gloom. The trees thinned, and a natural clearing opened in front of me.

A large grey wolf stood sentinel while his pack mates devoured their latest kill, the carcass trembling as they tore into its hide. Yellow eyes, wary and watchful regarded me. A low growl rumbled from the wolf's chest, a clear demand to leave them to their meal. I sheathed my dagger then turned and followed my tracks back to camp, adrenaline ebbing as I neared.

Kieran rushed to meet me as I stepped from the trees. "Captain!"

"Just a pack of wolves," I explained. "You likely heard them calling to each other during the hunt."

"But sir–"

"There is no one here but us, cadet. I swear it."

He opened and then closed his mouth, deferring to his superior officer like a good soldier. "Sir."

I clapped him on the shoulder and offered a warm smile. "Now. What's for breakfast?"

I stayed a few paces behind as I trailed him to the fire, mostly to give my racing heart time to calm. And for my shaking hands to still. Even though I hadn't found General Stark's soldiers, the wolf could have easily made a meal out of me, yet he'd let me leave. And live.

~ Chapter Twenty ~

Grace had made her fair share of rash decisions but still had no business traipsing after the army on their way to war, yet she couldn't let it go. She'd never forgive herself if something happened to Taryn without at least apologizing so she followed Rafe along the main road. He kept to himself, which she preferred, and led her ever farther from the garrison.

His grandfather had explained they'd need spend only one night outdoors. Rafe had brought plenty of cold weather supplies, yet she shivered in her wool cloak just thinking about it. How Taryn survived winter here astounded and impressed her. To see him, perhaps for the last time, would be a gift from the gods. One she would not squander just because her lips had turned blue.

With nothing else to do but plod behind her guide, she thought about how she could breach the gap between her and Taryn once she found him. Her last letter should've reached him before he'd left the garrison. She didn't have anything to say beyond what she'd written, other than apologizing enough to make it right. Perhaps he would have a few choice words to say based on her erratic and confusing behavior. She wouldn't blame him. Not one bit.

Rafe stopped and dismounted, nodding to Grace to do the same. Grateful, she slid from the horse and handed him the reins. Without a word, he strode away to tie them to a small tree. She frowned at his broad back. The strong, silent type had never appealed to her. She much preferred confident, assertive men. Like Taryn. Gods, she missed him. Every minute of every day it seemed. Well, she'd be with him soon enough. For now, she'd simply help Rafe prepare the camp and hope for a decent night's sleep.

❧

The sun had barely crested the treetops when Grace woke, opening her gritty eyes with a groan. Had she not slept at all? She had. On a rock, apparently.

She climbed from her tent, frowning at the unlit fire and Rafe's untimely absence. He'd likely gone looking for wood or some other camp-related errand, but she didn't trust the forest's deceptive innocence. Wolves roamed this territory, and she had no desire to meet one today. Though if Rafe met one, they'd likely shake hands and part as friends. Nothing seemed to rattle him. Facing a savage beast in the forest wouldn't either.

He trudged into camp, arms laden with sticks. Grace shivered while he started a fire then rubbed her hands against the heat, though it did little to ease the chill. She angled her head, watching him go about his tasks. His gaze flicked to hers every few minutes, but he remained silent. Social awkwardness? A physical deformity? Or did he find her company abhorrent? She studied him like a puzzle in need of solving, her healer's mind quickly assessing the problem, formulating ways to help.

He sat next to but not near her then handed her a stale roll. She took it and their eyes met. And held. "Thank you." She tried to start the conversation, to get him talking. But he only nodded and turned away to eat his food.

His grandfather hadn't mentioned anything about Rafe beyond his ability to see her safely to the checkpoint. Perhaps she should have asked. But she hadn't, and now the need to know what prevented him from talking outweighed rational thought. She wanted to fix it. "Rafe." His gaze flicked toward her, brows raised in question. "Why won't you talk to me?"

He stared as if no one had ever asked him. His mouth opened but nothing came out. Clearly no issues with his jaw, then. He blinked and the silence stretched on, but Grace knew how to wait. And she would, all night if need be. He snapped his mouth shut and shook his head, eyes downcast. She edged closer and touched his arm. He tensed but didn't brush her off. "Rafe. I only want to help. I swear it. I'm a healer, actually. And a good one. If you'd just–"

"I'm … fine."

The roughness of his voice startled her, and she jerked her hand away. A log popped in the fire, yet she remained motionless for fear of scaring him mute again. Patient and persistent to a fault, she waited.

They sat in silence for what felt like forever, yet couldn't have been more than a few minutes. Ever so slowly, he lifted his head to look at her. His eyes seemed to burn with secrets, hidden messages she wanted to uncover.

"Please Rafe," she whispered.

He leaned forward, his intense gaze traveling the length of her body. Not in a predatory way but as a curious child might examine a new toy. His eyes met hers again and she shivered, though not from cold.

"I …" His voice sent another shiver crawling up her spine and she sucked in a breath. Held it.

He cleared his throat. "I'm sorry. I apologize if I seemed … rude."

He didn't appear to be in pain or to struggle with speech. And though he'd paused, he had no trouble finding words. He just needed practice. She released a breath and flashed a bright smile. "No apology necessary."

His lips curled in a crooked grin, revealing a dimple. He looked quite handsome as his features softened. Her heart thumped, a reminder of how little experience she had talking to men. Yet she needed a friend. She'd approach this situation as a challenge, then. An opportunity to hone the skill.

He stood, gesturing toward her tent.

"Falling back into old habits already?" She gave a small shake of her head. "And after we've made such progress."

He laughed under his breath then louder until it boomed through the treetops. A song to lift her spirits, which she sorely needed.

"We should go." His quiet tone both soothed and surprised her. "Before the snow returns."

He extinguished the fire while she dismantled her tent. He took it from her and secured it to the back of her horse. "How much longer?"

He narrowed his eyes as if reviewing a mental map of the route. "Two hours."

She caught his arm before he could turn to mount his horse. "Thank you, Rafe. For talking to me." With a rakish grin, he swung up into the saddle. She did the same, and they set out once again.

She rode beside him this time, throwing smiles his way, which he returned. Pride bloomed in her heart at what she'd accomplished. And so quickly. Her mentor would be proud. If only she'd gotten through to Taryn with such ease. Hopefully, there would be plenty of time to work on his issues.

~ Chapter Twenty-one ~

Nothing but white everywhere. The thick cloud cover grew denser by the moment, barely penetrated by the sun's weak rays. I sighed heavily, sick to death of snow and cold and wind. And white.

I'd given the men leave to do as they wished, as long as they didn't venture too far from camp. And stayed together. The idea of losing one of them to a wild animal turned my stomach. Another night of solid rest and they would be ready for the next leg of our journey. But would I?

I paced like a caged beast, clenching my dagger in a white-knuckled grip while worry and doubt crowded the corners of my mind, pushing into every thought. The harder I tried to avoid them, the more aggressive they became in their assault.

I stalked to the edge of camp and stared across acres and acres of still life, blinding despite the indirect light. I shielded my eyes against the glare and almost dropped my dagger. Two riders, coming from the north. Not racing but traveling fast enough to worry me. I could dispatch them both. Probably. But I would need to be quick and agile and silent and stealthy. And take them by surprise.

Crashing through the trees, I bolted back toward camp to find it empty. I skidded to a halt near the dying fire and cursed, raking a hand through my hair. I shoved the dagger into my belt and shimmied up the nearest tree, practically invisible in its snow-packed boughs. I climbed as high as I dared then flattened myself against the trunk to wait.

Boot steps crunched on snow. Two hooded figures emerged from the trees. One tall and one not. They spoke in hushed tones, their murmured voices too low to make out words. I pushed a branch aside and peered down at the tops of their heads. They paused near the fire, just as I had moments ago. The tall one meandered through the camp, checking behind tent flaps while the other one waited.

"What do you see?" I almost didn't hear the soft-spoken question.

The searcher turned, his features lost in the shadows of his hood. "There is no one here now. But they were. Recently."

My heart thudded. I did not want to hurt these people. They looked harmless, really. And the short one could have been a woman.

The tall one walked back across the camp and stood just under my hideout. "They're nearby." His quiet voice radiated assurance. "We should wait. Sit down while I get the fire going."

A tense minute of silence dragged on then a heavy sigh. "Fine. If you think it's best."

At full volume, the voice undeniably belonged to a woman. She sat on a log and pushed her hood back. A long, golden wave of curls flowed over her shoulders and I almost fell out of the tree. *Grace?* Impossible. But also not a threat.

My relief lasted mere seconds. I tensed at the sound of voices behind me, my entire company slogging back to camp, chattering like a gaggle of ladies at afternoon tea.

My hissed warning fell on deaf ears and I jumped down to intercept them, almost breaking my ankle. The man leapt to his feet faster than humanly possible and Grace's head whipped around, her mouth open as if to scream.

"Hello, Grace."

"Tar … Taryn," she gasped, breathless, just as the boys crashed through the trees. They stumbled to a stop behind me, thirteen bristling warriors-in-training.

I sighed with ebbing patience and turned to face them, holding up my empty hands. "Lower your weapons, cadets. They mean no harm."

Kieran pushed his way to the front of the pack, ever my loyal protector. He'd make a fine steward. "Captain, sir. What's going on? Who are these people?"

I stepped toward the fire, beckoning the boys to come with me. I stood a few paces from where Grace still sat. She stared open-mouthed as if she didn't know what to make of us. The man hadn't moved an inch, but he also hadn't shot an arrow through my chest. My blood remained where it belonged inside my body.

"Grace, this is my company. Cadets, this is Grace." The boys shuffled their feet, most of them pink cheeked, though not from the cold. Grace's beauty had always enthralled me, but they hadn't seen a girl much less a woman in quite some time. She smiled, and Kieran swallowed hard. I laughed under my breath then turned back to the men. "Strike the camp. Dismissed." They gawked at me then at Grace. "Now, cadets."

Scrambling into action, they bounced off each other, jostling to obey orders. I inched forward, watching the man's hands but he stood with preternatural stillness. I covered the remaining distance to Grace's side. She smelled of horses and wet wool and something heady enough to send my pulse racing. And gods, her smile. One I would kill to see.

The man cleared his throat and she jolted to her feet. "Forgive me. Rafe, this is Taryn. Taryn, Rafe."

Rafe lowered his hood. "Hello, your highness."

"Rafe! Is it truly you? What in gods' name are you doing here?" He jerked his chin at Grace in response. "Ah, of course. And how is your grandfather?"

"He is well, your highness. Thank you."

"And you? How are things?"

"As good as can be expected. The north offers little in the way of entertainment, as you know, but I manage to keep busy nonetheless."

I turned to Grace. She glanced from me to Rafe and back again, brow furrowed. "Am I missing something? How do you two know each other?"

"We–"

"And Rafe." She pointed an accusatory finger at him. "Why are you all of sudden such a chatter box? You've barely said ten words to me since–"

"Grace." I gently clasped her elbow.

She scowled at me, chest heaving, eyes blazing. "What?"

"Calm down. Rafe has been at the garrison for years, helping his grandfather take care of it. And he's terribly shy. Especially around gorgeous women. Finds himself almost completely at a loss for words." I grinned at Rafe, who simply stared back, not bothering to deny it.

"Oh." She bowed her head. "I'm so sorry."

I lifted her chin. "No need to be. But I think we should sit down and talk about what in gods' name you think you're doing here."

"Agreed," Rafe grunted, slinging his bow across his back.

We sat around the fire, now roaring thanks to Rafe's tending, while the cadets roamed about the camp trying not to eavesdrop. "So." I beamed a smile, elbows braced on my knees. "What brings you here this fine winter's day?"

Grace glanced at Rafe, who shrugged with casual indifference. Then she turned back to me, an earnest expression on her face. "Did you get my letter?"

"Yes."

"And?"

I arched a brow. "And what?"

"Do you forgive me?"

"Did you truly come all the way here to beg my forgiveness?"

She crossed her arms and glared. "I didn't beg."

I angled my head, studying her body language. She may have had defiance pouring off her in waves, but her eyes glistened with unshed tears. I took her hand. "I forgive you."

All the fight seemed to rush out of her and she slumped. "Thank the gods."

"Now, tell me why you're really here."

She glanced around the camp then leaned to whisper in my ear. "I came to help you. I wanted to make sure you were all right."

I swallowed against the tightness in my throat. She'd come out of pity, a sense of duty to continue our sessions. Yet we couldn't simply pick up where we'd left off in her quest to heal me, to free me from my burden of guilt. And I didn't need her help, not anymore. Plus, I had a war to fight, and win. "I'm fine, Grace. Truly. And you shouldn't have come. It's dangerous."

Rafe snorted, shifting in his seat. He might not have been a soldier, but he had watched us train since childhood and could fight better than most. His deadly aim rivaled even a royal archer's. I shot him a look, which he interpreted correctly and kept his opinions to himself.

"But Taryn," she pleaded. "I only want …"

I felt Kieran's stare on the back of my head and turned. "Yes, cadet?"

He licked his lips, barely able to keep his eyes on my face instead of Grace's. "We're ready to move out on your command, sir."

"Wait with the others at the tree line."

"Sir."

Grace's eyes tracked him as he ambled off. "He's so young."

I nodded soberly. "Indeed. As are his fellow cadets. Some only thirteen summers, if you can believe it."

"And are you really going to war?"

I raked a hand through my hair. "I'm afraid so. Though I have to find my uncle first."

Rafe's head jerked up. "What happened to General Creston?"

"I'm not sure, exactly. One minute there, the next … Gone. No sign of them here when we arrived. And we searched the area. Nothing."

Rafe narrowed his eyes, drawing the same conclusion I had. "Taken."

I clenched and unclenched my gloved hands, the leather stretching tight. It felt like skin tearing. "Perhaps. I must find him, rescue him if possible. And then send my men to die." Grace shot to her feet, hand over her mouth as she stared at me. "Grace …" She turned and fled back through the trees toward the main road. I stood to follow but Rafe grabbed my arm.

"I'll go."

I nodded, and he strode after her. I briefly closed my eyes. Grace did not need to hear about war and death and slaughter, for gods' sake. *Idiot.*

~ Chapter Twenty-two ~

"Captain?" Kieran called from the other side of camp. "Are we going now?"

"Give me a minute."

I tracked Rafe's progress then stopped a few paces away, hidden by the trees. He stood with Grace near their horses, a large hand on her small shoulder. Her hands covered her face as she cried, her whole body shaking with sobs. Rafe gently stroked her back and I gritted my teeth, jealousy raging through me, though I had no right. Grace could do whatever she liked, with whomever she liked. Rafe gathered her into his arms, held her against his chest while he soothed her.

... Enough.

I growled low in my throat. "Rafe." He leapt away from her like she'd caught fire. Her head swiveled between us as she wiped her tear-streaked face. "I'm so sorry, Grace. I didn't mean to upset you."

She straightened her shoulders and leveled a stare at me. "I'm fine, Taryn. Perfectly fine. And I'm leaving."

"I think you should."

"Clearly," she huffed before stalking off to mount her horse.

I shook my head then turned to Rafe. Despite my mixed feelings at seeing him with Grace, I couldn't deny his abilities would be an asset. "Come with me?"

"Sorry?"

"I've seen you fight. I know you're not in the army, but you could still serve. I need warriors, not stable boys."

"I'm no warrior, your highness." His brows drew together. " And how will Grace get back safely?"

"I'll have one of my men escort her."

He squinted into the distance, indecision written all over his face.

"Please, Rafe. I could really use your help."

"All right. I'll come. But you must send someone who can protect her, not just some lackey kid you want to get rid of."

"Done."

"Grace?" he called over to her.

"It's your decision, Rafe. Though I'd rather have you accompany me."

His face burned crimson as he bowed. "I should go with them. But it's been a pleasure traveling with you."

"The pleasure is mine. I hope to meet again soon so we can continue your … lessons." She sat stiffly in the saddle, her gaze trained on the horizon.

I turned to Rafe and he squared his shoulders. "Captain?"

"Return to camp. Send Kieran Whitmore then move out. We're headed for the western border. I'll catch up shortly."

"Sir." He disappeared into the trees, and I nearly collapsed in relief. Now I wouldn't face this daunting task alone.

I stood at Grace's side and took her hand. She gazed down at me, hope burning in her eyes. "It will be all right. I swear it."

Her lower lip trembled. "Just … be careful. Please."

I kissed her hand. "As you wish."

We waited in awkward silence until Kieran stepped through the trees and jogged to my side. "You asked for me, sir?"

"I need you to do something for me, something of monumental importance."

"Of course, sir. Whatever you need, sir. Always."

Gods, this kid. So much like his brother. And like a brother to me. "I need you to see Grace safely back to the garrison."

"But, sir–"

"I know you want to fight with us, but I can't leave without knowing Grace is in good hands. You are the best man for the job."

His chest swelled. "It would be my honor, sir."

"I knew I could count on you." I clapped him on the shoulder. "Rafe is coming with us so take his horse."

"Sir."

Kieran climbed into the saddle and a tear slipped down Grace's cheek. I raised a hand in farewell, but she simply turned her horse's head. Away.

I stood at the side of the road, barely aware of the chill seeping into my bones. The ache in my heart burned by comparison. I watched until they were mere specks in the distance, far longer than I should have. Eventually, I forced myself to leave. One of the hardest things I'd ever done.

~ Chapter Twenty-three ~

I glanced at the sky for the thousandth time, trying to find the sun. But it had been completely obliterated, blotted from existence by a bank of menacing clouds.

"Captain." Rafe hadn't left my side, already proving his worth. "We should make camp while it's still light."

"I know. But where? This storm is almost on top of us. There's nothing here but trees."

"We'll have to make do."

I ordered a halt to the march, and twelve gaunt faces sagged in relief. This ordeal had taken its toll on these boys. The closer we got, the more anxious they became. I could feel their fear like a living thing stalking us. As it goes with war.

I dropped my pack and rolled my shoulders. Rafe had taken Kieran's and started to unpack his bedroll and rations. The others had done the same without a word from me. Just as well.

Bone-tired with hardly enough energy to keep my feet under me, I sank to the snow-packed ground and fumbled with the lacings around my tent. My fingers hadn't frozen, but they were numb with cold. Rafe reached over and took the bundle from me. "Thank you."

He nodded and assembled the tent as close to the fire as possible. The clearing we'd found wouldn't accommodate all of us, so I sent half the group with Rafe to find somewhere similar close by. The men needed no encouragement from me to settle down for the night, and soon the area rattled with their snoring. The sound always comforted me, and I laid on my back then closed my eyes. Sleep carried me away in its gentle embrace.

�֍

Rough mornings were standard on a march, but this one exceeded all expectations. My back ached, my head pounded, and my stomach growled an angry protest. I'd forgotten to eat at all yesterday. Whoever had come up with this idea should be stoned. To death.

The first one awake, I crawled from my tent and stretched to the clear blue sky. Shocking, given the near-constant cloudiness of the last several days.

I lit a fire then sat on my heels, rubbing my hands together as I stared into its flickering depths. I thought of Grace, of her smile and laugh and compassion. Kieran would defend her with his life and she'd be home safe in a matter of days. One less thing to worry about.

I closed my eyes, the fire's warmth thawing my face while life stirred around me. Boys ambled over, murmuring greetings to each other and preparing for yet another hard day of marching. But just one more and we'd be within sight of the front lines. And the western border, where we'd hopefully find my uncle.

How could I know for sure? Even if I convinced General Stark to meet with me, he would never divulge any information. Maybe we could persuade one of his scouts to talk. Rafe knew a thing or two about persuasion. Of course, we'd have to capture one first. An impossible task with us stumbling through the forest. I'd have to send my own scout ahead to get the lay of the land, yet I had no idea who. Rafe lacked the subtlety required for stealth, and I'd reassigned my best man elsewhere.

I sighed heavily. I had no other choice but to go myself. "Carson." His head snapped up, a scared rabbit look on his face. I rarely singled them out and when I did, it usually didn't bode well. "It's all right, cadet."

He scurried over, throat bobbing as he swallowed. "Sir?"

"Have Rafe assemble the company."

"Sir." He almost tripped in his haste to flee, as if I'd change my mind and punish him, though he'd done nothing wrong. Still, a healthy dose of fear never hurt anyone.

I dismantled my tent, and just about had it packed when Rafe and the others gathered. The men lined up, ready and waiting for me to motivate them, encourage them. I didn't have it in me, so I simply told them the reality. "We are one day's march from the border. Heavy fighting awaits us there. I also hope to find the general with the rest of the garrison. One way or another." I paused for a reaction but got none. "I'm fairly certain they were taken by General Stark, but I need to know before we attempt a rescue. Someone has to scout ahead and capture one of the general's men for interrogation."

They reacted as expected, heads turning with whispered speculations. Rafe crossed his arms over his broad chest and stared right through me, as if he already knew my next words. He'd make a good spy.

"I will be the scout."

Whispers turned to shock and disbelief as twelve pairs of eyes beseeched mine, silently begging to send someone else, anyone else. Rafe's eyes, however, held nothing but respect. "Rafe will lead the march to the border. I leave you here to do what must be done."

I nodded to Rafe and he stepped forward to address the group. "I am a stranger to you, but the Captain has placed his trust in me. I will not break it. I will see you safely to the border and then fight at your side. Now is the time for boys to become men, for warriors to rise and laugh in death's face as we cut down our enemies. You can fight. And you can win. To victory!"

I gaped at him, dumbstruck not only by his rousing speech but by the sheer number of words he'd used. The cadets gave a mighty roar and Rafe smiled like a wolf on the hunt. I couldn't help but grin back. If only I'd recruited him long ago. "Take care of them, Rafe. Please."

"As if my life depends on it, sir."

I grasped his forearm in gratitude then pulled my hood up. With a nod, I turned and darted toward the trees, melting into the shadows like a thief in the night.

~ Chapter Twenty-four ~

Shrouded in darkness, I made my way to the border. My lungs burned, begging me to stop but I pushed on, through the trees and into a clearing awash in moonlight. A battlefield, eerie and peaceful without a foe to fight. Memories rose to the surface, teasing and tortuous. I clenched my jaw and focused on the enemy camp looming ahead. Tents coiled around each other like a snake about to strike, small fires flickering among them. But only a handful of sentries patrolled the perimeter.

I released a shaky breath and scanned the tents for the telltale sign of command. If my uncle had been captured, I'd likely find him there. His men, however, could be anywhere. At least I hoped. I couldn't face the alternative. I spotted the largest tent, perched as far from the front line as possible. *Of course.*

Heart pounding a frantic beat, I crept to the outer edge of the clearing then across into enemy territory. I hid behind a tree, waiting for the nearest sentry to turn the other way. Once he did, I raced to the next hiding place, repeating the process until I reached the command tent.

I paused in the shadows to catch my breath, debating the wisdom of this plan. The chances of finding my uncle so easily were slim at best. But I had no other choice now. I inched toward the back of the tent, ears straining to hear any noise from within. I briefly closed my eyes and begged the gods for good fortune.

A rough voice inside the tent broke the silence. "There will be no negotiations, General. Only defeat. Yours." General Stark.

"Please. I only ask for the lives of my men in exchange for my surrender."

My uncle's plea surprised me, almost as much as his offer of sacrifice. I'd never heard him utter such a thing, though I understood his reasoning. I'd do the same in his position. More, probably. Then again, I'd never faced a situation such as this. Heart in my throat, I hoped General Stark would weigh his options and not simply kill my uncle.

"And what is your surrender worth? What will your king trade for you?"

My father would not take kindly to such threats. My uncle held his tongue, likely imagining the worst. Surely my life held more value, carried more weight. Would General Stark agree? Only one way to find out. I took a deep breath and a sword point pressed into my back.

"Turn around. Slowly."

I followed instructions, raising my empty hands for good measure. I pretended not to feel the weight of my dagger at my belt. The sentry's sword jerked in his shaky grip, and I fought a grin. "Well met, soldier."

His throat bobbed as he swallowed. "Who are you? What are you doing here?"

I reached up to pull my hood off, and he angled his sword toward my chin. "Easy. I'm not going to hurt you."

His eyes widened as my hood fell back. "You're … But what …?"

"Braxton," General Stark snapped. "What in the …" His face appeared around the corner of the tent. He grinned like a feral beast as his steely gaze landed on my face. "Well, well. Prince Taryn. I don't recall extending an invitation, but I'm pleased to see you here nonetheless. Won't you join us?"

Braxton lowered his sword but didn't sheath it. The general turned and I followed, Braxton right behind me. I stepped into the tent and strained to keep the shock from my face. My uncle sat slumped in a chair, bound hand and foot. He lifted his head and stared at me through bloodshot eyes. I refused to give in to the panic.

"Your weapon, if you please."

I tore my gaze from my uncle's lined face and handed over my dagger, jaw clenched.

"Would you like a drink? You look like you could use one."

I glared hatred at General Stark. "No, thank you. I'd rather you release General Creston. Then we'll be on our way and we can all get some sleep."

General Stark's rasping laughter scraped against my ears. "I'd forgotten what a charming young man you are."

I beamed a royal smile and bowed.

"But you're mistaken if you think I'm going to let you go. In fact, I believe I'll take you with me."

The smile froze on my face. "Take me where, exactly?"

"Home, of course. Your father will have no choice but to yield to me when I show up with you as my prisoner."

"No," my uncle croaked. "Please."

My mind whirled, struggling to come up with a valid argument against the general's plan. But then I realized the opportunity he had unknowingly given me. The chance to save them all, if I could bluff my uncle out of his bonds. "You might find the task difficult given the men surrounding your camp."

His eyes narrowed. "Impossible."

"I assure you, it's not. They're hidden, awaiting my safe return." My gaze flicked to my uncle, whose expression had hardened to granite. "But if you let General Creston and the others go, I'll remain in your custody." The silence stretched on while my heart threatened to explode in my chest. This had to work.

"Done."

I released a shaky breath as Braxton cut the ties on my uncle's hands and feet. He rubbed his wrists and stood, straightening to his full height. I stared at him with a silent plea to not do anything to jeopardize our bargain. With a curt nod, he strode from the tent. The flap snapped closed, leaving me alone with the enemy. I swallowed hard at the look of triumph in General Stark's soulless eyes.

Holy gods.

~ Chapter Twenty-five ~

Rafe's scalp tingled as if an unidentifiable evil lurked nearby. No doubt true, given their proximity to the border. His gut clenched every time he imagined what could've caused Taryn's delay in returning. He'd been gone far too long but Rafe couldn't leave the company. Frustrated, he clenched his jaw and prowled the tree line, bow gripped tight in his fist. *Where are you, Taryn?*

A branch snapped, and he whirled around, a heartbeat shy of launching an arrow at General Creston.

He paused a few yards away, gray hair ashen in the moonlight. "Rafe?"

"Sir." Rafe shouldered the bow. "I'm relieved Taryn found you." His head swiveled. "Where is he?"

He sighed heavily, then briefly glanced over his shoulder as if expecting his nephew to materialize from the trees. "General Stark has him."

"What?"

"It's a long story, and my men are exhausted. How far is your camp?"

"Not far."

He nodded then whistled a message. A reply came immediately, followed by two dozen beaten, half-starved soldiers. "Lead the way."

Rafe shook his head to clear it then plunged into the forest, the general and his men close behind. What had gotten into Taryn? Surely he hadn't been captured. He would've never been so careless. Or reckless. But Rafe could not for the life of him imagine any other scenario. But then what were General Creston and his men doing here? None of this made any sense.

The forest thinned, and the smell of wood smoke filled the air. A cadet rushed over as Rafe stepped through the trees. "Sir," he breathed. "What–"

Rafe held up a hand. "Gather the men." The cadet nodded then scurried off. "This way, general."

The entire garrison minus its most valued member gathered around the fire, faces tight with worry. The general squared his shoulders as he addressed them. "Captain Ellsbree is being held by General Stark. He traded his freedom for ours."

Angry murmurs rumbled through the group, Rafe's loudest of all. "Sir," he grated out through gritted teeth. "We can't leave him."

"We don't have a choice. We're too weak and outnumbered. We wouldn't stand a chance against General Stark's men. Captain Ellsbree bought us valuable time. I suggest we not squander it."

"But–"

"Let me finish. I do not mean to suggest we abandon our prince. We simply need reinforcements, strength of numbers. And a solid plan."

The low hum of agreement buzzed around Rafe's head, yet he didn't see the need to plan anything other than a brute force attack. A bully like General Stark would only respond to violence, but General Creston seemed unconvinced.

Rafe's head snapped to the tree line as Kieran ducked under a low branch. "Sir," he greeted, approaching the group.

Rafe struggled to control his temper. "Kieran. What are you doing back here? Where is Grace?"

"She's at the garrison."

"You left her there? Alone?"

Kieran seemed to shrink the louder Rafe's voice became, nearly shouting in the small clearing.

"Sir," Kieran stammered. "She's with your grandfather. She's safe, sir. I swear it. She wanted to … wait."

"Wait? For what?" Rafe steadied his breathing, willing his pulse to calm. If anything happened to her, he'd never forgive himself.

Kieran pulled at his jacket collar and shuffled his feet. "I'm sorry, sir. But she insisted. She can be very persuasive."

Rafe snorted. He could all too easily imagine how she coerced this impressionable youth to do her bidding despite orders to the contrary. "Fine."

Kieran beamed a smile as he glanced around at the assembly, gaze landing on General Creston's curious face. "General Creston, sir. Welcome back."

The general's lips twitched at Kieran's youthful exuberance. Rafe had to agree. The boy could coax a smile from anyone, yet his own faltered. "Where is Captain Ellsbree?"

Rafe placed a gentle hand on Kieran's shoulder. "He's with General Stark. Held as a prisoner of war."

"What?" he croaked, his shoulder tensing under Rafe's palm. "Why aren't we moving out to get him back?"

Rafe started to answer but the general cut him off. "Son, I understand your eagerness, but we need to be practical. We can't retrieve him now, not like this." He spread his arms wide, gesturing at the bedraggled soldiers, most of them swaying with exhaustion. "We need time to–"

"No," Kieran growled. "We have to go now."

Rafe blinked at Kieran's outburst, half-expecting the general to show him the back of his hand but he only sighed heavily. "It's all right, son. We'll get him back."

Kieran's chest heaved with labored breaths. "You swear it?"

"I swear it."

Kieran's look suggested he doubted the man would honor his word.

"First things first. Food and rest. We'll set out at dawn for the garrison. Once we've restocked our supplies, we'll return to Evanston and gather enough soldiers to fight our way back to Tar … Captain Ellsbree."

"Sir. Yes, sir," the men mumbled.

"Dismissed." The general waved a heavy hand then rubbed it over his face. "Rafe, a word."

"Sir."

"While I'm glad to see you, I have to ask what in gods' name you're doing here."

"It's a long story, sir, and I'll gladly tell it, but right now I'd rather concentrate on Taryn. Let me go after him, alone. I'm not in the king's army but I'm willing to give my life for his. Please, sir."

The general's face softened. "I admire your courage, Rafe, but I cannot allow it. Get some rest. You've earned it." He ambled away, leaving Rafe fuming with helpless rage.

❈

Rafe tossed and turned as he lay on his back, mind reeling with worry and doubt. His conscience balked at the thought of disobeying orders, but his heart ached to bring Taryn back. He had to do something, he just didn't know what. He sighed heavily and closed his eyes, willing sleep to claim him.

A branch snapped, and his eyes flew open. He stared out across the camp, straining to hear anything other than his thunderous heartbeat. A shadow moved among the trees, too solid to be a mere trick of the light.

He eased from his bedroll and slipped into his boots, never taking his eyes off the figure as it slowly crept from camp. Bow in hand, he stalked into the trees, following at a careful distance. A dark cloak hid the figure's features but not its frame. Slight. Young. And stupid. "Kieran?" he whispered. "Is it you?"

The figure spun around so fast the hood fell back, revealing Kieran's pale face. "Sir, I … I …"

"Save it," Rafe growled. "What are you doing? I could have shot you."

Kieran's slim throat bobbed. "I'm sorry, sir. I just couldn't leave without him, sir. I can't." Tears glistened in his eyes and Rafe's gut clenched.

"It's all right, Kieran. No harm done. Let's just head back to camp now."

"No, sir."

Rafe arched a brow. "Are you arguing with me, soldier?"

Kieran shook his head and wiped his nose on his sleeve. "I'm going to find him, sir. With or without you."

Rafe opened his mouth to bark a command but stopped at the hard set of Kieran's jaw. Determination rolled off him in waves, and Rafe doubted he could hold him back, despite his promise to Taryn. "All right, then. With me it is."

Kieran's mouth fell open, and hope shone in his eyes. "Sir?"

"Come on. It's almost dawn."

"Sir." Kieran's smile split his face and Rafe chuckled. No wonder Taryn liked him so much.

He led Kieran into the trees, forging a path through the tangled growth as they went. Eventually, the foliage gave way to a clearing, where the enemy camp should have been. Rafe's stomach dropped all the way to his feet. "Damn," he snarled under his breath.

"What now?" Kieran whispered.

"I don't know. We can't follow. They'd capture us too easily. Which means …"

"Which means we return without him." Kieran heaved a sigh. "Damn."

"As I said. But we did all we could. He wouldn't want us putting ourselves in danger to rescue him anyway. Best to follow through with the general's plan."

"Yes, sir."

Rafe frowned at Kieran's dejected tone but they didn't have a choice. Sometimes the way forward meant going back.

~ Chapter Twenty-six ~

We'd been on the march for two weeks, and I'd spent every night huddled in misery on the frozen ground with only my cloak for warmth. While I'd volunteered for this tour of duty, I didn't appreciate the mode of transport. Or the accommodations.

I stumbled along behind my captors, yanking on my leash every time my foot caught on a stone. The knot at my wrists chafed like mad, yet I couldn't scratch the itch. Its own form of torture.

I scowled at the soldier in charge of my comfort. If looks could kill, he would have been dead ten times over. Unfortunately, my murderous glare landed like a harmless butterfly on the back of his head, leaving him very much alive.

Hunger gnawed at my insides, and I scanned the area scavenging for food but it remained frustratingly out of reach in the wagon, yards behind me. So, I plodded, shuffled, tripped along the route while my brain worked at a furious pace devising an escape plan. But without a weapon, my hands were tied. Literally. I heaved a sigh and adjusted the bonds for the thousandth time as the men chattered, debating the merits of the local wine and women.

"No gardian girls are very hospitable," Jamison quipped in front of me. "My cousin said he could bed a different one every week if he wanted."

McAllister scoffed. "What a load of crap. No one would ever bed your cousin."

Guffawing laughter bounced between them and I frowned. No gardian girls were beautiful, amazing, charming. Like Grace. My frown deepened as I tried to push thoughts of her from my mind. Stubborn to a fault, she refused to budge and simply stood there with her arms crossed, a look of pure exasperation on her face. I briefly closed my eyes and stifled a groan. Thinking of Grace, of anyone from home would only lead to heartache. And I'd had more than my fill lately.

The sun arced across the sky, yet we continued. Apparently, General Stark cared about his men as much as his prisoners. They had to be just as hungry, just as tired as I felt. But no one complained, at least not in my hearing. They simply put one foot in front of the other as if they expected this journey to last the remainder of time. It wouldn't, of course. Soon enough we'd reach the castle. Home. I shuddered to think what my father would do. Part of me hoped he'd meet General Stark's demands, whatever it took for my release. But another part yearned for vengeance. I'd give my crown for a chance to run my sword through his blackened heart.

"Halt!" The command floated down the line, and my handler slowed to a stop. I hung my head in relief. Finally, a break to sit. And eat. I stood with ebbing patience, waiting to be dragged to a tree or a horse or a wagon wheel. But instead of transferring my tether, General Stark himself removed it altogether. I gently rubbed my raw wrists, trying to guess what he meant to do with me now. "Thank you," I mumbled.

He inclined his head then gestured to a spot off the road where his men had cleared the snow and set-up a makeshift camp. "Care to join me?"

I didn't need any encouragement and followed him to the fire. We sat side by side, awkward and quiet among the bustling sounds of the men as they unpacked supplies, including food. My stomach protested the delay and the general chuckled.

"Hungry, boy?"

I refused to engage in conversation and simply stared at the flickering flames. More chuckling as he handed me a tough piece of dried meat and an even tougher roll. I took them with as much dignity as I could muster. Not much considering the extent of my hunger.

We ate in silence, the entire company huddled together in front of the fire's meager warmth. If I hadn't known better, I'd have thought they were my own garrison, based on the similarities. War obscured the finer details, reducing us to mere men fighting to hold death at bay. It did not discriminate between friends or foes in the end.

My stomach soured, and I swallowed the last of my food with considerable difficulty. Memories of battles past still swamped my senses as the group broke camp. General Stark sneered at me before ambling off toward his horse. The rest of the men were otherwise occupied, and I remained miraculously alone and ignored on my log near the banked fire. I glanced toward the trees on the other side of the clearing, their beckoning branches promising freedom. I scooted down the log, one eye fixed like a hawk on the activity to my left, the other trained on the escape to my right. My heart crashed against my ribs as I prepared to flee. Now or never.

I shot off the log and bounded into the forest, hurtling through the trees as if my life depended on it. Branches caught on my cloak and roots grabbed at my toes, but I managed to put some distance behind me without falling. Cold air seared my throat and burned my lungs, yet I kept going, not daring to pause for even the slightest rest.

My dwindling energy supply forced me to slow then stop. I hid behind a massive tree, breath pluming as I panted. Eyes closed, I leaned my head back and calmed my racing heart. Then I smiled. A huge, beaming smile the likes of which hadn't graced my features in weeks, if not months.

Freedom intoxicated me to the point of giddy delight, but I held in my celebratory cheer while considering my limited options. Legs shaking, I picked my way deeper into the forest, expecting the crunch of a bootheel in the snow behind me at any moment.

My instinct for survival roared to the surface, and I let it guide me to a small creek. I stared at my reflection in the water's frosty surface then sank to my knees and scooped a handful of water into my mouth. I drank like I'd never get another chance. And then a bootheel crunched in the snow behind me.

Any hope of escape drained away like sand through an hourglass. I hung my head, too exhausted to run any farther.

"You," a rough voice snapped. "Stand up and turn around. Nice and slow."

I followed orders, not surprised to see Jamison and McAllister along with several unfriendly soldiers, all armed to the teeth.

Jamison stood directly in front of me pointed his sword at my chest. "How did you escape?"

I opened my mouth to answer but then snapped it shut. I had nothing to say to him, other than obscenities and insults.

He chuckled with dark humor and angled his head. "You don't look like a prince anymore. In fact, you look like a criminal. One who needs to be punished." He sheathed his sword, which did little to ease my anxiety. He could do whatever he wanted to me and General Stark would never know. His companions seemed more than eager to shed my royal blood.

Jamison, enjoying his role as the leader, pinned me with a predatory glare. "McAllister. You have any rope?"

McAllister pulled a length of rope from his belt then took an immense amount of joy in binding my wrists. I didn't protest. I didn't say a word, in fact. I simply let them haul me back through the trees. At least I'd have food and shelter if not my freedom.

I held in a sigh, my mind wandering as I tuned out the conversations around me. I had no desire to hear about their lives, though my ears did perk up at the mention of a northern garrison. *Ours? Or theirs?* I listened hard but they'd suddenly decided to lower their voices as if telling secrets. I tripped on a root and stumbled into McAllister.

He glared at me but then elbowed Jamison. "We should tell him. About the northern garrison."

Malice gleamed in McAllister's beady eyes. "You're right. He deserves to know."

Every word he said made my skin crawl. "Know what?"

They exchanged a look then Jamison grinned. "We burned it. To the ground."

I stared, mouth hanging open in shock. *No.* Please no. These bastards had to be lying, fabricating a tragic story to rile me. I shook my head. "The garrison is a fortress."

"Not anymore."

"Impossible."

He stepped forward to snarl in my face. "Are you calling me a liar?"

I leveled my gaze at him. "Yes."

His snorting laughter turned my stomach. "Believe what you will, prince. But it's true. Right, McAllister?"

McAllister nodded emphatically, and my stomach turned again, this time ridding itself of its contents. I wiped my mouth on my sleeve. "What about …" I cleared my throat. "Were the soldiers there?"

More vigorous head bobbing from them both. "We could hear the screams from miles away."

The men, my uncle. Grace. The ground tilted under me, and I braced my palm on a tree trunk while my brain and heart battled for dominance. Logically it made no sense. The entire garrison should have been there, three dozen men. Most of them highly trained and no match for these miscreants. Yet my uncle had been beaten and his men imprisoned, likely weakened from days with little rest and even less food. And the look of outright triumph on the faces swimming in front of me couldn't be ignored. Doubt receded, carried away by the tide of truth, leaving nothing but an all-consuming grief.

"McAllister!" someone barked from the head of the procession. "What is the delay?"

"Nothing, sir." McAllister tightened his grip and yanked me forward. "Time to go, your highness."

Darkness destroyed my will to live.

❧

"He's going to die if he doesn't eat." Rough hands pawed at me then hauled me upright.

"I know. We'll have to force him, then."

My vision focused, blurred, focused on two figures looming out of the morning mist. Monstrous and huge with glaring red eyes and gaping jaws dripping blood. I blinked once, twice, then shook my aching head.

McAllister frowned and grabbed my chin to force my mouth open. Water drenched my face, filling my nose and throat. I coughed and gagged and spluttered a stream of curses.

"At least he's awake," Jamison quipped. "Though he looks half-dead."

McAllister snorted. "I don't much care how he looks. He just has to live until we get to Evanston."

"Right. Let's see if he'll eat something."

A large spoon forced its way past my tightly clamped lips. I struggled against Jamison's iron grip as McAllister shoved the spoon deeper. "We're going to get this into you one way or another, prince. I suggest you cooperate."

Jamison grinned. "You won't like the alternative. Trust me."

I nodded, and the spoon scraped past my teeth, leaving behind an inedible blob. I forced it down with a grimace.

"Much better," McAllister cooed. "There's a good lad."

Jamison chuckled. "Hurry up. The general said we're moving out."

McAllister dropped the bowl into my lap and jabbed a meaty finger at my chest. "Eat it. *All* of it."

I watched until they'd crossed the camp then emptied the bowl into the brush behind me. Every cup of water, every plate of food had ended up in the dirt once my captors turned their backs. Without access to a weapon or anything sharper than a spoon, I had to resort to dumping my food at every meal and then wait for death. While starvation would no doubt kill me, it sure took its sweet time. If my body would just cease its relentless, stubborn refusal to give up, my suffering could finally end.

Day bled into night as shadows gathered, a welcome friend among a multitude of foes. Sleep offered release but not escape. Without alcohol to dull my senses, dreams became nightmares of wicked things hiding in the inky darkness, waiting to hurt, maim, kill. Their tormenting, teasing, mocking laughter overwhelmed me. Surrounded by pain and despair, I cursed, screamed, howled until my lungs ached and my throat bled. Then blissful release as the enemy withdrew, crawling, slithering, slinking back into its nightmare world.

~ Chapter Twenty-seven ~

My one purpose in life, to end it. To never again feel the agonizing pain of loss. To disappear, to not exist on any plane where my men were dead. I hoped, prayed, yearned for death to claim me. But of course, it didn't. *Bastard*. Instead it taunted me from the ground below, far beyond my reach. The rope wound tight around my wrists with not enough slack to take a nasty fall. There would be no diving, no splitting my skull open in a million bloody pieces.

… Relief.

I would not die today. Unfortunately. Another me would've never considered suicide. But my shredded heart lay in tatters, its weak bonds blown apart like a spider's web in a windstorm. I wanted only oblivion and distanced myself from recent events like a man obsessed, accepting the challenge with single-minded determination. Success relied on my ability to not care, about anything. Even thinking became obsolete in my quest for peace.

Time lost all meaning and reality soon blurred around the edges. I felt nothing other than acute boredom, mild curiosity as to our destination. Further and further I retreated into myself, until I could no longer see the way back. Someone or something had taken control. Stolen my personality, my identity. My sanity.

Every day I faded away.

Just …

a little …

more.

❈

The northern forest yielded to the southern plains, bringing milder weather. Gone were the freezing winds and driving snowstorms. Now we basked in sunshine under a cloudless blue sky traveling east. Toward Evanston, and the castle beyond. Would General Stark stop there? And if so, why? Surely he didn't plan to simply ring the bell and demand an audience with the king. I leaned forward, craning my neck to see ahead where he rode like a peacock strutting about the yard. His pride would be the death of him.

A command traveled down the line, and Jamison reined to a stop. He untied the rope then stood back to let me climb off the horse. Smothered by exhaustion and dizzy from the lack of food, I could barely stand but managed to put one foot in front of the other while he dragged me to a nearby tree. Hands bound once again, I sat and leaned against its mighty trunk. Voices floated around me as the men rested, joked, ate. I closed my eyes then cracked one open when a plate landed in my lap. Despite my hollow stomach, I chose unconsciousness.

❈

What are you doing here?

… What do you mean, what am I doing here? What are you doing here?

I live here.

... So do I.
Oh.
... Don't you believe me?
I do. I guess.
... You guess? You know I would never lie to you.
You don't have to be mean about it.
... I'm not.
Yes, you are.
... Sorry.
Don't be. It's not your fault.
... It isn't? Why?
I don't know. I deserve it?
... No, you don't.
Fine.
... Don't pout. It's childish.
I'm not pouting. I'm sulking. There's a difference.
... Do you want me to go?
You probably should.
... I'll be back. Now wake up.

~ Chapter Twenty-eight ~

"Wake up." A boot connected with my side, and I bolted upright, using the pain to fully wake. McAllister glared in my face. The sun framed his head like a halo, and I snorted. Not so much an angel, this one. To prove my point, he kicked me again, harder. In the same spot. A groan escaped my lips before I could stop it.

Rough hands hauled me to my feet. Despite my nap, I had no energy and struggled to stay awake. McAllister half-dragged, half-carried me to the horse then flung me onto its back like a sack of grain, my wrists bound once again. *As if I have the strength to flee.* I slumped forward, head bouncing along with the horse's clattering hooves on our way to the city gates.

I jolted from sleep and almost fell off the horse. We'd arrived. The general's men all clambered down, boots thudding on the cobblestones. I swayed on my perch, in no mood to move. Jamison seemed content to let me sit here while we waited. I fought to remember why we'd come, what the general planned to do with me. Something about leverage? A bargaining chip?

"Jamison," I croaked. "What's going on?"

"Quiet, you," he snapped with a hard tug on the rope. My arms jerked but the pain hardly mattered anymore.

A commotion at the gates drew everyone's attention, even mine, and I sat up tall in the saddle. Spearpoints pierced the air, bobbing and weaving as a small group made their way forward.

General Stark stormed ahead to meet them, chest puffed out in victory. "You see?" he barked as he stood abreast of my horse. "Here he is. Just as I said."

A guard stepped forward, eyes narrowed. Bleary-eyed, I blinked while he studied me. The guard shook his head. "It's not him."

General Stark spluttered a curse, shaking his fist in the air with impudent rage. "I demand to see the king!"

Impending violence crackled like a lightning bolt as the king's guards now surrounding us leveled their spear points ready for the killing blow. It wouldn't take much for one of them to run me through. I shivered, praying I'd meet my end as collateral damage.

The group parted, allowing another guard to shoulder his way to the front. "Stand down. That's an order."

I sighed in disappointment, wishing they'd just get on with it already. Kill me, abandon me. Anything to get me off this bloody horse.

The guard crossed his arms over his chest. "What is going on here?"

General Stark's face had taken on a nasty purplish hue. "Take me to the king. Now. Or he'll never see his son again."

I glanced around, looking for the prince. But he had even less reason to be here with this sorry excuse for an army than I did.

The guard glanced at me then back at the general. "Very well. But only you. Everyone else stays outside the walls, under heavy guard."

If he'd asked, I could have told him no good would come of this.

Shadows crept from one side of the road to the other as the sun continued its journey. A bird trilled from a nearby tree before it took to the skies. I watched it soar ever higher, idly wondering if flying felt as liberating as it looked.

The general returned, more determined than ever to prove his point. "Jamison," he barked. "Bring him." He strode away without another word, and Jamison yanked me off the horse. I landed awkwardly, legs buckling. His vise-like grip on my arm held me upright as he dragged me after the general. Where were they taking me? The castle likely had a dungeon but why turn me over to the king and not keep me? Half-formed thoughts collided in my head yet failed to form a coherent explanation.

The guard led us through the gates and into the castle. Rough stone walls, smooth marble floors, and heavy tapestries dominated the view as we followed the guard to a huge set of gleaming, wooden doors.

"Wait here," our escort instructed, disappearing through the doorway.

Two wide-eyed sentries stared with unreadable expressions. Perhaps they knew why I'd been brought here. General Stark paid them no attention as he paced like a caged animal, practically growling at the delay. Indifferent, my mind drifted in a sea of blissful ignorance.

The guard returned and motioned us forward. General Stark strode ahead, exuding the confidence of a king. Jamison followed, more ruffian than royalty, dragging me behind him like a hunting trophy. We stopped a disrespectful distance from the throne where the king sat regarding us with narrowed eyes.

"General."

"King Merrick," General Stark spat without bowing. "I am here on behalf of my king, the rightful ruler of this realm. His forces are spread along your borders. They will attack unless they receive word from me."

"Which is?" the king drawled, arching a regal brow.

"Surrender."

"And if I refuse?"

"I will slit your son's throat, right here, right now."

My head swiveled. *Whose throat?*

Every sword pointed at the general as the king slowly stood, towering over us. "First of all," he began as he stepped down the dais, "you are completely surrounded. And my men are simply waiting for the word from me. The word is *kill*." He paused, perhaps for effect. Like a spectator at the theater, I couldn't wait to see what happened next. "Second of all, this man is not my son. My son is at our northern garrison, miles from here. I heard from him just the other day, in fact."

Jamison gulped, and I glanced at him. A bead of sweat trickled from his hairline down his temple. General Stark's mouth fell open like the punchline of a bad joke. My barked laugh bordered on lunacy. He regained his composure and shot Jamison a look. His face paled, even beneath the layers of grit. Apparently, this northern garrison meant something to them. But what?

"Your northern garrison is nothing but ashes," he sneered with obvious contempt.

A tremor ran through my body and bile crawled up my throat. I swallowed hard, swaying as the room spun. A stern-looking guard at the king's right shoulder took half a step forward as if he to steady me. The king held up a hand and the guard stilled. I blinked, and the world righted itself.

The king's booming laughter bounced against the stone walls. "I assure you, General, the northern garrison stands." His gaze flicked to the guard and he nodded slightly. "Now I suggest you return to the hole you crawled out of before my anger gets the better of me. And consider yourself extremely fortunate I'm in such a merciful mood."

The general's face hardened as he glared at the king, at the guards. At me. Though I hadn't done anything other than stand here and keep my mouth shut. For the most part.

"Rafe. Secure the prisoner."

The burly guard hadn't moved from his position except to draw his sword with the others. Now he sheathed it and bounded across the marble floor. He loomed in front of me, taller than the tallest tree. His face blurred as my vision dimmed.

General Stark's eye twitched. "Don't touch him," he warned.

The king peered down his nose as if General Stark were nothing. No one. "He is my subject, and I have every right to claim him. You are in my kingdom, in my throne room and I will do as I please."

General Stark seemed to pulse with rage, but the look of violence in the guard's eyes convinced him to back down. "This is far from over," he snarled then turned and stalked from the room, Jamison scurrying at his heels.

My gut twisted, torn between calling out to them and collapsing on the floor. Exhaustion trumped any misplaced affections I had for my captors, and darkness claimed me.

~ Chapter Twenty-nine ~

Rafe's face betrayed no emotion when General Stark dragged Taryn into the throne room. His hand tightened on the hilt of his sword, however, itching to christen the blade with the general's blood. Taryn's head lolled as if he'd given up without a fight, and Rafe bristled with unchecked fury. His friend, his prince reduced to a tortured prisoner of war, enduring the gods knew what in enemy hands.

Every muscle strained with the urge to rush forward, yet he held himself back, waiting for word, any word from the king. He had to recognize his own son, see past the grime and filth and vacant stare. The general spoke, and Rafe's jaw clenched hard enough to crack a tooth. He barely heard what he said over the roaring in his ears.

"I will slit your son's throat, right here, right now."

Rafe's sword jumped into his hand without a thought, along with every other guard. He tensed as the king stood. A volley of heated words passed between him and the general while Rafe held his breath.

"Rafe. Secure the prisoner."

He didn't need to be told twice and sprinted toward Taryn. The soldier dropped his arm as if it had caught fire then backed away. The general made a weak threat of some kind. Rafe glared at him with lethal promise then slung Taryn's arm over his shoulder, easily holding him upright.

The heavy doors banged shut behind the enemy and Rafe could finally draw a full breath. "Taryn," he coaxed. "Can you hear me?" His eyes roamed Rafe's face but no recognition shone from them. Taryn's head rolled back, and he slumped in Rafe's arms.

The king hurried over and brushed the hair from Taryn's forehead. He gazed at his son with grief-filled eyes. "Oh, my poor boy. What have they done to you?"

The king's coarse whisper tore a hole in Rafe's gut. But Taryn had survived and returned home. Safe, if not yet sound. He would heal, in body and soul. Rafe would see to it personally. "Your majesty. He needs a healer."

"Yes, of course. Thank you, Rafe."

Rafe's bootheels echoed like thunder in the hushed silence of the throne room as he carried Taryn out past the guards' somber faces. He strode down the corridor, praying to every god he knew for Taryn's recovery. What had happened? Why hadn't he spoken? Fear gripped Rafe's heart and squeezed as he laid Taryn on his bed with reverence. If not for the dirt covering him from head to toe, he would have disappeared completely against the white sheets.

Rafe hurried out to find a healer. Grace came to mind, of course, but he didn't want her to see Taryn in this state. Best to get him cleaned up and coherent first. He took the stairs two at a time, feet practically flying underneath him. He banged on the healer's door and tried to calm his ragged breathing.

The door creaked open. "What is it?"

"The prince," he rasped in lieu of a greeting. "Now." The healer nodded and grabbed a satchel then followed him back to Taryn's rooms.

He left the healer to her art then retreated to the hallway, where he marched back and forth for what felt like days. If pacing were an award-worthy sport, he would have won first prize.

Taryn had to recover. Rafe would never forgive himself if he didn't. He should have never left without him. But he'd followed General Creston's orders like a solider. Instead of following his heart like a friend. And once the king realized General Stark planned to bring Taryn to his doorstep, he refused to waste resources on a rescue mission. Rafe should have insisted otherwise. Perhaps then Taryn wouldn't be in his current state of misery. And neither would Rafe.

The healer stepped out into the hallway with a brisk nod to Rafe. "His body is weak. He looks like he hasn't had food or water in days. We won't know the extent of his injuries until he wakes."

Regret surged up the back of his throat and he swallowed hard. "And when will he?"

"It's hard to say. In the meantime, you should try to rest yourself. You look like you could use it."

He didn't doubt it. Sleep had eluded him for far too long. "Thank you. But I'd like to stay with him."

She dipped her chin. "Of course. I'll let the king and queen know."

He scrubbed his hands over his face and took a deep breath. He'd let Taryn down and would do anything to make it right. Even sit by Taryn's bedside until the end of time if need be. Whatever it took to bring him all the way home.

~ Chapter Thirty ~

A candle burned low on a table nearby. Familiar shadows danced, crawled, writhed on the unfamiliar walls. I blinked in the semi-darkness, but my surroundings remained unchanged. Real, then. Not a dream or a nightmare, at least not yet.

Anxious dread skittered up my spine as a brisk knock sounded. My heart ricocheted against my ribs. Friend or foe? A foe would likely break the door down and barge in, not knock politely then wait for an invitation. Fear ebbed and flowed as I slowly sat up, wincing at the sting on my wrists. I glanced at the reddened skin, fingers lightly tracing the raised welts. Memories tickled the edge of reason.

A more insistent knock jolted me from my thoughts and the bed. My muscles shook with the effort to stand. I nearly fell then staggered to the door and cracked it open, one eye peering through the narrow space. *Do I know him?*

… Yes.

I opened the door wider and waited.

"Taryn." *My name?*

… Yes.

"Yes."

"Can I come in?"

"Yes?"

He arched a brow. Had I said the wrong thing? I started to panic then he placed his hand on the door and gently widened the gap. I stumbled back as he stepped into the room, his eyes never leaving my face. I knew him. I blinked and grabbed the door for support, my legs barely able to support me.

"You should sit down."

I nodded and he helped me across the room. I sat on the bed while he studied me with blatant expectation, as if we'd done this dance a thousand times. I remained still, not sure what he wanted from me.

"Taryn." My name. Again. "How are you?" *How am I? … Fine.*

"Fine."

"You look better."

I dared a smile. He seemed sincere, pleasant, nice but I couldn't remember his name. I kept smiling.

"What have you been doing?"

"I've been busy."

"Oh?"

"Yes. We … I do things."

"Such as?"

"Eat."

"And?"

"Sleep."

"And?"

"Other things."

He narrowed his steely eyes and I cringed, suddenly wishing I had never opened the door. "Taryn. Are you being honest with me?"

"Yes."

"Are you sure?"

"Yes?"

"Would you like me to leave?"

I hadn't voiced the thought. Had I? "No. Yes."

"Taryn."

He kept saying my name as if trying to remind me. As if I didn't know. "I … Yes. Can you? Go, I mean. Please?"

"Of course. I apologize if I upset you."

"You didn't. But I … want to be alone."

"Understood." He got up and I stayed in place, keeping my distance.

"It's good to see you." He smiled and recognition tugged at my memory. I knew him. I smiled back and relaxed a little, feeling less anxious than I had in forever.

"Let me know if there is anything I can do for you."

I nodded and he disappeared out the door. Alone again, I gazed around the room. Comfortable, yet completely unknown. I concentrated and focused but ended up with only a pounding headache for my efforts. The king insisted I should be here in this room, in this bed. My visitor knew me as well, surely a sign I belonged. And even though my own name still sounded foreign, I had to agree. Too tired to dwell on it any further, I simply lay down and closed my eyes. Hopefully given time and a chance to rest, I'd come to feel at home.

~ Chapter Thirty-one ~

Rafe slumped against the wall outside Taryn's room and closed his eyes, his breaths even despite his racing pulse. Taryn seemed so far from himself, from the carefree, charismatic young man Rafe knew. Something had broken inside him, sheared clean off, and Rafe couldn't do a thing about it. Except worry. Which he'd done every minute of every day since General Stark had dragged Taryn's limp body into the throne room. He raked a hand through his hair. "Damn."

"Rafe?" Grace approached from around the corner. "What's wrong? Is it Taryn? Is he–"

Rafe gently held her shoulders. "He's fine. At least he says he is."

She smiled weakly. "I wish I could do something other than wring my hands and wait. It's driving me mad."

"You and me both."

"Nothing in my training prepared me for this level of mental anguish. I can't reach him, at all."

Tears gathered in her eyes, and he drew her to his chest. "He'll come back. He has to."

With a delicate sniff, she pulled out of his embrace. "I hope you're right."

"I know I am. Are you here to see him?"

She hesitated as if something unsettling lurked behind the door. "I want to, but I'm afraid."

"He won't hurt you."

"I know. I'm afraid he won't recognize me. He still hasn't."

Rafe sighed heavily. "He hasn't recognized me either, I don't think. What about Natalie? Or his parents? Any luck there?"

She shook her head, her bottom lip trembling. "I've even given him blackthorn tea to help relax him, but he still doesn't seem to know where he is. Or who he is. I can barely stand it."

Her tears fell then, in great hiccupping sobs. She buried her face in her hands, and he stroked her back until she quieted, then raised her head.

"Better?"

"Some."

"Good. So, what now?"

She shrugged and wiped her damp cheeks with a lace handkerchief. "I suppose I should go home. My father is expecting me for dinner."

Rafe struggled to hide his disappointment. They'd spent a considerable amount of time together since they returned, consoling each other over Taryn's condition. "Oh. Well, have a good night."

He started to walk away but she caught his arm. "Come with me."

"What?"

"Have dinner with me. Please. I could use a friend."

He considered her a friend, of course. He'd come to appreciate her tender honesty and calming presence. She had an uncanny way of pulling him out of his shell and he found himself inexplicably drawn to her. And he wanted more.

Meeting her father seemed a positive first step. "Will your father approve?"

She breathed a laugh. "Are you kidding? He'll be thrilled I've brought a man home."

He felt his cheeks heat with embarassment. "All right. Thank you." He sorely needed a distraction from the constant worry over Taryn's state of mind.

She dipped her chin and took his offered arm. He managed to keep the idiotic grin off his face as they strode down the corridors, curious heads turning in their wake. Let them gossip. For once, he didn't care what they said, even if they said it about him.

He'd been the subject of many hushed conversations since he joined the royal guard, a stranger from north of nowhere trusted with protecting the king. A fitting reward, the king had assured him, for his efforts on Taryn's behalf. Whatever the reason, his new post meant more time at the castle and more time with Grace.

They reached the courtyard and Grace didn't even break her stride. She simply climbed into one of the many waiting coaches, smiling at him from the dim interior. "Are you coming?"

"What? Oh, yes." He settled onto the bench across from her and the coach lurched forward. His stomach lurched with it. He swallowed hard and forced the panic away. He served the king as his personal guard, for gods' sake. Surely he could face one young woman's father. His sweaty palms and thundering heart said otherwise. His jacket collar suddenly felt too tight.

"Rafe? Are you all right? You look a little pale."

He forced a smile. "It's warm in here."

She arched a brow, the cool breeze blowing in through the open window ruffling her hair. "We'll be there soon enough. Why don't you take your jacket off? It looks like it's choking you."

He peeled the heavy fabric away from his damp shirt, sighing in relief. Now he just had to deal with the nervous dread coiling in his stomach. Dinner. At her home. With her father. Before he knew it, the coach had clattered to a stop in front of a small bungalow.

"Rafe?"

"Yes?"

"You can get out now."

Under normal circumstances, her smirk would've coaxed one from him, yet he barely managed to step down without falling on his face. She grabbed his hand and tugged him toward the front door. *No turning back now.*

Once inside, his eyes adjusted quickly to the low light. A middle-aged man sat in a comfortable oversized chair, a warm smile on his lined face.

"Hello, Father." Grace bent to kiss his cheek. "This is Rafe. He's the friend I told you about."

"Sir." Rafe gave a brief nod.

"It's nice to finally meet you, Rafe. Grace hasn't stopped talking about you since she returned."

Grace swatted the old man's arm. "Stop teasing him, Father. He'll never come back."

His eyes twinkled as he smiled and Rafe couldn't help but smile back. Perhaps this night wouldn't be so horrible after all.

~ Chapter Thirty-two ~

Grace's nerves had become a tangled mess. Her father and Rafe carried on an amicable conversation but she heard the current of wariness in her father's voice loud and clear as he asked question after question. Rafe answered every last one, much to her relief. His typical stony silence would've only aroused her father's suspicions, which were quite high enough already.

She had come home from her trip north exhausted in every way possible and refused to talk about it until after a decent night's sleep. Her father demanded a full account the very next morning. She told him everything, of course, and he picked up on the way her voice softened when she spoke Rafe's name. To her mortification, he'd called her on it. She denied harboring any romantic feelings toward Rafe, but her father simply wouldn't hear it.

She cared for Rafe, she just didn't know how much. Yet. He hadn't shown an ounce of interest in her beyond her safety. Did she want there to be more between them? She honestly had no idea.

More than anything she wanted to see Taryn fully recovered. Only then could she truly move forward with her life, which had come to a screeching halt when Rafe had told her of Taryn's condition. Her heart had twisted even further to see him lying there so pale. A mere shadow of the man he used to be.

"Grace?"

Her head snapped up at Rafe's anxious tone. "Yes?"

"Are you all right?"

"Of course. Why?"

"You look quite sad, my dear." Her father's eyes shone with kindness. "Do you want to talk about it?"

She glanced at their twin expressions of concern then sighed. "It's nothing new."

"Taryn." Rafe's quiet voice seemed to shout regret.

She nodded and bit her lip to hold the tears at bay. Crying would not solve anyone's problems, least of all her own. She sniffed and straightened her shoulders. "But let's not dwell on such dismal thoughts. Should we play a game? I can get the cards or–"

"No, Grace. I'm far too tired for games." Her father grimaced as he stood. "But you two enjoy yourselves. Good night, my dear. Such a pleasure to meet you, Rafe. I hope to see you again soon."

He kissed Grace on the cheek then shuffled down the hall to his room, leaving her alone. With a man. She swallowed. "So, what would you like to do?"

Firelight danced across the planes of Rafe's face as he smiled. "Whatever you'd like is fine."

"Maybe we should talk. I feel like I don't know you very well."

He arched a brow. "Even after all the hours we've spent together?"

She laughed. "Most of the time we were either freezing to death or sick with worry. Not exactly conducive to pleasant conversation. And you are far from talkative." She leveled a gaze at him.

"True."

Her heart tripped as his smile broadened, a smile unlike any she'd seen from him before. Could this be the sign she'd been waiting for? An indication of his feelings for her? "I'd love to know more about your childhood. Where did you grow up?"

He settled back in his chair, hands clasped on his flat stomach as if about to tell a lengthy story. "Iredale."

"Really? You've lived near the garrison your entire life?"

He chuckled under his breath. "My entire life? How old do you think I am?"

"I … I never thought about it."

"And now?" He leaned forward and peered into her face. "What do you think, Grace?"

"Twenty-three?"

He sat back. "Very good, considering you've never thought about it."

She scoffed. "Perhaps I'm just a good guesser."

"Perhaps." His eyes sparkled in the low light.

The clock on the mantle rudely chimed the hour. Late, even for Grace, who'd been known to stay up half the night reading.

"I should go."

Neither of them moved, however. Grace perched on the edge of her seat, waiting for some unfathomable reason for Rafe to kiss her. But he didn't. He simply stood and shrugged into his jacket.

Grace walked him to the door. "Good night, Rafe."

"Grace." He breathed her name like a prayer and she almost didn't hear him. "Thank you."

He placed a featherlight kiss on her cheek then turned and walked away. She touched the spot where his lips had been, marveling at her fluttering stomach and thumping heart. She hadn't imagined such a simple kiss could elicit such a complicated reaction. Yet here she stood, breathless and weak-kneed like a schoolgirl.

Rafe had gotten under her skin, past her defenses and into her heart. He'd made the first move. Now she just had to decide what to do about it.

~ Chapter Thirty-three ~

I hated this room. And this bed. And all the flapping, nervous hands. The constant poking and prodding, fluffing pillows and straightening blankets. Suffocating to say the least. Entirely unwelcome, yet they insisted on visiting, a constant stream of strangers hellbent on annoying me, coddling me. If only one of them could break whatever spell I'd been under and restore my memory.

I didn't remember much in the early days. Only random images of soldiers. Fleeting thoughts of suicide. I relied on others to fill in the blanks, supply information. Who, what, where. But the pain came back with blinding ferocity, lingering like a haunted echo. A constant evil stalking me, refusing to leave my side as if its existence depended on mine. Late at night after my strength had waned, it turned my dreams into nightmares of blood and violence and death. Yet familiar in their darkness. Comforting. Safe.

Hoping for a distraction, I padded to the window. The view did not disappoint. Acres of snow-covered fields stretched far into the gray horizon, a blinding white expanse unblemished by the pain of the past, untainted by the hope of the future. It simply existed, much like I had since arriving here.

Resting my palm on the smooth glass, I swung the window wide open then stepped onto the windowsill. My bare toes curled around the cold metal frame as if hanging on for dear life. The frozen ground mocked from below, too far to jump. And survive.

I teetered on the edge, the cool breeze ruffling my shirt. A single step would bring blessed relief. Freedom. I would no longer feel pain. Or remorse. Or grief. Death waited just beyond my perch, whispering promises.

… Eternal peace.

"Taryn!"

I spun around and lost my footing, sprawling on the floor in a heap of curses. Strong hands under my armpits helped me up. I glared at my would-be rescuer like a thief caught in the act. "Doesn't anyone knock?"

"I *did* knock. You didn't answer." She reached past me and pulled the window shut then locked it for good measure. "What are you doing? It's freezing."

"I got hot."

I stepped around her, and she caught my arm. "Talk to me. Please."

"I don't have anything to say," I snapped. "Why can't I be left alone?" *To die.*

Tears spilled down her cheeks, glistening like diamonds on her porcelain skin. I blinked then shook my head. "Remind me who you are." A request I'd grown tired of making.

"Taryn, it's me. Grace."

A supposed ally, though her presence felt more forced than friendly. I bit back a sigh. "What do you want?"

She wiped her eyes. "I just want to talk. I swear it."

"No herbs, no tea, no magic attempts to heal me?" She shook her head and some of the tension rolled off my shoulders. "Fine. But not in here."

She followed me to the sitting room then perched on the couch with her delicate hands white-knuckled in her lap. Surely she didn't see me as a threat. I could barely walk, yet my words cut as deep as any sword. And I hadn't meant to hurt her. "Please forgive me. I'm ... not myself these days."

"There's no need to apologize. I can't even begin to imagine all you've endured and what you're dealing with now. I'm only trying to help. If I can."

You can't. "I don't know how you could. Unless you're willing to do me a favor?"

"Anything."

"Get me out of here."

She arched a brow. "And go where, exactly? You are far too valuable to be traipsing–"

I waved away her argument, the same one I'd heard countless times from everyone else. "I don't want to leave the castle. Just this room. Please."

"A fairly simple request. What would you like to do?"

I grinned. "Surprise me." A blush crept up her neck and my dormant heart thumped.

"All right. When?"

"Now works for me."

She narrowed her eyes. "You might want to bathe first. You smell atrocious." I blinked and she laughed. "I meant no offense, your highness."

I clenched my jaw. Learning my name had been hard enough. I still hadn't come to terms with my title. The wrongness of it bothered me, as if I'd stepped into someone else's body, stolen someone else's life. I couldn't argue with her astute observation, however. I'd neglected my personal hygiene in favor of personal reflection. "Very well."

"Shall I return in an hour? Or will you need more time?"

"Gods, no. Please don't make me spend another minute in this hell hole."

She glanced at the silk sheets, brocade curtains, priceless art then smirked. "We wouldn't want you to suffer." Breathing a soft laugh, she shook her head and left me to gather my thoughts. Which lay scattered in every direction as I tried to recall her voice, her laugh, her smile, yet the memories eluded me. She remained little more than a stranger. Sweet and kind and beautiful but still unrecognizable. Like everything else I'd ever known.

~ Chapter Thirty-four ~

My legs wobbled like a newborn foal as Grace paraded me around the castle grounds. Everyone we passed either bowed or curtsied, and I gritted my teeth in frustration. Even though being outside soothed my wounded heart.

She stopped at a small bench in the garden. "Let's sit for a while."

I lowered myself onto the bench, my thigh brushing hers, and sighed. "Thank you. For this."

"Of course, Taryn. Anything to help a friend."

"Are we friends?"

She blinked. "I'd like to think so, yes."

I nodded then studied the hills rolling away in the distance under an ice-blue sky. The landscape stretched for miles, slumbering under its blanket of snow, hidden for the winter. Peaceful and serene yet utterly foreign. I could've been on the moon for all I knew.

She laid her hand on my arm and I turned to find her staring at me, despair etched onto her face. I squinted at the pale winter sun. "I'm sorry. Again. I feel like I'm always apologizing, though I don't quite know why."

"I'm the one who should apologize."

"Whatever for?"

"For not helping you."

Tears glistened in her eyes and her lower lip trembled. I reached up to touch her face but hadn't yet earned the privilege. "You have helped. More than you know. Being here with you has made a huge difference."

"Really?"

I pulled a brilliant smile out of nowhere. "Yes."

She seemed to relax then laid her head on my shoulder. Just two people enjoying each other's company in the garden as if our continuing friendship were a foregone conclusion. But we were soldiers battling an invisible enemy, fighting to free my imprisoned heart. Would she stay the course or give up?

Light footsteps crunched in the snow behind us and I glanced over my shoulder. The guard who'd visited me the other day strolled with casual grace down the path with a young man chattering like an excited child. They stopped a few yards from where we sat. The guard stared open-mouthed, but his companion seemed unaware and kept talking. Then he too noticed us, and snapped his mouth shut with a clack of teeth.

"Taryn." The guard beamed a smile as he bowed. "Your highness. I'm so pleased you're up and about."

"Hello," I greeted with automatic politeness.

With a soft laugh, Grace beamed a smile. I peered sideways at her, pretending her flushed cheeks had nothing to do with the way he smiled back. The young man shuffled his feet, looking like he wanted to run in the opposite direction. I knew the feeling.

"Rafe," she breathed, her beautiful smile still stamped on her beautiful face. "Kieran. How nice to see you again."

Rafe. Kieran.

My head began to throb as gruesome images of blood and gore flashed in my mind. I squeezed my eyes shut, thoughts and feelings and memories colliding. Jaw clenched, I fought the pain as it roared through me with more ferocity than ever before. *Agony.*

Claws tightened like an iron band around my chest, threatening to crush me, forcing my breath out in shallow gasps. I swayed and almost fell off the bench.

"Taryn!"

I opened my eyes and must have looked worse than I felt, though it seemed impossible.

Grace crouched next to me, her face a pale oval. "Rafe, help me."

Rafe hauled me to my feet. "Kieran, grab his other arm."

They staggered and lurched under my weight as they ushered me to my room. My entire body screamed in protest, a thousand points of misery I couldn't defeat. Bile crawled up my throat and I swallowed hard, forcing it back down. *Darkness save me.*

❈

Light woke me, searing my eyelids, flooding the room with cheerful brightness. I scowled at the intrusion then rolled over, every muscle groaning.

"You're awake."

I tried to sit up but thought better of it. "I am, though I have no desire to be. Even my hair hurts."

A low laugh rumbled through the room. At least someone found my situation amusing. I did not.

"How are you feeling?"

I managed to roll onto my back. "Dead."

Another laugh. "If you were dead, you wouldn't be in pain."

"True." With a disappointed sigh, I turned my head to find Rafe sitting in a chair near the bed, elbows braced on his knees as he leaned toward me. A lopsided grin softened his otherwise hard features, which I now remembered with crystal clarity.

"Can I get you anything?"

"Help me sit up."

He sprang into action, easing me upright against a mountain of pillows then sank back onto his chair. His jacket had lost a button, and his boots needed a shine. And by the looks of his stubbled jaw he hadn't shaved in days. Stuck here watching over me, no doubt.

"So, what happened? In the garden?" He studied me like he feared for my sanity.

"I have no idea."

He arched a brow. "I don't believe you."

"Well, it's the truth. Grace and I were perfectly comfortable one minute, then you and …"

"Kieran."

I swallowed hard. "You two showed up."

He pinned me like a rabbit in a trap under his steely gaze. "And then?"

I picked at a loose thread on the blanket, not meeting his eyes. Seeing Rafe and Kieran had brought back all the other memories, a past I didn't want to face. But it crowded my mind, callous in its quest to take over every waking thought.

The episode, while brutal, had fully restored my psyche, scars and all. I didn't know how to explain it or if I even could. And I didn't want to try in case the confession triggered a regression. I shook my head, tears building behind my eyes. "I can't. Please, Rafe."

He sucked in a breath and stared at me wide-eyed, a slow smile blooming. "You … know who I am?"

I nodded and his smile turned into laughter. Rich, booming and full of joy. I smiled in return, though his far outshone mine.

"What else do you remember?"

Pain. "Everything."

"Oh." His smile slipped, replaced by profound sadness and regret.

I knew exactly how he felt. "But I'll be fine. I swear it."

"Taryn, I–"

"It's all right, Rafe. Honestly."

He sighed and leaned back in his chair, exhaustion personified. "What now, then?"

"I have no idea. More of … this, I suppose though the very thought of spending another second in this room grates on my nerves."

"Is it really so bad?"

"Yes."

He studied me with a critical eye. Did he doubt my word? Had I fallen so far? I fought the urge to squirm under his assessing gaze and held my chin high.

He nodded as if he'd made a decision. "You're ready."

"For?"

"What comes next."

"Which is?"

"Life, Taryn. You get to live your life."

The idea did not appeal to me, a fact I kept to myself. The less he knew about my vulnerable mental state, the better. I refused to be seen as beaten and broken and sick, on the brink of spiraling into lunacy. I would remain strong, confident and take each day as it came. One at a time.

~ Chapter Thirty-five ~

Rafe banged on the door a second time, anxious and excited and bursting with pride, though he had nothing to do with Taryn's improvement. Still, he claimed at least partial responsibility. And Grace would feel the same. He raised his fist to knock again and the door creaked open.

One green eye peered at him through the small gap. "Rafe." She threw the door wide open, caution replaced by cheerful recognition. "What are you doing here?"

"Taryn." Breathless for all kinds of reasons, he smiled like an idiot.

"Is he …"

He grabbed her hands. "He remembers me. You. Everything. Come on." He started to drag her from the house, but she pulled back.

"Rafe, wait. I can't just leave."

"But–"

She laughed. "I'm coming with you, of course. I need a minute." Tugging on his hand, she urged him inside. "Wait here."

He stood in the tiny alcove near the door, watching as she hurried down the hall on bare feet. He swallowed and adjusted his jacket collar. What would she say and do and feel once she talked to Taryn? He knew she cared for him, he just didn't know in what capacity. Rafe only hoped her feelings for him went deeper.

"I'll be back this afternoon," she called to her father over her shoulder. She flashed Rafe a bright smile, eyes sparkling like emeralds. "Let's go."

The ride to the castle passed by in a blur of questions, all about Taryn. Rafe answered with minimal emotion, not wanting to get her hopes up. Taryn hadn't exactly jumped for joy during his last visit. Rafe doubted his reaction to Grace would be much better, yet he couldn't help but respond to her excitement.

She didn't wait for his help and bounded out before the coach had even come to a complete stop. He followed at a more sedate pace, knowing she'd want to see Taryn alone. His gut clenched at the thought, but he kept it to himself as she disappeared behind Taryn's door.

He paced while he waited, ears straining to hear just one word of their conversation. But the castle's thick stone walls made it impossible, so he stewed in speculation instead.

Worry gnawed at him and he chewed his lip to keep from wringing his hands in nervous anticipation. He hadn't realized his true feelings for Grace until this very moment. All his life he'd struggled with women, avoided them, but Grace had helped him overcome his shyness. They'd formed a cherished bond and he'd rather die than give her up without a fight.

The door opened. He skidded to a stop, breath held and pulse thrumming. Grace stepped into the hall and eased the door closed, her smile radiating like the sun on a cloudy day.

"I can't believe it." Her voice held nothing but breathless wonder, much the way his had mere hours ago.

He knew then he'd lost the fight before it had even begun. Why had he ever thought he could compete with a prince? *Stupid, arrogant idiot.*

"Rafe? What's wrong? I thought you'd be happy. He knows me, and he said–"

"I don't care what he said," he growled.

"What?"

He raked a hand through his hair. "I'm glad he knows you, but I can't …"

She stepped toward him, crowding his space, overwhelming his senses, and laid her hand on his arm. He jerked, and she pulled away, hurt splashed all over her face. "Are you angry with me? What did I do? I don't understand."

He stared, trying to erase the sight of her disgusting happiness about another man's affections, but it had been branded on his brain, carved into his heart. Turning on his heel, he stalked away as fast as his feet would carry him.

A frown took residence on his face, and he scowled at everyone he passed. Servants scurried out of his way as he stormed by, anger rolling off him in waves. He'd been unmoored, cast out into a sea of despair. He only had himself to blame, of course. He had dared to get close to her, had allowed himself to care for her.

He slammed his door closed, rattling it in its frame then crossed to the window, bracing his hands on its edge. Clouds had gathered, blocking out the weak winter sun and turning the sky a somber shade of gray. The perfect complement to his inner turmoil.

If only he'd stayed at the garrison. He'd give just about anything to be back there now, far away from this agonizing heartache. Perhaps he should leave. He could resume his duties with his grandfather. But he'd sworn an oath to the king and would honor it, despite his shattered heart.

His mood plummeted, spiraling down into a disappointment so deep he didn't know if he'd ever crawl out of it. He'd dared to hope, a fool's quest, and ended up on the wrong side of hell.

~ Chapter Thirty-six ~

Grace returned home to find her father eager and waiting for news. He all but pounced on her the minute she closed the door.

"How is he, Grace? Will he be all right?"

She bit her lip and blinked away tears. "He's doing much better. And he remembers me."

Her father breathed a sigh. "Finally. But something is bothering you. What happened?" He patted the space on the couch next to him.

She sank onto the cushion. "Rafe."

"What about Rafe?"

"He's angry with me for some reason. He refused to say."

"Are you sure? He seems like such a nice young man."

"I agree. I'm confused and don't know what do to. What do you think, Father?"

He leaned back and clasped his hands. "I think Rafe cares for you a great deal, more than he's willing to share right now. He may be threatened by your relationship with the prince."

She arched a brow. "I see. And I thought you weren't a healer."

He shrugged a narrow shoulder. "I'm just an astute observer of human nature. And a father. I used to be a young man, you know. Once upon a time."

"True." She chuckled. "Well, I suppose I'll just wait for Rafe to talk to me."

"Until then?"

"Spend more time with Taryn, since he remembers what happened. He'll surely need someone to listen."

"And Rafe?"

She huffed an exasperated breath. "I can't worry about him right now. Taryn is my priority. If Rafe doesn't understand my loyalty, then he's not a true friend."

"How wise you are, my sweet daughter. Just like your mother."

Her mother had been a saint and Grace, though skilled, would never consider herself her equal. She merely strived to do the best she could for whoever needed her. Right now, Taryn needed her, and she'd try until her last breath to ease his pain and help him regain his mental balance.

❋

"Good morning, Taryn." Grace smiled with abundant cheer as she breezed past him into the room. "You're looking well."

Taryn glanced at his rumpled clothes and bare feet then grinned. "No doubt."

Her heart soared to see him in such good spirits. And he did look well, considering recent events. More color in his cheeks, fewer shadows under his eyes. He still needed to put on weight but overall, she couldn't have been happier with his physical recovery. His fragile mental state, however, troubled her.

His pain must have been staggering to drive him so far away from everyone. From himself. But now he'd returned.

Different, of course, but no less the man she'd known. The precise reason for her early morning visit.

He padded to the couch and plopped down, every inch the lazy, carefree prince, yet she knew better. She could see it in the tightness of his shoulders.

"What brings you here, Grace?"

The sound of him saying her name thrilled her. "You, of course. Can we talk?"

His jaw hardened. "About what, exactly?"

"Whatever you'd like."

"I …"

"How about you tell me something you've never told anyone else?"

"A secret?" She grinned and he narrowed his eyes but nodded. "I'm afraid of snakes."

She stifled a laugh at his serious expression. "Snakes? Honestly?"

"Yes. Why?"

"No reason."

He crossed his arms and pinned her with a look. "Your turn."

What? She hadn't considered he'd expect the same from her. But he'd confessed a minor secret, a small fear. Maybe if she admitted something deeper, he would too. "I dreamed of you every night you were gone." His mouth fell open, a look of shock she would cherish for the rest of her days.

The tips of his ears turned pinked, but he arched a brow. "Every night?"

She swallowed hard. "Well …"

"I thought of you, too. Quite often, actually, before …"

He seemed unable to finish but she could fill in the blank easily enough. She'd have wanted to banish all thoughts of him if he died. A normal reaction to loss and grief.

She took his hand in both of hers. "It's all right, Taryn. I'm here." Their eyes met and held in the sudden silence. Her heart fluttered as he leaned toward her, close enough to kiss. A loud knock shattered the spell.

"Yes?" Taryn sounded as annoyed as she felt.

The door opened and Rafe stuck his head in. "Taryn, I …" He stared at Grace, sitting thigh to thigh with Taryn, his hand still clutched in hers. She jerked up from her seat, her father's warning words blaring in her head.

Taryn smiled with warm affection. "What is it, Rafe?"

Rafe cleared his throat as he stepped into the room. "I wanted to ask if you'd go on a ride with me. But you're busy. Perhaps another time."

He turned but Taryn called him back. "I'd love to. Just give me another minute with Grace."

Rafe's eyes flicked from Taryn to Grace and back again. Then he nodded and disappeared out the door.

"Do you mind? I haven't been on a ride with Rafe since … Well, in a while." He rubbed the back of his neck and sighed. "But I'd be happy to talk with you again soon."

"Soon it is." Her voice remained steady despite the rejection. "Whenever you'd like."

She hurried from the room, crashing into Rafe's broad chest in the hallway. He caught her by the arms as she stumbled, holding her so close she could see the faint scar on his eyebrow. She blinked, and he stepped back, releasing her like she had the plague.

"I'm so sorry, Grace," he stammered. "I didn't mean to–"

"It's fine. Truly." He seemed calm or at least not as angry. "Rafe, can we talk? For just a minute?"

"I don't think so."

She winced at his harsh tone, one he'd never used with her, ever. "I understand if it isn't a good time."

"You're right. You don't understand. It will never be a good time."

Her breath caught and Taryn's door opened. He stepped out, head swiveling as he took in the scene. "What is it?"

"Nothing," Rafe confirmed.

She suddenly couldn't bear the sight of either of them. She turned and fled, heels clacking on the marble floor as she ran, not caring about her destination. She simply wanted to distance herself as much as possible from the look on Rafe's face, the callousness of his voice. Tears fell wild and free, coursing down her cheeks as pain squeezed her heart.

She had thought Rafe cared for her, had developed feelings for her but his actions now told another story. She'd upset him, though she couldn't imagine how other than by being Taryn's friend. If Rafe truly couldn't see past his jealousy, then she didn't know him at all, which somehow hurt more than anything else.

~ Chapter Thirty-seven ~

The sun finally came out of hiding, a bright star in a cobalt sky. I breathed in the scents of wood smoke and horse. Familiar and comforting. Rafe sat rigid beside me, all but glowering as if this perfect day offended him.

"Rafe." I used my friendliest tone. "What's wrong?" He grumbled an incoherent stream of words under his breath. "Sorry. I didn't catch that."

He turned to me, his eyes like chips of granite. "Nothing you can do anything about."

"Well, if you change your mind, I'm here."

He grunted and stared into the distance. Something had happened, and I wished he'd tell me what. This ride had been his idea and a good one, a way for me to life my life as he pointed out. But it felt more like a trip to the gallows than a pleasant excursion. And silence only invited introspection, a dangerous pastime I'd rather avoid. "You and Grace seem to have gotten close."

Silence.

"You must be comfortable talking with her."

More silence.

I huffed a breath. I did not have Grace's skill with prying the truth out of people, especially those who balked at sharing it. And Rafe's stoic demeanor did not lend itself to random confessions. He'd talk when he had something to talk about, hopefully today.

We walked on and on, and still Rafe refused to utter a single word. I gave up and started talking to my horse instead. He at least seemed interested in the conversation. His answers were just as guttural and nonsensical as Rafe's, but I'd take what I could get. "It's quite warm for this time of year, don't you think?" A quiet snort. "I agree. Perhaps we've seen the last of the snow. I'm ready for–"

"Stop. For gods' sake, stop talking to your stupid horse."

I grinned, more than pleased he'd spoken, even if to insult my horse's intelligence. "So, I can talk to you now?"

He groaned as if I'd just asked him to cut off his sword arm and then fight without it. "Yes."

"Sorry boy." I patted my horse's neck and beamed a smile at Rafe. "What should we talk about, then?"

"Anything but Grace."

"Why?"

"Taryn, please. I don't want to talk about it. Her. *Gods*." He raked a hand through his hair, a gesture reserved only for the most frustrating of circumstances.

"Whatever happened, you can tell me. I might be able to help."

He scoffed. "Impossible."

"Rafe, my good man, haven't you learned by now? Anything is possible! I am a prince, you know. Surely we can figure this out. Now tell me. What happened?"

Rafe's gaze slid to me, and I held my breath. Clip, clop went the horse's hooves while I waited patiently.

"Fine," he relented. "I'll tell you. But if you breathe a word of this to Grace or anyone …"

"Understood, brother."

"I … I'm in love with her."

I barked a laugh and he hung his head. "I'm sorry. I didn't mean to laugh. But you're simply in love with her? I can't say I blame you but why the dramatics?"

"Love is never simple."

"No, I suppose it isn't. But it can't be so complicated, not with Grace. She's the most accommodating, understanding person I've ever known. In fact, just the other day, she—"

"Taryn, stop. I do not ever want to hear about what you two do … together. I just … can't. Please."

Brow furrowed, I studied his slumped shoulders, his woeful expression. "Gods above, Rafe. Please look at me." He slowly raised his head and my heart sank. But I could fix this. Him. Them. "I swear on my honor nothing happened with Grace and nothing will. There was a time when I thought otherwise but … she is only a friend."

Several emotions flashed across his face, one after the other, ending with hope. He released a shaky breath. "Truly?"

I nodded. "Have you even asked her how she feels?"

"Well, no." He frowned. "I just assumed …"

"Ah. Therein lies your problem, my friend. You assumed to know a woman's heart. A mistake of epic proportions."

He arched a brow. "I'm beginning to see it now."

"Just talk to her. Tell her how you feel. She probably feels the same about you, you dolt."

He bit his lip. "I don't know. What if she doesn't?"

"Rafe." I flashed a grin. "What if she does?"

He stared at me for so long I began to question his true affections, but then he smiled. "What if she does."

"I knew you had it in you. Rafe Grant, slayer of dragons and women's hearts everywhere," I proclaimed with a broad sweep of my arm. He threw his head back, laughing as we rode side by side into the sunset. Perhaps I'd survive after all.

~ Chapter Thirty-eight ~

The throne room looked exactly as I remembered it. The man seated on the throne, however, did not. His face had aged ten years since I'd seen him last, yet he smiled as I came to stand in front of him. "Father."

"Taryn."

"You asked for me?"

"Let's sit in the council chamber. This room is too drafty for my old bones."

I followed him from one grand room to another. He sat at the head of the large table and I took my customary seat on his right, feeling a bit awkward alone with him. He'd visited my sick bed only a handful of times and hadn't sent for me until now, weeks after my return.

"How are you feeling?"

"I've been better. But also, worse. Recovering well, if that's what you mean."

"Indeed, it is. Have you spoken to your uncle? Your men?"

"Uncle Niall, yes. But not the men. I … can't."

"They've asked to see you. I heard you gave orders to not let them near your room. Why?"

I sighed and rubbed my temples. "Seeing them reminds me of … everything. It's too painful, Father. Surely you understand."

"Of course Taryn, but they're your men. They simply want to thank you. You sacrificed yourself for their freedom. They owe you their lives."

"I'm not ready, not yet. Soon."

"Very well. Are you talking to anyone? A healer?"

"Grace has visited a few times, and we've talked, but I'm not sure it's helping. It is good to have a friend, though. Friends, actually, with Rafe here as well."

"I hope he's adjusting to his new position."

"It's an honor I'm sure he's grateful for. And he seems happy. Although he and Grace had a falling out."

"I'm sorry to hear it. Perhaps we should lighten the mood, since you're feeling so much better. A celebration of your return. What do you say?"

"I don't know, Father. A party seems awfully … loud."

His booming laughter rang against the stone walls. "I'm sure there will be music. But you love parties. Or at least you used to."

"No, I do. A party sounds fine. If you think it's a good idea."

He nodded. "Your mother and sister will be over the moon. Any excuse to wear a new dress."

I laughed under my breath. "Some things never change."

"Thank the gods." He stood, signaling the end of our discussion. "Let me know if you need anything, Taryn."

"I will. Thank you, Father." I bowed and left the room, feeling like I'd lost a game I hadn't realized I'd been playing.

❦

The party started like any other, with toasts and cheers and endless applause for my bravery. My face started to throb from all the smiling, and my shoulder ached from all the backslapping. Gods, these people never ceased to amaze me, though I should thank them for teaching me how to compartmentalize with phenomenal success. I'd learned from an early age the art of ignoring everything going on, going wrong outside these walls. To smile and laugh and dance as if nothing else mattered.

"Taryn, dear," my mother purred at my elbow. "You should be celebrating. This is your party, after all."

I scoffed. This party had never been about me. My mother used it as an excuse to wear every piece of jewelry she owned, reminding her subjects who sat next to the king. As if anyone would ever forget.

I gazed around the ballroom, music blaring as couples twirled and teetered their way through dance after dance. I felt no desire to join them, but then Grace floated in at Natalie's side, her gossamer dress leaving little to the imagination. Almost every male head turned in her direction as she swept toward the royal table. I couldn't tear my gaze from her golden hair or her emerald eyes.

She flashed a stunning smile and dropped into a curtsy. "Your majesties. Your highness."

My father dipped his chin. "Grace. Please, join us."

She sat at the opposite end of the table, not near enough to engage in conversation. Her laughter made my heart lurch. My palms sweat, my pulse race. Like an untested youth. A familiar feeling I remembered from the night I'd held her in my arms as we danced. We'd gone out to the courtyard afterwards and I'd almost kissed her but then something happened. The memory eluded me, yet it didn't matter. I simply had to recreate the magic under the stars. I rose from my seat to ask Grace to dance, and Rafe burst into the room, striding for the dais like a charging bear.

My father shot to his feet. "What is it, Rafe?"

"The northern border, your majesty. It's under attack."

"When?"

"Two days ago."

"The garrison?"

He shook his head. "No word yet."

The room started to spin, and I sat down before I fell down, stomach heaving with dread. No. Not again. Not now. *Please.*

My father clenched his jaw, looking for all the world like a king about to obliterate his enemy. Which I hoped he'd do and leave me the hell out of it.

"Sir. Your orders."

"Find a captain. Take two, no three companies north. And bring me General Stark's head."

Rafe glanced at me then bowed. "Sir."

I watched him rush from the room, aching to call him back. I needed him here. With me. *Safe. Alive.*

"Taryn," Grace's soft voice coaxed me back to reality. She'd come over to stand beside me at some point. I shook my head, unable to speak, to voice the fear clawing up my spine. "He can't go, Grace. I can't lose him too."

"Don't worry. He'll be fine."

If only it were true.

~ Chapter Thirty-nine ~

A winter storm lashed through the trees, whipping around the castle with a furious roar. Chill winds blew gusts of icy air along the stone walkways and chased anyone brave enough to venture outside back indoors. Soldiers trained to endure such conditions stood tall and straight, waiting for the order to march. A young officer had been hastily promoted and sat in his saddle, eyes wide and hands shaking. Not the best start for a new captain but war levels the playing field. All men are created equal when death calls.

The order rang out in the courtyard and the soldiers filed past beneath my window. Part of me balked at staying behind but my soul would not survive another battle. My career as a soldier had come to a bitter end, and none too soon. Surely I could find something worthwhile to do with my time. A position on the king's council, perhaps. Anything to keep me away from the front lines, from the death and chaos of war. *Never again.*

I sighed and pulled the blanket tighter around my shoulders. The huge fire blazing in the hearth did little to warm the chilling thought of the northern garrison under attack. And

Rafe, a solid man yet not truly a soldier, going off to fight a war he shouldn't be fighting. I hadn't seen him or my father since the party. Avoiding me, perhaps, though I hadn't sought them out, either. I had no desire to get swept up in whatever military campaign they had planned.

... Coward.

I took solace in the library alone to sort through my feelings. About everything. I could no longer wallow in self-pity, mired in self-doubt. Time to face whatever demons still tormented me and slay them. Once and for all.

Grace found me, though I hadn't been hiding. "Hello, Taryn. I've been looking for you."

I grinned, more for her benefit than mine. "And here I am."

"Here you are." She glanced around, the library blessedly empty but for a few scurrying mice. "What are you reading?"

"I'm not, really. Just trying to act the part." I slipped the book back onto its shelf and started toward the door. "You said you were looking for me?"

"I wanted to check on you, see how you were doing. You seem well. Are you?"

"Surprisingly, I am. I've done a lot of soul-searching these past few days and I've come to realize something."

"Oh? Something good, I hope."

"I'm an idiot."

She failed to stifle a laugh, earning a scathing look from the librarian as we passed her desk. I ushered her into the hallway, where she burst out in a fit of giggles. "I'm sorry," she gasped between guffaws. "I'm just so pleased I'm not the only one who thinks so."

"I thought you might be."

She wiped her damp cheeks. "But why do you think you're an idiot?"

"Isn't it obvious? Because I haven't listened to anything you've said about my recovery. And I have some serious work to do to get past … what happened."

"I'm so pleased to hear it, Taryn. Would you like my help?"

"Absolutely, if you're willing."

"I'd love to. And we can start now if it suits you."

I escorted Grace to my room, where she sat on the edge of her seat as if expecting something. A breakthrough? A breakdown? I didn't know which I dreaded more. But either way, I needed her. I couldn't do this with anyone else. Her presence calmed me enough to see past the arrogant pride blocking my path to wellness.

"So." My voice remained calm, though I felt anything but. "Where do we start?"

"Wherever you'd like."

I frowned. How could I adequately describe my feelings when I'd yet to understand them myself? Still, I'd brought her here for this very reason. I swallowed the lump of anxiety. "My mother never wanted me to be a soldier," I blurted.

She nodded in agreement. "Naturally."

"She claimed I had no right putting myself in such danger. As heir to the throne."

"But I take it you didn't listen?"

"At first, yes. I love my mother and she had a valid point. But year after year, I practiced with wooden swords and then with blunt-tipped steel, watching soldiers march out to fight, to claim their glory. They often returned home heroes, and I ached to be one of them." Her gentle smile encouraged me to continue. "Eventually, I just couldn't stand on the sidelines anymore and told my mother I planned to join the army. She argued and wept but never begged. In the end I think she realized my mind couldn't be changed, so she simply relented. I left for the northern garrison the next day."

"And you trained there? In that snow-blasted wasteland?"

I nodded. "But I thrived there. From the moment I set foot inside those walls, my uncle treated me like any other soldier, like I belonged. Soon they all did. And then I pledged my life to the military." I shrugged, not sure where to take the story next. My first battle? My last? Everything seemed monumentally important yet inconsequential at the same time.

"What do you love most about being a soldier?"

Her question caught me off guard, jolting me from my thoughts. Yet answering had never been easier. "Camaraderie. Being a part of something larger than myself."

"Not the glory or the heroics?"

I blinked. "I had wanted those things as a boy, but the brotherhood mattered more. Especially my men. I respect them, trust them. Fighting shoulder to shoulder on the battlefield …" My throat tightened with emotion.

"You can do this, Taryn. Just try."

I took a shaky breath. "I cherish every soldier under my command. Know their names, their dreams, their fears. As they do mine. They all hold a special place in my heart." Tears streaked down my face, but I had to continue. I'd never get it out otherwise. "We fought successfully together for years, side by side, returning with only a few minor bumps and bruises. Until Haverton. Too many died. Thirteen of my own men. Brothers, friends. Pieces of my soul."

"I'm so sorry," Grace whispered.

I wiped my cheeks. "I returned home, grieved and mourned. Accepted their losses as a harsh reality of war. But I still saw the battlefield every time I closed my eyes. I held myself responsible for their deaths."

"It isn't your fault. Truly."

I blinked the last tears from my eyes. "I know. Now. But the knowledge doesn't lessen the pain or bring them back." My chest still ached with loss but the pain seemed bearable now.

"No, it doesn't. But it helps you go on, to honor their sacrifice by living your life."

I stared at her as if she'd just exposed the secrets of the universe. Perhaps she had. I'd been too heartbroken to do anything other than blame myself. I hadn't seen the truth, the error of my ways. My selfishness. "You are absolutely right. And brilliant."

She shook her head, wiping at her damp cheeks. "I only listened."

"You did so much more, helped me in ways I can never explain. You cared about me, and I took advantage of your kindness and your friendship. Forgive me."

A faint blush stained her cheeks. "I'm so pleased I could help. And of course I care about you. You don't need to apologize. You were hurting and scared. Lost. And it's hard to find the light when you're trapped in the dark. But we still need to talk about what happened with General Stark."

"Why?"

"When you returned, you didn't know me or Rafe or anyone, really. You didn't even know yourself, Taryn. There has to be more to the story."

"I suppose there is. But I'm exhausted. Can we talk about it tomorrow?"

"Oh, yes. You need your rest." She smiled brightly as she stood. "Shall I come after lunch?"

"I'll be waiting."

She dipped a shallow curtsy then hurried out the door. I took several deep breaths, willing my heart to calm before it burst. I still couldn't speak of my time with General Stark, mostly because I didn't know how. The words refused to be said, failing me when I tried to express my feelings. A heavy burden. Like a boulder lodged in my gut. A stain on my soul I would never fully cleanse.

~ Chapter Forty ~

Rafe hated snow. Had hated it his whole life, despite growing up surrounded by its fluffy whiteness. His boyhood friends had all loved it. They'd hurled snowballs at each other or raced down snow-packed hills on battered shields while Rafe stood on the sidelines, scowling his silent scowl. And now the blasted stuff only added to his misery, covering every trace of the enemy's presence and muffling all sound. Sneaking up on them would be nearly impossible.

Captain Lawson rallied the men in a valiant effort to improve morale. The three companies marched with grim determination across the broad plain, through the narrow valley and into the woods, hoping to catch the enemy there. But they'd moved on, likely toward Evanston.

They finally reached Iredale. Captain Lawson ordered a halt, his voice cracking in the bitter cold. They'd sleep at the garrison then move out at dawn.

"Thank the gods," Rafe mumbled to himself. The northern garrison still stood, as did the village. General Stark's men wouldn't have had time to destroy either if they hoped to reach the castle before Rafe and the others intercepted them.

Rafe blew a warm breath into his hands, which only made his throat burn. The air itself seemed to be against them, pushing back with arctic temperatures. He could handle just about anything Mother Nature threw at him and simply wrapped his cloak tighter around his shoulders while the others shivered next to him, huddling close to the fire's meager warmth.

The night wore on, yet no one ventured into the barracks to sleep. Either too cold or too anxious to relax enough, so they all sat watch, eyes narrowed to slits.

❧

Dawn's early light broke through the trees, feeble and watery in the frosty air. Rafe creaked to his feet, stamped snow from his boots and shouldered his pack.

No one said a word as they marched ever north, colder and colder the farther they went. Soon all vegetation disappeared, any signs of civilized life long since blown away by the frigid winds. They marched for what felt like days, and Rafe's toes went numb, but frostbite didn't worry him nearly as much as the looming battle. Their untried captain would lead them in sure enough, but would they come out the other side? Or die somewhere in the middle? Rafe would give his life for his kingdom, but he had unfinished business. Starting with Grace.

He'd left without saying goodbye, taking the easy way out. *Coward.* A move quite out of character, yet he couldn't face her. Not after the way he'd behaved, like a jilted lover, insecure and weak. He'd tried to tell her how he felt, had started to several times, but his mouth betrayed him. Jaw clenched around aching teeth, he pushed those thoughts from his mind. He'd own up to his failures when he returned. *If* he returned.

"Sir?" Kieran tapped his shoulder, jolting him from his self-hate session.

"Kieran. You don't have to call me sir. I'm not your superior."

"Sir," he repeated, breath pluming. "Do you know how much farther until the next checkpoint? The others are wondering."

Rafe squinted at the darkening sky then shook his head. "And I know you're all tired, but we don't stop until the captain gives the order. Just tell them to keep moving. They'll freeze to death otherwise."

"Sir."

He bounded away to the rear of the pack and Rafe sighed. Kieran had been through enough, as had his family. Both Rafe and Taryn had argued with him, urged him to stay behind but he refused to listen. Taryn almost resorted to commanding him as his prince but Rafe had talked him down, promising to see Kieran safely home.

Rafe swore under his breath as a brisk wind kicked snow into his face. The sooner they found these bastards, the better. Anything to get out of this gods' forsaken wasteland and back home. Where Grace waited, probably wondering if Rafe had ever cared for her at all. *Stop it, you fool.* He couldn't afford such distractions. He needed to keep his head in the game for them to win it.

A sharp crack tore through the night, halting his steps. He signaled the others to stop and the forest quieted. Breath held, he listened, waited. Another sharp crack and he bolted, unshouldering his bow as he crashed through the trees.

Anxious shouts nipped at his heels and branches snapped as he thundered past. Chest heaving, he burst into a clearing. The enemy camp.

Time seemed to slow even as his pulse accelerated. Every head turned, all eyes widening as realization struck. Rafe did not belong.

He slowly backed away, hoping the cold had dulled their senses and slowed their reflexes enough for a safe retreat. Unfortunately General Stark's men were smarter than they looked. The sharp tip of a sword poked his back.

"Stop there," commanded a rough voice behind him.

He stopped.

"Drop the bow and turn around."

He dropped the bow and turned around.

The soldier eyed Rafe's cloak, boots, sword, and belt. "One of King Merrick's, eh?" he sneered. "What are you doing out at this time of night? Shouldn't you be home in your bed?"

Rafe shrugged. "Couldn't sleep."

"You can sleep now." The pommel of his sword met the side of Rafe's head.

He slept.

~ Chapter Forty-one ~

Grace ran through the maze of corridors, legs pumping and lungs bursting. But she couldn't outpace the fear charging after her. It tackled her with rib-crushing force, her feet sliding on the slick cobblestones. She tumbled then landed with an awkward bounce in the courtyard. The snow cushioned her fall, but her pride would bear a nasty bruise just the same.

She hung her head and cried harder than she had when her mother died. She'd been a girl then. Now as a woman she should have more self-control, more composure, but she simply could not stop.

"Grace," a gentle voice called from across the courtyard.

She forced herself to at least sit up if not hold the tears at bay. Natalie walked toward her, eyes full of sympathy. She knelt at Grace's side and offered her a lace handkerchief. Grace took it with a trembling hand.

"You poor thing. What can I do?" Natalie rubbed her back in soothing circles.

Grace wiped her eyes then blew her nose. "Nothing," she whispered. "Nothing at all."

"But he might be fine. We don't know any–"

"He's dead! I just know it!" Cradled in Natalie's arms, she dissolved into chest-heaving sobs. With despair eating at her soul, she cried until her eyes were red and swollen. She took a shuddering breath and wiped her cheeks. "Thank you."

"Of course. You're my dear friend, and I would do anything for you. Including ruin my new dress."

"Oh, I'm so sorry!" A furious blush raced across her face, but Natalie simply grinned.

"I'm only teasing, silly. I hate this dress."

Grace managed a small smile.

"There. Feel better now?" She nodded, and Natalie helped her to her feet. "Come inside. Let's get something warm to drink."

Mute with grief, she let Natalie guide her past curious servants and whispering courtiers. Grace hardly noticed. *Rafe. Oh gods.* She'd never again see his crooked smile, hear his rumbling voice. Feel his heated gaze. Pain splintered her heart into a thousand bleeding fragments. She whimpered and bit her lip as Natalie dragged her into her rooms.

"Sit," Natalie commanded.

She sat.

Natalie shoved a glass into Grace's shaking hand. "Drink this."

She drank.

Natalie took the empty glass with brusque formality. "Now." She settled onto the couch next to her. "Let's be logical, shall we? What do we know?"

Of course Natalie would approach the situation like a problem in need of solving. Why couldn't she just accept it as the world's most devastating news? Grace shook her head. She simply refused to voice her thoughts because if she did, they'd become real.

"All right. I'll start. We know General Stark's men captured Rafe fifty miles north of the garrison. A three-day march, I think." Natalie's brow furrowed as she calculated the distance in her head. "Yes, three days. So then …" She trailed off, mumbling as she added and subtracted, though Grace couldn't imagine what they'd do with the information. Rafe had been in the enemy's hands for almost a week. Suffering. Likely dead.

She closed her eyes, wanting nothing but to lie down and never get up again. The thought of living her life without Rafe exhausted her. How could she, while he didn't? Unthinkable. Unimaginable. And far too painful to contemplate.

Air. She needed air immediately. Lurching to her feet, she startled Natalie from her arithmetic. "I have to go," she tried to say, only it came out as a strangled sigh. Natalie's wide-eyed stare faded from view as darkness claimed her.

❈

"Grace."

Grace cracked open an eye, regretting it instantly. Her head throbbed in pain with every beat of her stubborn heart. She struggled to sit up, and strong arms braced her, laying her against a pile of pillows.

"Better?" Taryn's smile pierced through the fog of grief.

"Yes," she croaked. "Thank you." He held out a glass of water, but she shook her head.

"Are you all right? Natalie told me you fainted."

She swallowed past the tightness. "Where is she?"

"With Father. She's trying to sweet-talk more information from him."

"About Rafe?"

He nodded soberly. "But I'm sure he's fine. If anyone can survive, he can. I managed to, so it can't be all bad."

She smiled weakly at his attempted humor. "I don't think so. In fact, I'm sure of it."

"You can't be sure, as you well know. Did you ever once give up hope for me?"

"Well, no. But–"

He held up a hand. "Exactly. So why wouldn't you do the same for Rafe?"

Tears filled her eyes. "I don't know."

He blew out a frustrated breath. "He will get through this. I swear it. What can I do to convince you?"

"Nothing."

He tapped his chin with a forefinger. "There has to be something."

She shook her head and wiped her cheeks. "Just leave me be, Taryn. Please."

"Absolutely not. You know how stubborn I am. We don't have to talk but I'm not leaving." His voice rang with regal authority as he leaned back in his chair.

She sighed. "Fine, you can stay. And we can talk. Just not about …"

"Fair enough. What should we talk about?"

"How have you been? I've hardly seen you lately."

"Ah, yes. I've been extremely busy, you know. Council meetings, affairs of state. I'm a very important person."

His eyes glittered, and she smiled. This felt good, to banter with him as if nothing had happened. Exactly what she needed right now. Just seeing him so happy, so healthy warmed her heart. Her stomach, however, rumbled in protest, and she glanced out the window at the twilit sky. "How long have I been in here?"

"A few hours, I think. Why?"

"I'm starving."

He laughed, one of her favorite sounds. "Something I can surely remedy. Come with me."

He stood, and she blinked at him before climbing to her feet. His warm hand cradled hers as they walked to the dining hall, yet she couldn't face the court, not in her current state.

She pulled him to a stop as they reached the doors. "Taryn, I can't …"

"Don't worry. You're safe with me."

He opened the door and urged her inside. She cringed but no one laughed or mocked or jeered in the empty hall. "Where is everyone?"

"It's Wednesday."

She stared at him as if he'd spoken a foreign language. "And?"

"Oh." He grinned like an imp. "We don't dine in the hall on Wednesdays."

"Why not?"

He shrugged, pulling her across the marble floor to the servants' entrance then into the kitchen. The scent of baking bread wafted around them, and cauldrons bubbled merrily on the cooktop. Venison stew, if her nose hadn't deceived her. Saliva flooded her mouth.

"Your highness." The cook dipped a curtsy. "What brings you here?"

"I'm sorry to intrude but Grace would like something to eat."

"Of course. Please, sit." She gestured to the scarred wood table.

With mischief in his eyes, Taryn helped Grace down onto a bench. He clearly enjoyed these clandestine adventures. She had to admit the thrill of excitement enticed her as well. And just sitting here with him in the cozy kitchen, eating from chipped earthenware bowls reminded her of happier times. She smiled and one of the cracks in her heart sealed closed, forged together by the strength of Taryn's friendship.

~ Chapter Forty-two ~

I walked among the corpses, numb to the gory scene. Dense fog encircled my ankles as it slithered across the battlefield. Bodies lay broken and battered as far as the eye could see. I glanced at the faces I passed. All strangers, all dead. Carcasses waiting for a hungry scavenger to pick their bones clean. A lone wolf howled, its eerie sound an echo of the ghostly wailing all around me.

… Taryn.

I stopped, head angled. *Yes?*

… Why are you here?

I don't know.

… Yes, you do.

I frowned, trying to remember how I'd gotten here, why I'd come. *Do you know why I'm here?*

… Yes.

Why?

… You need to see this.

What? Why?

… To remind you.

I will never forget.

... You already have.

I jolted awake, chest heaving in the moonlit room. Gods, what a horrible dream. I raked a trembling hand through my hair and swung my legs over the side of the bed. The dream image refused to fade, as if it were a memory. Of course I'd seen a similar battlefield, but I had known those men. The men in the dream were all strangers to me, yet the gruff voice sounded like Rafe's. Why would he speak to me in a dream? He'd been in my thoughts often the past few days with good reason, but I'd never dreamt of him. Why now? I shrugged it off as another trick of my cruel subconscious. Some things just cannot be explained.

I proceeded with my day as usual, refusing to acknowledge the worry edging its way into my heart. Rafe would be fine, just as I'd told Grace. We'd win this ridiculous battle and bring him home, safe and sound.

I eased into the council chamber, only a few minutes late for the morning session. My father raised a brow but otherwise ignored my tardiness. I stood at Lord Carlisle's shoulder as he droned on about troop movements, gesturing to a large map spread out on the table. Wooden figures dotted its surface, scattered across the kingdom. I sucked in a breath, hardly able to believe my eyes. The enemy had not only grown, but had made considerable advancements. Why hadn't I seen this before now?

"Lord Carlisle." I interrupted his report and he frowned, his gray mustache quivering against his jowls. "Please tell me this is a hypothetical representation."

"I'm afraid not, your highness. This is, as far as we know, the current state of affairs."

I gaped at him then at my father. "What are we doing about it?"

My father shook his head, a sober admission of defeat. "We are doing all we can, Taryn. Fighting hard and pushing back, but it isn't enough."

I searched the other faces, hoping for some sign of hope or flash of brilliance. Even a long-shot military strategy would calm my racing heart. Nothing?

"I'm sorry, Taryn. But we must face facts. King Rendon has men to spare, and General Stark has a score to settle. He's fueled by vengeance, a powerful ally in battle. Our own forces are depleted after Haverton, and General Creston's men are still recovering."

"But they are your soldiers, Father. They will follow where you lead them. Please." The look on his face answered my plea easily enough, yet I wouldn't be persuaded to give up just yet. Not with Rafe still in enemy hands. He wouldn't have been captured if he hadn't come here in the first place. And he came for me. I couldn't sit here and not try to do something to stop it. For good.

A plan began to form. One which would force me to face my demons head-on, alone. Reckless, dangerous and beyond stupid. Taking a life for vengeance with malice in my heart could shatter me beyond recognition. I'd only ever raised a hand in violence when defending myself, my men, or my kingdom. Yet it remained the only logical course of action.

"Let me do it, Father. I'll take my men. They will follow me." He blinked as if I'd just suggested I jump off a bridge.

Lord Carlisle barked a laugh. "Your men? You mean those boys you abandoned?"

White hot anger pulsed through me. "You forget your place, sir. And yes, I mean those men. I trained them myself." I turned to my father, who would ultimately decide. "Please. Let me put an end to this." *Permanently.*

He blew out a heavy breath, glanced at the map, and nodded. "Very well. I want reports every twelve hours. And no heroics. Understood?"

"Of course, Father. Sir." Placing a hand over my heart, I swore a silent oath, a solemn vow. This would serve as my way to honor the fallen. Their deaths would not be in vain.

I left the council chamber, mind whirling. My own death didn't concern me, but anyone else's filled me with dread.

A shudder ran down my spine as if a presence had rubbed against my soul. I stopped in the middle of the corridor, head angled. Listening. An offer of support whispered from deep in the shadowed corners of my mind. With a sigh of relief, I continued to my room. Anticipation replaced doubt and my path became crystal clear. I knew what I had to do and how to do it. Despite the shadow on my heart.

I rounded a corner and collided with Grace. I gripped her elbow to steady her. "Grace, my apologies."

She flashed a genuine smile. "I'm fine Taryn. But where are you off to in such a hurry?" Her smile dimmed. "Has something happened?"

"No. Well, yes. Sort of." I grabbed her hand. "Come with me."

I parked her on the couch then explained the situation as clearly as I could without divulging my secret intentions. She'd never let me go through with it if she knew. And I needed someone to believe I'd come back to keep me tethered to reality.

She nodded and took a deep breath. "And you truly think your company can make enough of a difference?"

"I do."

"Well, then so do I. But I'll worry about you every minute you're gone."

I sat next to her and took her hand. "I know you will, and I can't tell you not to. But have faith in me, believe in me, Grace. I can do this."

"Of course I believe in you. I've never stopped." She squeezed my hand then hung her head. "Do you think … Is it possible you'll find Rafe?"

She didn't whisper, but she might as well have. A tear slipped down her cheek, and I wiped it away. I never wanted to see her cry again. I vowed to do everything in my power to bring Rafe home, for her sake as well as his. And mine. I lifted her chin, and her gaze met mine. "Yes."

The time had come to finish this, no matter the cost. I could not fail. I would not allow myself to even think of the possibility. Darkness smiled with eager malevolence, promising refuge. A place to hide from the pain. A way to shield my heart from destruction. I'd found a true ally at last and my confidence soared to new heights.

… *The time is now.*

~ Chapter Forty-three ~

I sat back in my chair, wary in the resounding silence. I hadn't held back with the details. The men were either rigid with resolve or shocked speechless. "Any questions?" Not a single comment or grumble or whisper of dissent.

"Sir." Kieran spoke first from his seat in the front row.

"Yes, Kieran."

"When do we leave?" The group gave a collective sigh as if they'd all been wanting to ask but didn't know how.

I grinned, which seemed to break the tension. "Dawn tomorrow."

Kieran nodded then stood along with the others. They saluted as a cohesive unit, per their training. "Sir. Yes, sir!"

"Dismissed." Tears of pride pricked my eyes. We could do this.

The group ambled out, talking in twos and threes, but Kieran hung back. I clapped him on the shoulder. "What is it?"

"It's nothing, sir."

"Kieran." I pivoted him to face me. "You can tell me."

"The others, sir. They've been … different towards me. Ever since you were captured."

I raised a brow. "Different in what way?"

He studied the toes of his boots, shuffling his feet on the gleaming marble floor. "They ignore me. I can't … they won't …" He blew out a breath and looked up at me. "They said it's all my fault."

The others shouldn't blame him. I certainly didn't. He and Rafe had taken a huge risk when they came looking for me. I held General Stark entirely responsible. "But you didn't do anything wrong."

He shook his head, biting his lip. "I couldn't convince General Creston to go back for you. And then Rafe and I didn't make it in time, and we had to tell everyone we failed. We … lost you and–"

"It's all right, Kieran. I'll talk to them."

"But, sir–"

"It's done. Dismissed."

He trudged out the door, his feet as heavy as my heart.

This all or nothing operation required everyone's participation. Those who weren't up to the challenge could stay behind. My plan did not allow for hesitation or doubt. And I had to get this job done without letting emotion distract me. Anything less would only lead to capture. Or disaster. *Disaster may be my destiny.*

I kept to myself as I usually did before battle and ate a quiet dinner in my room where I could retreat into my head in peace. Solitude also ensured no one would witness a potential break down or other sign of mental instability. I didn't want to suddenly find myself stripped of command and chained to my bed. Worry probed at the edge of my thoughts yet strength and determination flowed through me in equal measure. A spark ignited by the unquenchable blazing desire for action. For violence.

Evil swam in my veins, prowling in my head like a demon to be tamed. I harnessed it, honed it to razor sharpness. The perfect weapon.

... First the general. Then the king.

❧

I slept in increments and woke well before dawn. The castle grounds slumbered on, deserted except for the night watch as I strode toward the stables. The horses greeted me, expecting an early breakfast. "Sorry to disappoint," I whispered. My horse stood proud and tall, watching me with calm eyes. I saddled him, stroking his mane and praising his speed. I'd need every ounce of it on the road ahead.

The most recent report from the field indicated General Stark's men had advanced as far west as Landon, a small but prosperous city near the coast. A valuable target for King Rendon as all our trade entered and exited through its ports. But he'd never acquire it. Not if I had anything to say about it.

General Stark and his men were my top priority. I hoped by cutting off the snake's head the rest would lay down their arms and surrender. More of a wish than a hope, but I had to try. I'd proceed with the second part of my plan regardless of what happened with the general. It would just be a bit trickier.

Dawn broke over the stable roof, and the men arrived, eager to be on their way. I knew the feeling, and led my horse from his stall. "Good morning."

"Good morning, sir."

"I won't thank you for coming as I know it would be somewhat of an insult, but I will say I'm proud to command every one of you. The last several months haven't been easy, and I expect the next few weeks to test us in ways we never imagined. But we are soldiers, bonded in brotherhood to support each other no matter what. We each act according to our own conscience, but as a unit we strive towards a single goal. We are united in this effort and because of our unity, we will succeed."

I swallowed hard, determined to remain strong for them. For myself. We weren't at war, not yet, and I'd do everything in my power to prevent it. Anything to keep these men safe. I swung up into the saddle to lead them onward, to victory.

~ Chapter Forty-four ~

Rafe would give anything to just close his eyes forever. But every time he tried, Grace's face appeared in his mind. She'd smile or smirk or pout, and he'd open his eyes, forcing himself to stay alive. He had to live so he could tell her how he felt. He loved her. Even if she didn't love him in return.

Heavy boot steps echoed down the corridor, and he tensed. Anyone who had visited his cell brought with them a new wave of misery, adding to his already miserable life. This time, his usual tormentor entered with a young man, a noble by the sneer of contempt on his face. If Rafe had known to expect such exalted company, he'd have tidied up. Though the nobleman couldn't complain about much other than the stench of waste. And despair.

"This is the one?" The nobleman pointed a slim finger at him and the tormentor nodded. "Very well. Clean him up then bring him to me."

Rafe wanted to crush his haughty voice right out of his throat. He clenched his jaw and swayed, wincing as the chains suspending him from the ceiling bit into his wrists.

The nobleman turned with a swirl of his heavy cloak, leaving Rafe alone with the tormentor. Every bone in his body ached, yet he lashed out when he came near.

"Relax, big man. I'm only going to unlock your chains."

Rafe blinked and tried to swallow, his throat clicking with the effort. He swayed again, and the chains slithered to the floor with a dull thunk. He had never heard a more beautiful sound and collapsed to his knees, moaning as the circulation returned to his weary shoulders.

"Here." The tormentor pushed a bucket of water under Rafe's nose. "Drink."

The water smelled foul, but he drank in heaving gulps. He retched then drank again with more patience, and managed to sit up. The tormentor held out a towel and a clean set of clothes. Rafe took them with shaking hands, wondering if he were dreaming. Or hallucinating. "What ..." he started to say but ended up coughing instead.

"I'll be back." The tormentor stomped out the door, locking it behind him.

Rafe sat on the cold, stone floor, rubbing feeling back into his wrists. He swallowed a few dozen times, though his throat felt raw, as if he'd been screaming. Perhaps he had. His first few days here were lost in a haze of pain and blood. But he hadn't broken, hadn't said a word about anything to anyone. Yet even the strongest man will crack under enough pressure. Including Rafe. So why release him now? And for what purpose?

He should be grateful, but his suspicion had risen to paranoia. Deep in enemy territory, he couldn't let his guard down despite the cool water on the back of his neck or the soft shirt against his chafed skin. He'd bide his time, play along and figure out a way to escape.

The tormentor returned to escort Rafe to the nobleman's rooms. Any hope of freedom withered and died the minute he stepped inside. The man sat in a gilded chair, idly toying with a jeweled dagger. Rafe did not want to test its sharpness or the nobleman's generosity. He simply kept his feet underneath him and waited.

"You may go." The nobleman waved a lazy hand at the tormentor. The door clicked shut, like a key in a lock. From one prison to another, it seemed. "Well, well." The nobleman grinned like he'd just won a prize. "You certainly are a big fellow." He stood and prowled around Rafe as he assessed him. For what, Rafe had no clue. "I suppose you're wondering what you're doing here instead of rotting in that horrid cell."

Obviously.

"I am Lord Harlesby of Verlandia." His tone suggested the name should mean something to Rafe. It didn't. He scoffed as if annoyed and not a little affronted at Rafe's indifferent reaction. Did he expect Rafe to bow? He only bowed to royalty and this man fell far short. "My personal guard recently left my employ, and I need another. King Rendon generously allowed me to replace him from the stock in the dungeon. You are by far the burliest of the lot."

Pressed into service? To this man? Rafe would rather die. Still, he held his tongue. He might use this to his advantage.

"You do speak, do you not?"

Rafe nodded but remained silent. His throat pulsed with pain every time he swallowed, and he didn't want to speak with this sorry excuse for a lord, anyway.

"I see. Well, in time you will accept your sentence. Until then, we should have you properly dressed. I cannot be seen about town with you in this state."

Rafe glanced at his clothing, a far cry from the pristine uniform he'd donned, yet cleaner than he'd been in weeks. He thought he looked decent enough. Apparently not.

Lord Harlesby rang a small bell. The door opened a mere second later, and a young girl stepped in. Rafe fought the urge to roll his eyes as she curtsied.

"Yes, my lord?"

"I need a tailor. Now." He snapped his fingers in her face and she scurried out. Rafe's new mission became showing this man some humility. He swayed then grabbed the back of a chair for support. His stomach heaved from too much water and not enough food.

"Sit down before you fall down." Rafe sank onto the chair. Lord Harlesby huffed an exasperated sigh then examined him with a critical eye, like a side of beef at auction. Like property. Rafe bristled, yet easily imagined throttling him to death.

"What is your name?"

Rafe blinked. "Rafe Grant."

"Rafe, did you say?"

He cleared his throat with painful effort. "Yes."

"Yes, what?"

"Yes, my lord." He almost choked on the words but would need to get used to saying them eventually.

Lord Harlesby smiled and clasped his hands behind his back. "Very good." A knock sounded. "Enter."

A stooped man shuffled in, laden with fabrics. "My lord."

Lord Harlesby gestured for Rafe to stand. He creaked to his feet, every muscle screaming in protest.

"I need this man properly outfitted as my personal guard. Three uniforms, an extra jacket and a cloak. Two, no three pairs of boots, all black. And …" Lord Harlesby narrowed his eyes, stroking his chin as he peered into Rafe's face. "That is all. I leave you to your work." He flounced out the door without a backwards glance.

Rafe stared after him. He'd left him alone, unguarded, unchained. With a *tailor*. Luck? Or a test? He didn't particularly care. "I'm very sorry, sir, but I have to go. Now."

The tailor's mouth fell open. "But, sir. Lord Harlesby–"

"I don't give a damn what Lord … *he* said. I. Am. Leaving." He lurched toward the door, limbs warming to the task with each halting step.

"Sir!" The tailor called after him, but he didn't break stride and bolted toward freedom.

~ Chapter Forty-five ~

Grace hummed a quiet melody as she swept the last ashes from the hearth. The days had grown milder, but the nights still warranted a fire, and the warmth helped ease her father's aching joints. She carried the pail out the back door and tossed the contents into the garden. She'd need to plant soon for the spring harvest. Her mother had done the planting and taught Grace well, a skill she hoped to pass on to her own daughter someday. If she ever had children. Or got married. She rolled her eyes. Of course she'd do those things. She still had plenty of time. Young and healthy and according to her father, beautiful. She could wait. And she would wait. For Rafe.

She smiled and returned to the kitchen where she'd set a pot of stew to heat for dinner. The pleasant scene of her upcoming reunion with Rafe played through her head as she stirred. She hadn't lied when she told Taryn she believed in him, in his ability to bring Rafe home. Taryn's unwavering confidence inspired the same in Grace, and she found herself hoping more than praying since his departure.

Every night she dreamt of Rafe. And every morning she woke with a joyful spirit. She'd found someone to love who she hoped loved her in return. Now she just had to tell him.

Her heart ached whenever she recalled their last conversation. She should have told him then, told him sooner despite his misplaced jealousy. But he'd left so suddenly, without even saying goodbye. Well, she'd get her chance to set things right soon enough. She'd run into his arms, hold onto him and never, ever let go. Then she'd kiss him. And not just any kiss. The kind of kiss she'd only read about. The kind of kiss Rafe would not misunderstand or misinterpret or misconstrue. In no uncertain terms did she want him to doubt her feelings ever again. She certainly didn't. Not anymore.

"Father! Dinner is ready!" she called over her shoulder. She ladled two servings of stew and set them on the table with a loaf of bread. "Father!" She wiped her hands and headed for the living room.

Her father slept in his favorite chair, a peaceful smile on his face and a book propped open in his lap. She gently pulled off his glasses then placed a kiss on his cheek and covered him with a blanket. What would he do without her? What would she do without *him*? Perhaps he could live with Grace once she and Rafe married. Married? Good gods, she didn't even know if he loved her, let alone wanted to marry her. Her errant thoughts had traveled far, far ahead. Best to rein them in before they got her into trouble. She did not want to chase Rafe away or pressure him into a lifetime commitment.

❈

Grace strolled through the garden arm in arm with Natalie, talking of idle nonsense. They kept their conversation light on purpose. Grace didn't want to dwell on Rafe, and Natalie didn't want to dwell on Taryn. Despite her claims to the contrary, Grace knew Natalie worried. Her training and her skill allowed her to see things others didn't. Natalie had every right to be concerned. Taryn had been through an arduous ordeal recently and should not have been marching out to battle in his frame of mind. And so, they spoke of the weather and dresses and parties with not one mention of the men they loved.

"Do you know Lord Carlisle?" Natalie switched subjects with practiced ease as they reached the courtyard.

"No, I don't think so. Is he the tall skinny one who looks like a crane?"

Natalie laughed into her gloved hand. "No, but what an astute description. Lord Carlisle looks like a walrus, if we're keeping with our animal theme."

"Yes, I do believe I've seen him waddling about."

"Grace! Shame on you!"

Grace smiled at Natalie's teasing. They'd become such good friends since first meeting on this very lawn. "Well? What about Lord Walrus?"

"His son has asked to court me."

"I see. And is he a junior walrus?"

Natalie snorted then clapped her hand over her mouth. She shook her head.

"A penguin, perhaps?"

"Grace, stop!" she wheezed. They entered the castle by the side door, their slippered feet nearly soundless in the corridor.

"All right, but what does he look like? Short? Tall?"

"I have no idea. I'm simply praying the son bears no resemblance to the father."

"Oh, dear."

Natalie nodded and pulled off her gloves then opened the door to her room. Grace always marveled at Natalie's eclectic tastes. Fabrics of every style and color covered the windows, walls and furniture. None of it matched but it all seemed to belong. Grace fit right in.

Natalie flung herself onto the red velvet couch while Grace sat in the green leather chair, just two young ladies enjoying their afternoon. Grace couldn't imagine being happier, unless Rafe were here. The thought of him flitted in and out of her head like a wayward butterfly. Just as well. "So, when do we meet this mysterious, young Lord Carlisle?"

"His name is Grayson. Can you believe it? Grayson! Though it does have a nice, lordly ring to it. Lord Grayson Carlisle," she trilled. "His lordship, Grayson Carlisle."

Grace giggled. "And to think one day you could be Lady Carlisle."

Natalie groaned. "True. But I do hope he's a little handsome. At least he's young. Nineteen, I think."

Grace arched a brow. "You're nineteen."

"Old enough, then." Natalie breathed a sigh. "Mother assures me he's kind and thoughtful, which hardly makes up for a weak chin and sloped brow."

"Please don't tell me you're all about looks?"

"You should talk, Grace Dupont! Rafe Grant is one of the most gorgeous …" She stumbled over her words, a faint blush tinting her cheeks. "I'm so sorry. I completely forgot we're not supposed to—"

"It's all right. Truly. And you're right. Rafe is devastatingly handsome."

Natalie rolled her eyes. "Don't gloat. It's not becoming."

Grace snorted, which turned into a laughing fit. She rocked in her chair, clutching her heaving sides while tears streamed down her face. Natalie joined in, adding her own musical laughter to their symphony of joy. Grace couldn't have been happier.

~ Chapter Forty-six ~

I strained to hold my anger in check as my eyes swept the enemy camp. They'd had the audacity to set up their tents within mere miles of Landon's city limits, a ploy meant to frighten the citizens into a full-blown panic. Innocent civilians fleeing in haste would only make our job harder. Peace must be kept at all costs.

One small consolation. I'd spied General Stark's tent. I'd thought he'd be here, given the value of this target. Of course he'd want all the glory for himself. *Pompous ass.* Well, I had a different outcome in mind. And then I'd introduce him to the sharp end of my sword as I ran it through his blackened heart.

My men stood at attention eager for orders. "Right. Two things. First, we need everyone kept inside the city. No matter what happens, no one leaves. Second, General Stark is here. Or at least his tent is. You know what to do." Nods all around. "Good. Then get to work. Kieran, you're with me."

"Sir. Yes, sir!" A dozen well-trained, yet inexperienced soldiers descended the hill, heading toward the southern valley. I watched them go, my heart in my throat. *Let them be safe.*

I turned to Kieran. "I need you on my left, guarding my weak side. Should I fall, you are to press on and finish it. Do not falter, under any circumstances. Clear?" He nodded soberly, and we set out.

Darkness had been a constant companion, my one true friend for months, always with me in case I needed it. And I needed it now more than ever. It cloaked our progress down the hill, hid us from sentries as we crept toward the enemy camp. We paused on the outskirts, sheltered by the trees.

"The red tent is the general's." I kept my tone low. Kieran shivered beside me, though not from cold. "We will stay here until moonset. Most of the soldiers should be asleep then."

We settled in position to wait.

❧

Kieran's head dropped onto my shoulder. Exhausted, of course, yet we couldn't afford sleep. Not yet. "Kieran." He jerked, awake and alert in an instant. "It's time."

He nodded, his mouth set in a grim line, and followed my lead from the trees, through the camp, to the general's tent. We kept to the shadows, listening. A soft snore rumbled from behind the tent's rear wall. I signaled for Kieran to check the front. He returned seconds later, shaking his head. Another hand signal and Kieran drew his sword with a whisper of steel. He stood guard while I unsheathed my dagger and slit the heavy canvas.

I eased the fabric apart then poked my head inside, praying it would stay attached to my neck. A low lamp burned on a table beside the cot where the general slept. Quite at peace it seemed, given the lack of guards posted outside. Arrogant to the bitter end.

I slipped through the opening and froze, waiting. Steady snoring covered my footsteps as I crept toward him. I gazed down at his sleeping face, hate pouring from me in waves, so strong my hands shook yet my grip didn't waver. The grooves in the dagger's hilt bit into my palm.

... Kill him.

With a wicked backhand motion, I slit his throat. The wound gushed blood, hot and pungent in the stale air. His eyes didn't even open. They simply fluttered and then he went still. *Dead.*

Adrenaline surged through me. My chest heaved as I sucked in huge lungfuls of air. I stared down at the corpse with a sick smile. Dark laughter echoed in my head while blood dripped from my dagger, staining the dirt crimson. Mesmerized, I watched in morbid fascination as it pooled, lamplight flickering in its glossy surface.

I jerked my head up at Kieran's low whistle. Grinning like a feral beast, I exited the way I'd entered, a thief in the night. I wanted to sing, to dance. Kieran paled as he eyed me up and down. I glanced at my cloak then at my hands, freckled with blood. *Devil's paint.*

An owl hooted, and we bolted for the trees, crashing through the underbrush like a hundred galloping horses. I ran, leaping over roots and dodging branches, the boy in me giddy with the urge to whoop for joy. Kieran followed hot on my heels, breathing hard as we raced to safety.

The forest thinned then stopped altogether, depositing us in a broad meadow awash in moonlight. We'd left our horses tethered to a tree and quickly mounted then spurred them into a run. Miles and miles we rode, pushing them as fast as we dared until we reached the checkpoint. Clean clothes, food and water.

"Sir," Kieran croaked, breathless and wide-eyed. "Are you all right?"

I must have looked as crazed as I felt. "I am perfectly fine, Kieran. Though I am starving." I rooted through the food bags and pulled out a hunk of dried meat, tossing it to him before biting into one of my own. I chewed around a toothy smile, which I couldn't wipe off my face even if I wanted to. "What?"

He blinked then took a bite of his meat. "Nothing, sir. Just glad we're safe."

"We are, my boy. Without doubt."

We finished the food and drank our fill. My clothes had stayed clean, but blood saturated my cloak, a dark stain I hadn't even noticed until now. I exchanged it for another with my captain's badge, in case the enemy needed a show of authority once they discovered their fallen leader.

The pink glow of dawn heralded our departure. I swung up into the saddle and turned to find Kieran staring at me. "Yes, Kieran?"

"You have blood on your face. Sir."

I wiped my cheek. Red smeared all over my palm, evidence of the life I'd taken. Easier than I'd ever dreamed. I smiled with wicked promise.

… Now the king.

~ Chapter Forty-seven ~

Enemy soldiers marched toward the city gates with murderous intent but soon realized the futility of their plan and laid down their weapons almost without my asking. I simply sat atop my horse, a menacing presence fueled by vengeance, and took them into custody. We crammed the senior officers into the jailhouse and chained the rest together in a pit reserved for slaughtering swine. Quite fitting.

I needed reinforcements to bring these miscreants to the dungeon. Per my father's orders, I sent him a message, letting him know of the general's death. The details of how he had died could wait.

Now on with step two of my plan. I'd never been across the border into enemy lands, much less its king's evil lair. No one there would know my face. At least I hoped. And I assumed the castle's layout and design were like ours. Spiked drawbridge, guarded turrets and what have you. I just had to sneak in undetected, under the cover of darkness, and kill the king. Easy. Simple. Seemed like mere child's play after what I'd just done.

Laughter interrupted my thoughts. The men sat around a huge bonfire, talking and joking, eating and drinking.

Celebrating. I smiled and lifted a mug at Kieran, who had caught my eye from the other side of the fire. He raised his own mug with a crooked grin and we drank. And drank even more until the sun set and then rose to shine its golden light upon us.

I leaned on the stone wall, blinking against the glare. Gods, my head hurt but I pushed through the pain. Nothing could dampen my spirits or diminish my joy. *Alive.* So very alive, every muscle poised and ready for what came next.

I closed my eyes, letting the morning sunshine warm me. A dark chuckle rumbled in my chest. Blood thrummed in my veins, my pulse throbbed in my ears.

"Sir?" I opened my eyes to find Kieran in front of me, a mug in his hand. "Coffee, sir?"

"You are a godsend, Kieran. Thank you." I took a sip and groaned with pleasure. Steaming hot coffee, the likes of which we couldn't have on the march.

"The men are wondering, sir …"

"Yes?"

"They're wondering what to do, since we've secured the city. Are we simply to wait?"

He fell in step beside me as I strolled through the square. "Yes, wait for the king's guard. They will be here in two days. But enjoy yourselves in the meantime. This city is wonderful. I used to spend weeks here in between campaigns. The locals are very friendly." I winked and flashed a suggestive grin. He blushed, and I clapped him on the back. "I'm leaving you in charge, Kieran. Help get the prisoners back to Evanston. I'll meet you there. After."

His eyes widened. "But, sir. I cannot let you go alone. You could be killed. Or captured. It's too–"

I leveled a stare at him and he snapped his mouth shut. "Those are my orders, cadet."

"Sir. Yes, sir."

I nodded. "Can you do me one last favor and prepare my horse? I need to wash up before I get on the road."

"Of course, Captain. Right away." He hurried off, dodging and weaving through the sleepy throng.

"Captain Ellsbree." I turned as the city magistrate jogged to a stop. "Your highness," he amended as he bowed. "The guest house is prepared and at your disposal per your request."

"Thank you. I'll be leaving shortly and have given temporary command to Kieran Whitmore. Please see he is granted every favor."

"Absolutely, your highness. Anything for the crown."

I strolled along the main street up to the guest house. I longed to collapse face-first onto the down-filled mattress or at least immerse myself in a tub full of scalding water but had no time for such luxuries. I settled for a quick sponge bath and a change of clothes before heading back out into the light.

To kill a king.

~ Chapter Forty-eight ~

Rafe's feet hurt, his head ached, and his stomach rumbled as he trudged through the city, looking for a way out. In the hours since he'd left the castle, he'd done nothing other than go in circles, becoming hopelessly lost in the process. His usual excellent sense of direction had failed him, with spectacular results. He could barely tell up from down let alone east from west. If only he could pinpoint the sun's position in the sky. Then he'd know which way to go. But only stone walls and towering buildings surrounded him here in the heart of the city. He needed to find the outskirts, the slums. Somewhere he could see the blasted horizon.

Hours of searching later, he finally found it. His mouth went dry, and he stumbled to a stop then sat on a low stone wall, watching the last rays of light paint the sky. Darkness often proved a soldier's best ally but he couldn't see in the dark. And he still had no idea where to start. *Damn.*

He sighed heavily, which hurt his bruised ribs, and tried not to think of home. Of Grace. Gods, he missed her. More than anything. He didn't know if he'd ever see her again, not at his current rate. He'd probably die trying to get back to her. He staggered up on blistered feet to seek shelter for the night.

He slept in a barn with several accommodating goats and woke much later than he'd intended with straw in his hair and sunshine in his face. He jerked upright, smacking his head on a low beam, and cursed. He couldn't afford to waste daylight, yet he'd spent it like he had an infinite supply. A quick glance at the sky lit a fire under him. His kingdom lay to the west, so he set off, as fast as his injuries allowed.

He reached the city gates, heart thumping. If anyone recognized him, he'd be thrown into the dungeon to rot. Or be killed for spite. He adopted an air of casual nonchalance, simply out for a stroll as if he didn't have a care in the world. The soldiers on guard spared him only a glance and he resisted the urge to run as he passed them. He released a breath once he'd reached the other side and even dared a small smile. *Free*.

In the distance, a forest beckoned with the promise of food and shelter. His steps lengthened with every stride toward the haven then ducked into the trees and nearly wept. After a brief search, he found a small stream and splashed his face and neck with cool water. Nearby berry bushes yielded a handful of food, though not enough to dull the sharp-edged hunger in his belly. But he could find more and perhaps even trap a squirrel.

A branch snapped behind him, and he shot to his feet, eyes scanning the shadows. Silence reigned except for the roaring in his ears. He sat back down and shook his head. Surely hearing things. Next he'd start seeing things. Like venison stew with roasted potatoes. Or Grace. Or Taryn.

He choked on a breath and fell backward off the log as Taryn's face loomed from the shadows, like a ghost conjured from his subconscious. But then it spoke and Rafe knew he'd gone insane.

"Rafe?"

He swallowed and tried to scoot away but only managed to shove pine needles down his pants. "What …" he croaked.

"Rafe, is it really you? What are you doing here? How did you escape?" Taryn's figure floated into the clearing and narrowed its gaze on Rafe like a predator about to pounce.

"Who …"

"Gods above, man. Snap out of it already." It bent over and stretched its pale arm, waving a hand in Rafe's face.

"What …"

"All right, I've had just about enough of this. Get up." It grabbed Rafe's arm, and he yelped, trying to pull away, but the apparition yanked with supernatural strength. Or Rafe had become too weak. He sat on the log, panting and praying he hadn't wet himself while it squatted at his feet. It laid its hand on Rafe's knee. He expected cold, but warmth seeped through his thin pants. He blinked and noticed its face, not nearly as translucent as it should be. In fact, bright spots of color dotted its cheeks, and its blue eyes glittered. Not a ghost, then.

"Taryn?" He lifted his arm as if to touch him. Taryn took his hand. Warm, solid. *Real.*

"Rafe. It's me. Are you all right? You look like you've seen a ghost."

He would have laughed but still couldn't quite believe it. Taryn. Here, right in front of him. "What …" He cleared his throat. "What are you doing here? Why aren't you in Evanston?" The insane notion Taryn had come for him flitted around in his head.

Taryn sat on the log, his elbows on his knees. "It's a bit of a long story, my friend."

Rafe glanced around. "I don't have anywhere to be just now." Taryn laughed, and Rafe's heart almost burst with relief.

"I killed General Stark." A simple fact spoken with mild interest as if he'd just commented on the weather.

"What?"

"Slit his throat. From here to here." Taryn mimed the motion with obvious relish. "You should have seen it. Truly magnificent."

Now Rafe thought Taryn had gone insane. "What are you talking about?"

"He is dead!" Taryn jumped to his feet. "So very dead, Rafe. And now I'm going to kill King Rendon."

Taryn looked like he might just storm off and do it so Rafe grabbed his arm. "No, you're not."

"Ha!" Taryn shouted. "But I am!"

Taryn smiled with maniacal glee and Rafe tensed. Could he really stop him from doing such a thing in his state? Not likely. Taryn outranked him as both his captain and his prince. *Gods help them both.*

"But what are you doing here, Rafe? How did you get away?"

"Later. First explain what the hell you think you're doing."

Taryn blinked at Rafe's insolence, but he'd shoved protocol aside in favor of stopping his friend from ruining his life. Much good it did him.

~ Chapter Forty-nine ~

I explained the plan to Rafe again, for the millionth time. He nodded as if he understood but then tried to talk me out of it again, for the millionth time. "Rafe, you're not listening to me."

"I am, I swear it. I'm just not sure it's a good idea."

"It's a brilliant idea, you mean."

"No, it's not what I mean."

I sighed heavily and closed my eyes. Finding Rafe in this forest had been a dream come true. One less thing to worry about. Now I only had to get in, kill the king and get out. Simple and clean. But Rafe wouldn't listen to reason. Or to me. *Gods above.*

"Look," I continued with as much patience as my raging impatience would allow. "You cannot stop me, nor will you try. So, come with me instead. Watch my back."

"I would love nothing more, your highness, but I'm not quite fit for service."

I waved a hand. "Please. You've fought in worse conditions, and there won't be a fight, I promise you."

Rafe shook his shaggy head. "I don't like it. It doesn't feel right."

"Of course not. Which is why it's such a good plan. No one in their right mind would ever think I'd do such a thing."

"Perhaps because you shouldn't," Rafe countered. "Please, Taryn."

"I'm sorry, brother, but there's no turning back. The king must die."

Rafe sighed in defeat, and I clapped him on the back. "It's getting dark, which means it's almost time to go. Let's eat something now, and you can tell me everything you know about the castle." I dumped the contents of my pack onto the ground and smiled as Rafe dove for the food.

He chewed and swallowed then chewed again, closing his eyes. "Thank you."

"Of course. Now. How can I get in?"

Rafe's eyes flew open and he stared at me. "You don't have a plan for getting in?"

I shrugged. "How hard can it be? I'm a complete stranger here."

"You cannot be serious." Rafe pinched the bridge of his nose. "This is insane."

"Do I sound like I'm joking?"

"Yes."

I snorted. "Just help me. Please."

He bit off another hunk of meat, studying me with alarming intensity. As if I still had blood on my face. "What?"

"I'm trying to decide how crazy you are."

"Wicked crazy." I punctuated it with a wicked grin.

He grunted a response then washed down his food from the water flask. "All right. I'll help you. But you must do what I say. This won't work otherwise."

"Understood."

"There is a nobleman, Lord Harlesby, who pressed me into his service. Or at least he tried to. The dolt made the mistake of leaving me alone. With a tailor."

I arched a brow. "As in taking measurements and stitching fabric? A *tailor*, tailor?"

"Yes. Anyway, I left as soon as I could. Unfortunately, I ran myself in circles for an entire day. I spent the night in a barn then just waltzed out the castle gates. Either Lord Harlesby didn't care enough to send a search party, or I had luck on my side."

"Perhaps both. What does this Lord Harlesby have to do with me getting into the castle? Surely you don't think he'd help us?"

"No, but if I'm humble enough and appeal to his considerable vanity, he might take me back. Once I get into the castle, I'll let you in."

I rubbed my hands together. "Brilliant."

He nodded. "And I'll find out where the king is or at least where he'll be, so you can …"

"Don't worry, Rafe. This is going to work."

"Have you thought about how your father will react when he finds out what you've done? He must know about the general by now."

"I sent word the general had died, but I sort of … misrepresented how. Only my men and I know the true nature of my plan and they would never betray me. So, he has no idea where I am. As for what he does to me, I don't really care as long as King Rendon is dead."

"If you're sure, so be it. I'm with you all the way, Taryn. But what if–"

"Rafe, stop. No what ifs. No maybes or shoulds or anything else. I will do this." He nodded, and I grinned. *Finally.*

✤

Darkness covered the land between the forest and the city gates. I paused at the tree line, waiting for Rafe to gather his courage. He didn't fear for himself but for me, my safety and well-being. As if my life meant more than his. Or anyone else's. I wanted to live but not at the expense of another. Something I desperately wanted to avoid.

Rafe appeared at my shoulder and I took a deep breath. "Ready?"

"No."

"Good. Let's go."

I led the way across the meadow, a shadow among shadows with Rafe strong and silent at my back. I'd offered him my sword since the dagger would suit me better in close quarters. Plus, I'd used it to kill the general and the symmetry appealed to me. Rafe had argued vehemently, his mouth pulled down in a very unattractive frown. I kept the sword.

We approached the gates, arms around each other's shoulders, lurching side to side like drunkards home late from a night of revelry. I belted a bawdy song at the top of my voice. Rafe joined in, off tempo and off-key, and the guards scowled but let us pass. We swerved and tripped along the main street toward the castle. Once we were out of the guards' sight, we charged up the hill then paused at the corner across from the entrance where Rafe would plead his case for re-entry. Hopefully he'd convince Lord Harlesby to see him now instead of in the morning. Either way, I'd stay behind until Rafe signaled the all clear.

"Taryn, I'm–"

"Rafe, please. Have a little faith. We've made it this far. We're almost done."

He grimaced then strode for the castle. The guards stopped him, their murmured questions and Rafe's stilted answers floating on the breeze. He said whatever magic words the guards needed to hear, and they let him in. He didn't glance back of course. I grinned just the same then melted into the shadows.

~ Chapter Fifty ~

Rafe cringed but refused to cower under Lord Harlesby's considerable ire. The man knew how to throw an insult like a punch to the gut. Rafe bore it all, stone-faced and silent. Finally, he ran out of words and sat in his gilded chair, glowering while Rafe waited for judgement.

"Very well. I am a desperate man in a desperate situation. But you are warned. Do not disappoint me."

"Yes, my lord," Rafe mumbled.

"It is too late to call the tailor in. We will take care of it in the morning. For now, the castle steward will show you to your quarters in the servants' wing."

"My lord, if I may ask a question?"

"Certainly."

"What exactly is my role?"

"Ah, yes. I am here on a diplomatic mission to ease tensions between King Rendon and Verlandia. Since we aren't a monarchy, the king has his sights set to conquer us, a fate my chancellor wishes to avoid. You can imagine the danger someone such as myself might encounter. I simply need you to protect me from whatever harm comes my way."

"Have you spoken with the king, my lord?"

"Not yet, no," he huffed with an imperial frown. "Though I've been promised an audience any day now."

"Is the king not in residence?"

He sighed heavily. "He is here, which makes the delay so much more of an insult. He simply sits on his throne day after day, hearing complaints from his subjects in favor of speaking with me, an honored guest. Can you imagine?"

"I cannot, my lord."

"Of course you cannot!" His vigorous nod almost snapped his neck. "The man has no sense of propriety, no social graces, yet he calls himself a king!"

"I believe he inherited the title, my lord."

He waved a bejeweled hand. "Hardly an excuse."

Rafe stifled a yawn, feeling every minute of the past twenty-four hours weighing on him like a ton of bricks. Surprisingly, Lord Harlesby noticed and rang the bell. A steward opened the door mere seconds later.

"Yes, my lord?"

"Please make sure Rafe is given a comfortable place to sleep."

"Yes, my lord."

Rafe bowed and followed the steward from the room. Each step felt like a mile as they trudged down the stairs, through the corridors and into the servants' wing. The steward didn't say a word, which Rafe appreciated. He could barely form a coherent thought, let alone speak one.

They stopped at a closed door. "Servants dine at dawn in the kitchen. Down the hall and to the left. My name is Ross, should you need anything else."

Rafe blinked at the man's retreating form, fighting past the exhaustion. He had to let Taryn know he'd made it inside. And knew the king's whereabouts. He crept back the way they'd come, trying not to get lost in the labyrinthine fortress.

Rafe just had to find a window facing west. Taryn would be waiting at the corner.

He found several windows, but no Taryn. Had he been discovered? Or had he grown too impatient to wait? He hoped for the latter as he rushed around the castle, peering out of every window like a lunatic. Finally, he spotted Taryn's pale head among the shadows below. He tossed the golden coin Taryn had given him out the window. It arced and turned over, glinting in the moonlight before it struck the ground with a metallic clink. Taryn hurried forward and grabbed it, briefly glancing up at the window. His face split in a crooked smile then he disappeared into the night.

✺

Rafe slept like the dead and woke to persistent knocking on his door. Groaning like a hibernating bear, he opened his eyes, briefly wishing he'd chosen a different path in life. "Come in," he growled.

The same young girl summoned to Lord Harlesby's rooms opened the door and stuck her head in. "You're late for breakfast."

Rafe grunted a reply, and she closed the door with a quiet click. She'd only tried to help, yet his mood would not be improved by mere courteous attention. He needed more sleep and even more food. Food first.

He trudged into the kitchen then stood under the baleful gaze of the cook. She eyed him for a moment before turning to her work at the stove with a huff. He grabbed one of everything on the table then snuck out the back door to meet Taryn.

Rafe stood in the early morning sunshine, munching on a sweet roll. Taryn would show at some point. In the meantime, he leaned against the stone wall and enjoyed his breakfast. He licked the last crumbs from his fingers and Taryn turned the corner, hands shoved deep into his pockets as if he strolled around the castle grounds on a daily basis.

"Rafe." He flashed a dazzling smile.

"Taryn."

"So, what do we know?"

"The king is here, receiving visitors in the throne room all day."

"And likely sleeping in his chambers at night." He craned his neck, squinting at the upper floors of the castle. "I wonder where?"

"Come with me and find out."

He arched a brow. "Sorry?"

"What are you wearing under your cloak?"

"Rafe, I never knew you cared." He unhooked the clasp. His plain black jacket and pants would blend in perfectly with the other servants. The sword, however, would have to go.

"No one will look twice at you dressed like this. Just rub a little dirt on your face and hair and we could be brothers." Rafe grinned despite the dire circumstances. He'd always wanted a brother. "You'll have to find a place to hide your sword, though. Too obvious."

"Fine." He unbuckled his sword belt as he glanced around then tucked it under a holly bush. "Lead the way."

Rafe turned and led his prince through the back door, into the wolf's den.

~ Chapter Fifty-one ~

The servants occupied a wing as far from the castle proper as possible. I'd have to cover twice as much ground to access the king's chambers. But I could do it. Invincibility thrummed in my veins as I studied every stone, memorized every turn. Not so different from home, just more outlandish decor as if the king were overcompensating for something. I stifled a laugh and hurried to keep pace with Rafe's long strides.

His sparse room reminded me of him even though he'd been here less than twenty-four hours. "Nice room. Clean."

He stood in the center, looking around as if he hadn't taken the time earlier and grunted a reply. "Now what?"

"We wait for moonset. I want to be sure the castle is asleep. In the meantime, I assume you have work to do for Lord Harlesby."

"I'm supposed to see the tailor." His voice dripped disdain.

I laughed and shook my head. "Don't be so dramatic. You could do with some new clothes. Plus, you'll be able to take them with you when we leave. A souvenir."

He snorted. "As if I want a reminder of any of this." He raked a hand through his hair. "I'll be back as soon as I can with food. Try not to murder anyone before then."

He shut the door with a firm thud, all but locking me in. I'd made it inside and my plan had begun to unfold exactly as designed. Now to wait for dark.

❧

"Taryn."

I woke to find Rafe's face inches from mine. "Yes?"

"I brought food."

I sat up, rubbing the grit from my eyes. He set a plate of bread, cheese and fruit onto my lap then leaned against the wall looking resplendent in his dark gray uniform. Clean-shaven too. I grinned around mouthfuls and he scowled.

"Don't say a word."

I shrugged. "What? You look quite handsome."

He rolled his eyes. "Whatever."

I set the plate aside. "Did you find the king's chambers?"

He reached into his vest pocket and pulled out a folded piece of paper. "Here."

I unfolded it, eyes skimming over the hastily drawn map. "Which floor?"

"The top floor, of course. Where else would a king sleep?"

"True." Straight lines formed a grid, hallways and doorways and windows all clearly marked. A large red X in the upper left-hand corner drew my attention. I pointed to it. "Where are we in relation to this?"

"We're two floors below, in the opposite corner. The servants use an unguarded back stairwell to access all the floors. It's here." He placed a blunt fingertip on a square a few inches from the X.

"Perfect. You've outdone yourself, my good man." I met Rafe's steely gaze. "Thank you."

"Don't thank me yet."

"Oh, come now Rafe. Where's your optimism? Your can-do attitude?" He shook his head, but the corners of his mouth twitched. I beamed a smile, already feeling the thrill of victory, the elation of success. Soon this would all be over. Forever. King Rendon had no wife, no heirs, no reason to challenge my father ever again. No one else would die fighting another useless war. A peace worth any price, even my soul.

"Lord Harlesby is attending a dinner party tonight and requires my … services. But I'll come back straight after and then we–"

I shook my head. "I know what you're going to suggest, and I can't allow it. This is for me alone. Just perform as expected so you don't arouse suspicion. Wait here for my signal."

He looked skeptical but nodded. A loyal soldier to the end. "And then we'll go home?"

"I swear it."

~ Chapter Fifty-two ~

The moon rose higher and higher into the midnight sky, grinning like a madman hellbent on destruction. Much like myself. Darkness had come again. I felt a sense of home as it wrapped around me. A shadow guarding my soul.

I should have felt anxious or afraid. Or hesitant. But my heart beat a steady rhythm, my hands laid still in my lap. Not a nervous tic to be found. Calm and cool and collected. Anyone who looked at me would see only bored indifference on the surface. Yet underneath, my mind whirled with chaos. Somehow not a worry but a comfort.

I reviewed the distance between Rafe's room and the king's chambers in my head, counting the steps from here to there. I visualized my arm arcing through the air, my dagger slashing his throat, spilling his royal blood all over the silk sheets. I gave my dagger a reassuring pat. *Time to move.*

My bootheels echoed in the deserted hallways and empty corridors as I stalked through the castle. Where were all the guards? And servants? Suspicion flared but I chalked it up to paranoia and moved on to the stairwell. I bounded up two flights, my breathing even despite the excitement building in my chest.

I paused at the landing and peered into the hallway. Torches burned low, lending warmth to the otherwise cold stone walls. Measured footsteps echoed from around the corner. The night watch.

This floor would not be as easy to navigate. No king in his right mind would sleep without a bevy of guards in place. Two or three I could dispatch with ease but any more would create enough noise to raise the alarm. I whispered a prayer for the former and stepped into the light. Two guards strode into view and I walked toward them, eyes downcast per my lowly status. *I am a servant, nothing more.*

They nodded as they passed. Fooled by my disguise? I grinned and hurried the rest of the way. I rounded a corner then skidded to a stop. The sentries outside the king's door blinked in surprise. Apparently the king did not receive visitors in the middle of the night.

I swallowed hard, scrambling to think of an excuse for my presence. Nothing came to mind so I fled the other direction. Shouts rang out behind me but I didn't break my stride. I pushed harder and their boot steps faded just as I slipped into the stairwell.

Breathless with adrenaline, I panted in the darkness, waiting for the inevitable sword point to the chest. Loud voices argued beyond the door.

"I saw him go this way."

"Well I saw him go into the stairwell."

It seems my pursuers were at an impasse. All the better for me. I pressed myself into the corner and prayed. The door yawned open, spilling torchlight onto the landing. A guard stepped inside, glancing left and right. Wrapped in shadows, I held my breath. The guard scowled then returned to the hallway.

"There's nobody there, you idiot. Now let's go."

I remembered to breathe and slumped against the wall. Perhaps this plan needed some improvements. Not as foolproof as I'd thought. Or hoped. Still, I'd made it to the king's chambers. Now I just had to get through the door.

I sat in the stairwell for what felt like hours, listening for any hint of movement. Silence reigned and I risked a glance into the hallway. Empty. Quiet.

I stepped out then picked up my pace, determined to make it all the way this time. The sentries had gone off duty it seemed and I met no more resistance. The heavy oak door loomed in front of me. I ran a hand over the iron studs then reached for the handle, cool and smooth against my palm. With no one to stop me, I pushed the handle. Unlocked.

I eased the door open and slipped into a space devoid of light. I couldn't see my hand in front of my face, yet I welcomed the darkness. It had never let me down and surely wouldn't now.

One careful step at a time, I navigated through the inky black, feeling my way past rough outlines of furniture. Couch. Chair. Low table. The sitting room, perhaps. I trailed my fingers along the wall then met the recessed surface of another door, hopefully the bedchamber.

The handle gave way and the hinges whispered. Firelight cast flickering shadows on the king's hulking form. He slept on his stomach, greasy hair plastered to his forehead, bulky frame dominating the sagging mattress. The massive bed trembled with his snoring.

I'd hoped to slit his throat from the front, just like General Stark. But I couldn't roll him over, at least not without waking him. While part of me reveled in the idea of my face as the last thing he would ever see, I couldn't risk him calling for help. I'd have to stab him in the neck instead, if my dagger could even pierce his many folds of flesh.

I burned with the need to rid the world of him and slid the dagger from its sheath.

… Kill him. Now.

No. Wait.

What if killing him didn't solve anything? What if his death only made matters worse? Killing another while fighting for my life I could justify. But this? Cold-blooded murder? Regicide? What had I been thinking? My father would never forgive me and my soul would never recover.

I dropped the dagger and clenched my fists in my hair. There had to be another way.

… There is no other way. Killing him will bring you peace.

Peace. All I'd ever wanted. To be untethered from the anchor of pain and guilt and heartache weighing me down. At any price. If his death paid for my freedom, so be it.

I bent to retrieve the dagger then turned it over in my hand. The blade winked as I plunged it into his neck, burying it to the hilt. I yanked it out with savage force. Blood sprayed in a crimson arc, soaking my shirt, coating my hand, salting the air. A satisfying gurgle rang in my ears, the sweetest sound I'd ever heard. Euphoria flowed through me as the pale sheets darkened with blood. I backed away, searing the image of the dying king into my mind, a memory to cherish forever.

Out the door, along the hall, across the floor to the stairwell. Down the stairs I flew, my steps lighter than air. I'd never felt so ecstatic, so overcome with emotion. Tears of joyous relief spilled down my cheeks, and I burst onto the first-floor landing, breathless and giddy. I rushed through the kitchen and out into the night, grinning like a jackal at the moon, the stars, the darkness all around me.

I circled the castle, flipping the gold coin over and over in my hand until I reached the spot below Rafe's window then hurled the coin into the air. It clanked against the window frame. His dark head appeared a second later, and I waved then retrieved my sword belt. I paced at the corner, bursting with energy, eager to share my victory.

Rafe's hurried footsteps preceded him. He skidded around the corner, his cloak flapping behind him like a rebel flag. He didn't break stride as he barked at me to hurry. I ran after him, sword banging at my hip like the booming of my triumphant heart.

I could've swam all the way back to Evanston but Rafe needed to rest. We stopped a few miles from the castle, hidden in the forest where he could catch his breath. My restless energy demanded release. I prowled while he panted.

"Taryn," he croaked. "Sit down. You're making me nervous."

"I can't sit down, Rafe! I want to fly!"

He shook his head, a less than pleased look on his face. "Will you at least stop bouncing around like a deranged rabbit?"

I stopped. "Better?"

"Some."

"Oh, come on Rafe! Admit it. My plan worked with flawless brilliance. No one knew me and Lord Harlesby would never suspect you, so we're both in the clear. And the king is dead!"

"Keep your voice down!" he hissed. "You're going to get us killed."

"Sorry," I whispered. "I'm just so … so …"

"Crazy?" Rafe offered.

I grinned. "A good a word as any."

He shook his head again but kept any other opinions to himself. He climbed to his feet, determined to see this through despite his physical condition. I couldn't ask for a better friend.

"Ready?"

"No."

I laughed and clapped him on the shoulder. "Let's go home."

~ Chapter Fifty-three ~

Grace had practically worried herself into an early grave. As soon as Taryn's company had returned without their captain, she'd feared the worst for him and for Rafe. No one would tell her anything, which only fueled her nightmares and soured her stomach. She'd barely eaten or slept in the last week and didn't know if she would ever again. At least not until she knew what had happened. She tried to distract herself with training, with work. Even with idle gossip but nothing seemed to ease her distress. Instead she wallowed in grief, mired in anxiety, dreading yet yearning for news.

"Grace." Her father's gentle voice pulled her from her morbid thoughts.

"Yes, Father? Do you need something?"

"I need you to stop moping about. No good will come of it."

"I know, but I can't help it. Worrying is in my nature."

He chuckled softly. "So it is. But still, you need to relax. Isn't there something I can do to take your mind off your troubles?"

Her thin smile felt weak. "I don't think so. But thank you for trying. I just want–" A heavy fist beat on the front door and Grace nearly jumped out of her skin.

"Who in the world would be calling at this time of night?" Her father started to rise from his chair.

"I'll get it, Father. Sit down." She smoothed her skirts then pulled the door open.

A messenger stood on the other side, his jacket bearing the royal crest. "A message for Grace Dupont." He held out an envelope.

"Thank you." She took it with a trembling hand, heart thumping as she closed the door.

"Grace, sit down. You're as white as a sheet."

With an absent nod, she sank onto the couch. She stared at the envelope as if reading its contents would burn her eyes.

"Well? Are you going to open it, or should I?" She blinked and handed him the envelope. "It will be all right, Grace. Whatever it says." He cracked the seal then unfolded the paper. Unable to watch, she turned away, hands clenched in her lap. Her father exhaled a long breath and she closed her eyes, refusing to cry. "Grace." She shook her head, biting her lip hard enough to draw blood. She couldn't face him, couldn't hear it. "Grace, look at me."

Something in his tone had her lifting her head, meeting his steady gaze. "What?" she whispered. "What is it?"

"Read it for yourself." He handed the paper back to her. She glanced at it and then him. "Go on, my dear."

Her eyes skimmed over the words, barely registering their meaning. The familiar slanted handwriting, the stilted, concise sentences made her heart lurch then gallop in her chest. *Rafe*. Tears blurred her vision as she turned to her father. His eyes shone bright with promise. She jumped to her feet at his encouraging nod then placed a hasty kiss on his cheek before rushing out the door.

She ran until she thought her lungs would burst, yet she pushed on, only slowing her pace once she'd entered the castle grounds. The note had been brief, and to the point, just like Rafe, but didn't specify where to find him. She stopped the first servant she saw. "Where is Rafe?" The servant blinked, and Grace blew out a breath. "The king's guard? Just returned with Prince Taryn?"

"Oh, yes, miss. He's in the infirmary. He's–"

"Thank you!" Grace called over her shoulder, feet slapping on the stone floor. She didn't need to hear anything more. Only two words mattered. *Here. Alive.*

She slowed to a stop at the infirmary, smoothing her hair and her skirts. Nervous anticipation skittered up her spine as she opened the door. Blinking in the dim interior, she scanned the area for Rafe. She weaved through the room toward the only occupied bed. A still figure gazed out the window, as if lost in thought. She stepped closer, heart hammering in the near-silent space. "Rafe?"

His head snapped toward her, and she sucked in a breath. Dark circles marred the skin under his eyes, and his face had lost its usual ruddy color. "Grace."

At least his voice hadn't changed, though he sounded a bit hoarse. She jerked into motion, rushing to sit at his side. "Thank the gods you're safe!" Her smile nearly cracked her face in half, but she didn't care. His answering smile seemed forced. "What's wrong?"

He swallowed with a slight grimace and shook his head. "Nothing other than the obvious. I'm ... tired."

"Oh." Her happiness drained away like water from a sieve. "Are you not glad to see me? I thought–"

He took her hand. "Of course I'm glad to see you. We are friends, are we not?"

She tried to ignore the sting of his words. "Yes, we're friends. But something else is bothering you. What is it?"

He sighed heavily as if they'd had this argument a thousand times. "I'm so sorry, Grace. For everything."

She shook her head, confused at his odd choice of words. "What are you talking about? You have nothing to apologize for."

His eyes widened. "You're not … angry with me? For what I said? For leaving like I did?"

"Of course not." She smiled, placing her hand on his cheek. "Haven't you figured it out yet? I love you, Rafe."

He closed his eyes and released a shaky breath. When he looked at her again, her heart almost burst with happiness. Love shone there, deep and true and hers.

He swallowed hard, opened the closed his mouth. "And Taryn?"

"What about him? He doesn't have anything to do with us." She laughed softly. Just like Rafe to think she had feelings for Taryn instead of him. She cared for Taryn, deeply, but had realized long ago a romance between them could never be. Which left her heart more than open, more than ready for Rafe. He'd taken up every inch of it and then some. "You should rest. Apparently you don't think straight when you haven't slept well."

He refused to release her hand, however, and pulled her toward him. "I love you, too."

"I know."

He gaped at her. "You do?"

She nodded, tears gathering behind her eyes. "I think I knew before you did, though."

He shook his head with a lopsided grin, a look she cherished and thought she'd never see again. But he'd come home to her, the same man she'd fallen in love with. "Rest now." Her smile radiated joy and wonder and hope. "I'll return in the morning."

He nodded and laid his head down on the pillows. Moonlight gilded the side of his face as he smiled. Her heart swelled with the promise of a bright future, full of love and happiness. With him.

~ Chapter Fifty-four ~

My heart overflowed with victory and purpose and I could not stop smiling. Perhaps I never would. I didn't care. For the first time in my life, I felt satisfied, content with the choices I'd made, the steps I'd taken toward peace. With a single act, I'd ended the conflict between two kingdoms, generations' worth of animosity gone. Snuffed out like a candle. And every one of my men had survived.

I strode into the council chamber full of swagger. My father rose to his feet, his steely gaze tracking my progress from the door to my seat. I greeted the assembled lords then sat and placed my clasped hands in front of me. "So, what are we talking about today?" I quipped. "Expanding the kingdom, perhaps?"

My father stared at me, his face a blank mask. "Taryn. Do you have any idea what you've done?"

"Of course I do. I am a hero, am I not? You can thank me now, if you'd like."

His jaw tightened and the assembled lords all gasped at my impudence. "Taryn, remember your place," he growled.

"My apologies, Father. I meant no disrespect. I'm just so … so …"

"Cocky? Arrogant? Selfish?" he offered. "Taryn, you have committed a crime, punishable by death."

"Two crimes," I amended.

"And you've stirred the hornets' nest in Regnevar," he continued as if I hadn't spoken. "The citizens are demanding justice."

"But they have no idea who did it," I countered with a smug grin. "And you did tell Rafe to bring you General Stark's head. I just took it a step further. Why are you so worried?"

He sighed through his nose, the vein in his forehead pulsing at an alarming rate. "They may not have any evidence, but they suspect us. A lord from Verlandia, Harlesby I believe, confirmed a prisoner escaped his service the night of King Rendon's murder. How are we to refute his claim? He could easily identify Rafe."

"So, we'll send Rafe away." I shrugged as if it were nothing. "Or we'll take care of Lord Harlesby. In fact, I'll do it myself."

He gaped at me, his jaw falling open like an unhinged lid. "My lords. Will you please excuse us?"

The lords, who had been watching our exchange wide-eyed, all stood and shuffled out. The door closed with a soft click behind them.

"Father, please. Your emotions are clouding your judgement. If you would just listen to reason–"

"No, son. You listen to me. I am beyond relieved to have you home, where you belong. But you made a grievous error in thinking you could even do such a thing, let alone get away with it. Your mother is beside herself with grief, afraid for your life."

I leaned back in my chair. "I still don't see the problem."

He held up a hand. "I am not finished. When you first told me what you'd done, I thought you needed help. Now I'm sure of it. Whatever is going on with you must stop. Immediately. I will protect you but my generosity only goes so far. Do not test me. You are the heir to the throne, Taryn, not an expendable, royal assassin."

I blinked, not sure I'd heard correctly. "But I only meant to help. I thought–"

"What, exactly? I'd be proud? Grateful? No, Taryn. I am furious." He practically vibrated with it and I swallowed hard. "Get out. I cannot stomach even the sight of you right now."

"Father, I–"

"Get. Out."

The look on his face stung even worse than the reprimand, and I slunk from the room with my heart in my throat. He had managed the impossible and erased my smile.

I paced in my room, back and forth along a dizzying route while my mind grappled with the implications of what my father had said. I replayed the conversation in my head, realization dawning with startling clarity. I had been delusional, cataloging my actions as mere indiscretions, like being caught with a servant girl in my room. How had I thought otherwise? I'd made a mistake so vile, so contemptable I deserved whatever consequences resulted. Unless I could make it right.

If the power to destroy everything rested with Lord Harlesby alone, then removing him would end it. And the citizens would calm down, their thirst for vengeance would diminish over time. My father ruled with a kind heart and a generous spirit, much more so than King Rendon. Surely our new subjects would come to love him as I did, as everyone did. And the severity of my crimes would lessen in the wake of gratitude and become acts of valor. I'd be a hero. Admired, revered, loved by the people. The stuff of legends and stories and songs sung round the campfire. But only if Lord Harlesby no longer posed a threat. Senseless murder appealed to my darker side, yet I couldn't indulge it without damaging my soul beyond repair.

... *Unless.*

If it served the greater good and righted a wrong, then it would be worth the risk. I wanted to help, to do whatever I could, which meant Lord Harlesby had to die. By my hand. I couldn't allow anyone else to take on this task. And I'd done it before. Surely I could do it again. Determination roared, a call to arms I answered with my whole heart. But how to convince my father? His tone earlier suggested I never go behind his back again or he'd throw me in the dungeon himself. No part of me wanted to disappoint him, yet what he didn't know wouldn't hurt him. And he'd forgive me. Someday.

First, I needed a plan. Vanishing without a trace, especially given my criminal status, might start a civil war. And the thought of my father assuming I'd turned tail and run soured my stomach. But I also couldn't risk him sending someone after me, to talk me out of it. The truth remained my only option. I just hoped I'd get the job done before anyone could stop me.

Decision made, I basked in the resulting calm. Peace settled over me as if an outside force guided my hand, influenced my decisions. Relieved at the respite, I followed where it led, abandoning all control to a wiser power. I might end up on the wrong side of right but the serenity of letting go far outweighed the agony of holding on.

I scrawled a note to my father then packed a bag with only the essentials. I didn't expect to return. At least not anytime soon. I'd wait until the dust settled, until things quieted enough for the council to see reason and agree I'd acted with my kingdom's best interests at heart. My deeds may never be considered noble, yet I soldiered on. For the greater good.

Like a lone wolf slinking through the shadows, I made my way to the docks. I boarded then settled at the rail. The breeze ruffled the hair at my collar and gentle waves lapped against the ship as I gazed at the night sky. Darkness stretched in every direction. A deep velvety blackness where stars glittered. Winking, blinking, shining down on the water.

I stared across the sea toward Verlandia, where I planned to end Lord Harlesby. His death meant little to me on paper. On a grander scale, his demise heralded the coming of a new dawn, an era free of war and death and constant bickering over who should rule which kingdom. Without his testimony against Rafe, Regnevar's citizens couldn't substantiate their claims. And we would find peace. At last.

~ Chapter Fifty-five ~

I slipped inside Lord Harlesby's unguarded manor house with ease, tip-toed through his quiet hallways. Entered his bedchamber and slit his throat while he slept. I stared down at his lifeless body, feeling nothing at all. No remorse, no regret. Not even satisfaction of a job well done. And it had been perfect, executed with razor-edged precision.

Cue the fanfare! Let the trumpets sound my success! All remained quiet. Yet my efforts hadn't been in vain. Rafe would stay out of prison and the kingdom would unite under my father's rule. Nothing else mattered. Not even my own satisfaction or anyone's appreciation. Needless to say, the luster of my heroism had tarnished, leaving a bitter taste in my mouth.

And Lord Harlesby's blood on my hands. I studied the crimson leather on my palms as I took to the streets. Shadows cloaked me and darkness beckoned, my true haven. A wolf howled in the distance, a kindred spirit. Contentment surged through me as if I'd found a missing piece of my soul.

If only the feeling could last.

❋

Lies, nothing but lies everywhere. Chasing me down alleys and through forests, relentless in their pursuit, steadfast in their quest to convince me I'd done something wrong. I held fast to my convictions and clapped my hands over my ears to block out the constant droning, but they were in my head. Screaming, clawing, tearing at my soul. "No," I rasped, jaw clenched tight with raw fury. "Stop." Silence. Eerie, absolute, blissful silence.

I opened my eyes and the nightmare faded. It had started innocently enough, only mild fear and lukewarm panic. But then it erupted, spewing hate and violence into the air. The fear became a monster, nothing but shark teeth and razor claws, chasing, snarling and snapping as it sought only to destroy.

I shuddered in the darkness yet took comfort in its presence as always. Like a warm blanket on a chilly night. Or a soft voice, whispering reassurances after a troubled sleep, soothing away the ache in my bones with a gentle caress.

❋

Lazy dust motes danced in the morning light, spiraling through the air before settling on the floor. Just as lazy, I stretched like an indulgent cat. With Lord Harlesby out of the way forever, I had nothing but time. Nothing on the agenda. No meddling lords to assassinate. So what would today bring?

I sauntered through town, feeling like I belonged. I smiled a pleasant smile, one I'd honed to perfection during years at court. Everyone smiled back. I stopped to say a few words to the rotund baker, then the hawk-nosed banker, all the while imagining what they'd do or say if they knew what I'd done. Would they congratulate me? Doubtful. They were more likely to clap me in irons than slap me on the back.

I'd spent the better part of the past two weeks plotting and preparing. But I hadn't thought much past the task at hand and didn't know how to proceed from here. Perhaps the time had come to move on, though I certainly couldn't return home. Which left me with no idea where to go or what to do once I got there. Out of my depth and out of my league. Some would even say out of my mind.

... *Royal assassin.*

My father's voice echoed in my head but I ignored him in favor of the whispers calling to me. Urging me toward a path of destruction. I could do this. I could stay in Verlandia where no one knew me. Anonymity had its perks after all.

Yet how to market myself as a killer for hire? Counterproductive to say the least. And did I even want such a life? Hiding, staying one step ahead of the law. Spilling blood without caution or cause. But my unique skill set hardly qualified me for honest labor and I had to earn money somehow. Why not this way?

A gentle tugging on the hem of my jacket jerked me from my thoughts. I gazed down at the most adorable little girl, her blue eyes round with innocence.

"Sir?"

"Well, hello there."

"My mother wants to speak with you."

I crouched in front of her. "She does? And who might your mother be? Is she nearby?"

"Yes, sir." She reached for my hand. "I'll take you to her."

Curious and intrigued, I let her drag me off the street, down an alley and into a large warehouse full of boxes and crates.

"Far enough, Chelsea. Thank you."

My ears perked. Had the darkness finally found a way to speak to me outside my head? The thought made me grin as I stood in the dimness, watching, waiting, yet no one materialized from the shadows. The girl bobbed a curtsy then scrambled out the door.

"Who are you?" The voice again, no more than a rasping whisper.

I blinked. "No one of interest. Why?" I perused the space, inspecting boxes as I went.

"Someone recently killed a lord in his home."

"I heard. So tragic. My condolences to his family." I shook my head and opened a box. Linens. I resumed my inventory. "What does a lord's death have to do with me?"

"You recently came to town."

"Another rumor proved true." The voice fell silent, and I stopped, angling my head. "Why am I here?"

"I could ask you the same question, sir."

"Yet you didn't. Why?" The silence deepened, settling all around me. "Hello?"

"Your arrival coincides with the lord's murder."

I arched a brow and turned in a slow circle. "Quite the coincidence."

"I do not believe in coincidences."

"Do you believe in dragons?" More silence, heavier this time as if weighted by anger. I laughed under my breath. "I do, though I've never seen one. I'd rather believe in something I haven't seen than disbelieve something I have. Wouldn't you agree?"

A deep sigh bounced off the rafters. "You are a strange man."

I shrugged and opened another box. Sugar. I made a mental note to consider coming back for it. "What do you want?"

"I want you to leave."

"You invited me here and I came, yet now you want me to leave? And you say I'm the strange one."

"Leave this city and never return."

"How very ominous, but why should I? I've done nothing wrong. Paid my way like everyone else. I'm also a very generous tipper. Just ask the barmaid at the tavern."

"It is my job to keep this city safe."

"Your job? Interesting." *Who is this person?*

... Enemy.

I almost laughed out loud. As if I had enemies here. Or anywhere. "I understand–"

"No, you don't. I believe you are dangerous, and so you must go. Now."

Shadows writhed with manic energy but I brought them to heel. "Why do you believe I'm dangerous?"

"I do not like the way you look, or the fact you showed up when you did."

I glanced at my cloak, my pants, my boots. All high quality and in excellent repair. My hair needed a trim but otherwise, perfectly respectable. Regal, even. "Well, I'm not leaving. I've barely been here a fortnight, as you know, and I intend to stay a bit longer. Perhaps forever."

A figure strode forward into the light, clad entirely in black. I expected a guard or at the very least a man. Not the vision of loveliness now standing in front of me, hand resting on the hilt of her dagger. My own weapon snuggled against my thigh. Easily accessed and wickedly sharp. She made no move to draw hers as she studied me from behind a black mask. Smart. I'd have to get one for myself if I lived long enough.

... Kill her.

Shut up.

... Kill–

Not now.

Her gray eyes narrowed. "What are you doing?"

"Me?"

"Yes."

"Waiting."

"For?"

"You."

"To?"

"This is fun," I quipped. "Back and forth, one word at a time. How long do you think it would take us to have an actual conversation at this rate? An hour? A day?" She drew the dagger but didn't throw it or point it in my direction. A beautiful weapon for a beautiful woman. "Look." I held my hands in plain sight. "I'm here because your adorable daughter—if she even is your daughter—beguiled me. I'm not looking for a fight. Even if you are."

She twirled the dagger with mesmerizing smoothness as if she'd been doing it her entire life. I watched the light play off the blade, handle, blade. "I have no desire to fight you, either." All trace of whisper vanished from her voice.

"Why reveal yourself, then?"

"What do you mean?" Her fingers played with the edge of fabric against her cheek.

"You stepped from the shadows and no longer have a frog in your throat. Why?"

She shrugged. "I changed my mind."

I arched a brow. "About me? Why?"

"Do you always ask so many questions? My reasons are my own. Do not test my patience more than you already have."

"All right, calm down before you hurt yourself."

"Before I hurt you, you mean."

I grinned and rocked back on my heels. A dark look crossed her face. "You are free to go. But I will be watching."

"I certainly hope so." I slipped out the door before she could challenge me again.

~ Chapter Fifty-six ~

I ran a hand through my cropped hair. Shorter than I'd asked for, but it would grow back. The weather had changed anyway, and less hair meant a cooler head in the heat. Perhaps now I would measure up to whatever standards the warehouse woman had held me to. She didn't like the look of me? What did she know anyway?

... *Nothing.*

True, yet I spent my day prowling the streets, the alleys, the wharf hoping to run into her, to show her how wrong she'd been. But she had made herself scarce or invisible, and I returned home dejected, denied all satisfaction of wiping the smugness off her face.

I flopped onto the mattress, restless and itching for something to do. Surely someone in this town could use my services given all the wickedness in the world. I'd settle for delivering a heavy-handed chastising at this point. I heaved a sigh and rolled onto my stomach. Bored. So very bored. Perhaps I simply needed to look harder, farther. Or return home.

A shudder ran down my spine. Home offered nothing for me, not anymore. A bridge I'd burned to the ground then buried the ashes. No hope of resurrection. Only one person likely still cared, still worried but I couldn't face her. Or anyone. Not after what I'd done.

... Enough.

I clenched my jaw and forced my thoughts away from her, from there, to more pressing matters. Money. I'd frivolously spent almost all I'd brought. Now I barely had two coins to my name. If I couldn't find night work, I'd have to look for day work. With my strength restored and then some, I could and would do anything. Anything but go back.

I studied my palms, smooth even after years of wielding a sword. Apparently hacking through enemies until I thought my arm would fall off only built character, not callouses.

A soft knock on the door dragged me out of my reverie. "Who is it?" I sang in the voice my landlady loved. But only silence responded.

I slowly climbed to my feet, hand on my dagger, and crept to the door. Two of the six floorboards I stepped on squeaked in angry protest and I rolled my eyes. *Gods above.*

I yanked the door open, prepared to give whoever had disturbed my pity-party a piece of my mind. But instead I found myself staring slack-jawed with no social graces whatsoever.

Rafe flashed a crooked grin. "Well met, Taryn. May I come in?"

Words failed me, but my muscles obeyed, and I opened the door. He strode past me, tracking road dust all over my clean floor. He stood with his hands on his hips, then turned in a full circle.

I closed the door and my mouth then waited for him to either vanish or explain why in gods' name he'd come here and how he found me. *And what in the hell?*

"Rafe," I managed to squawk out. "What are you doing here?"

"I could ask you the same thing, your highness."

"Keep your voice down!"

He arched a brow. "Using an alias. Why, might I ask?"

I stood right in front of him, equally matched in height if not in weight, and poked a finger at his chest. "What are you doing here? How did you even find me?"

He snorted. "You paid for this room with a gold coin. From your father's treasury. Not exactly inconspicuous."

I groaned and scrubbed a hand over my face, the same face stamped on the coin. "Whatever. You shouldn't be here. Don't you know how dangerous it is? Are you trying to get yourself killed?"

"You mean the way you are?"

"I–"

"Don't you dare deny it," he snarled in my face. "You and I both know what's going on."

I stepped back as if he'd pushed me then started pacing. I raked my fingers through my hair, wishing I had more of it so I could tear it out. Of all the stupid, idiotic, addle-brained things to do. Showing up here, like this. Now. I muttered curses under my breath while Rafe simply watched with hooded eyes. I finally ran out of ways to insult him, his entire family and his dog. "I give up, Rafe. You win."

"This isn't a game, Taryn. Or a competition. It's your life."

"I am well aware."

"No, you're not. Look at you. You're living here under a false name, doing the gods know what after abandoning your duty, your family, your kingdom." His tone softened. "Taryn, please. Come home with me."

I narrowed my eyes, a blatant accusation. "So, you're here to take me back? I won't go. And you can't make me."

He matched me glower for glower as the tension climbed. "How old are you?"

"Old enough."

His shoulders tensed but he wouldn't fight me. I had the upper hand there. Yet the look on his face told me he wouldn't back down, either.

He grinned. It looked anything but friendly. "But I know someone who can make you."

Suspicion reared its monstrous head. "What are you talking about?"

"Do you really want me to say it?"

He leveled a stare at me, and I swallowed. He couldn't possibly mean her. No. She wouldn't. Would she? My head started to throb. I massaged my temples and sighed. "Rafe, just say whatever it is you have to say and then get out. I've had a long day, and I'm tired."

"Grace."

I froze as if her name alone compelled me to listen, to agree. A knee-jerk reaction. I stood my ground and held my tongue, my silence all but daring him to say it again. Just once, so I could punch the smirk right off his face. He had picked the wrong day, the wrong time to come here demanding I go with him, scolding me like a child who'd run away from home. Even though I had. Darkness sang in my blood, a siren calling my name, luring me towards violence.

… Hurt him kill him hurt him now–
STOP.

"Rafe." I clenched my jaw against the pressure building in my head. "You have to go. Now. Please."

Something in my voice or in my eyes convinced him. With a curt nod, he headed for the door. He turned back, opened his mouth as if to argue further then shook his head and walked away. Without another word.

Gods, what a mess. Legs shaking with unused adrenaline, I sank onto the bed. My hands, so recently coated with blood, trembled. Bile surged into my throat, and I lurched up just in time for my dinner to splatter into the sink. I clutched the cool porcelain, breathing in through my nose and out through my mouth until the sickness passed.

Ever so slowly my clenched fists opened, my tight shoulders relaxed, and my jangled nerves steadied. I glanced up, staring back at the man in the mirror. He looked how I felt. Lost. And alone.

~ Chapter Fifty-seven ~

Rafe stood on the dock, watching the ships sweep across the bay. He'd take one of them home, as soon as he convinced Taryn to come with him. Which might take a while, he realized with a heavy sigh. Why had he thought it would be easy? Nothing with Taryn lately had been easy. Not since he regained his memory. He'd act familiar one minute, distant the next. Strange and erratic and slightly insane.

The note he'd left sounded like the ravings of a lunatic. Nothing but hunting prey and righting wrongs and doing whatever it took to protect the kingdom. But at least he'd been honest about his intentions and his destination. Rafe hadn't hesitated when the king asked him to track Taryn down. And he had, only to find his friend gone, as if part of his soul had been replaced by a violent evil.

He didn't know what to think or do about it other than try to bring him back. But how? He couldn't just snap his fingers and undo whatever damage had been done. The only person capable of attempting such a thing had no business being here, not with him in this dangerous state. Who knew what he'd do next? Killing the general had been bad enough but then to kill the king?

No. Rafe refused to put Grace in danger, even if it meant saving Taryn from himself. And based on his behavior tonight, Rafe doubted Taryn would or could recover.

So Rafe would stay a little longer, remind Taryn of all the wonderful people in his life, people who loved him and only wanted his happiness. Taryn did not strike Rafe as happy here, despite whatever arguments he made to the contrary.

❈

Rafe woke with a renewed sense of purpose and decided to make the most of his time here by following Taryn. He strode through the city at a discreet distance, keeping a watchful eye. Yet Taryn did nothing out of the ordinary. He window shopped on the main street, tried on a pair of boots and then sat at the fountain in the town square, looking peaceful and content and far too relaxed for someone who recently committed regicide. Another warning sign. A bad one.

Taryn stood and stretched in the sun like a cat then meandered through a small park. Several children played in the grass and he stopped to watch them, a wistful smile tugging at his mouth. Rafe had almost grown bored enough to call this whole thing off when a woman approached Taryn from the other side of the lawn.

Her mouth curved in a warm smile as if they were friends, but the subtle shift in Taryn's posture, the sudden tightness in his shoulders spoke otherwise. Rafe watched from behind a row of hedges, wishing he could hear their conversation. He tensed when she briefly placed her hand on Taryn's arm and whispered in his ear. Her smile never faltered, as if etched in place.

She strolled away, and Taryn watched her go, looking almost as flabbergasted as Rafe at the women's uncommon behavior. Then Taryn's gaze landed on Rafe's hiding spot. He smiled as if he'd known all along he'd been followed. Rafe sighed. Best to get this over with now.

"Well met," Taryn drawled as Rafe came to stand at his side. "I thought I told you to leave."

Rafe ignored the obvious attempt to start an argument. "Who's the woman? How do you know her?"

"She's a friend."

He arched a brow. "What kind of friend?"

"The none of your business kind."

"Taryn, I'm only trying to help. Whatever happened doesn't matter. Everyone is worried about you and wants you to come home."

"I. Don't. Care."

"Yes, you do. You just think you don't for some insane reason. But we all love you and want what's best for you." Rafe had promised himself he wouldn't beg but now couldn't seem to stop. "Please, Taryn."

"Have you ever wondered what death is like?"

Rafe blinked at the abrupt change of subject, not to mention the subject itself. "Taryn …"

"I imagine it's quite peaceful. I've seen death often in my dreams and even when I'm awake. Yet it doesn't scare me or worry me or keep me up at night. Not anymore. It waits for us all, the only inevitability in life. Eternally patient and forever welcoming. A gift of blessed relief."

Rafe gaped at his friend, his prince, unable to believe what he'd said. Taryn had lost his mind.

"What?" Taryn blinked as if he hadn't just gone off on a rant of epic madness. "You don't agree?"

Rafe had no words to describe his feelings, so he simply shook his head.

"Well, no matter. I'm off. Things to do, people to kill. I mean see." He laughed to himself and shoved his hands into his pockets before strolling away.

Rafe stared at his back, wishing he'd wake up from this nightmare. Nothing made sense here, as if the world had turned inside out. He felt out of his depth navigating this bizarre situation. But he couldn't give up. Not yet. He needed to figure out what the hell had happened to Taryn. First, a stiff drink. He might even glean some information in the process. He turned and headed toward the town square then stepped inside the first tavern he saw. He released a long breath in the dimness and sat at the counter.

The barkeep sidled up to the counter. "What'll ya have?"

"Ale."

He nodded and poured while Rafe fished a coin out of his pocket. He took the mug then swiveled on his stool to study the other patrons, but he didn't expect much from the small crowd. At the end of the work day, the place would fill to the rafters. He could wait until then.

He nursed his ale while the shadows lengthened. A bell rang outside, and people started pouring into the tavern like fish from a barrel. He drained his mug then ordered another. Men of all shapes and sizes crowded the counter, yelling over each other. He listened to the chatter, hoping to hear a clue regarding Taryn and what he'd been up to. Mostly they talked of the harsh workday or the stale ale, but then someone said murder.

"They still haven't caught the guy," a burly dockworker mentioned to his mate.

"Not to worry. He only kills lords!" Laughter rippled down the counter.

"Lord Harlesby deserved to die, the pompous ass. Good riddance!"

Rafe felt the blood drain from his face. *Holy gods.* What had Taryn done? He lurched to his feet, pushed through the crowd and staggered from the tavern. He breathed in the cool night air, trying to keep the ale in his stomach. This could not be happening. Taryn would never kill in cold blood. Would he? Then again, he had killed both General Stark and King Rendon. But those were crimes of passion fueled by revenge and fury. And if they weren't? He had to know for sure, one way or the other.

~ Chapter Fifty-eight ~

I paced my room like a caged animal, replaying the conversation from the park in my head. Not with Rafe but with the woman. *Lady Amelia Ravencrest.*

She'd approached in broad daylight with a dozen witnesses, wearing a dress but no mask. She must have known any efforts to deceive me would never succeed. I would have recognized her voice, not to mention her eyes, anywhere. Mysterious and vague and utterly charming.

And then she started talking. Threatening, really, claiming she knew not only my true identity but also my crimes. I'd feigned shocked outrage at such an insult but my mind refused to focus on anything other than kissing her. I couldn't take my eyes off her exquisite mouth while she'd blathered on about evidence and treason and justice served. None of it mattered. She could've read my death sentence right then, and I wouldn't have batted an eye. Gods, her lips begged to be kissed, nibbled, nipped at until they bled.

… Enough.

She'd made her speech, her threat crystal clear then smiled as if she'd seen right through my flimsy charade.

Which meant I had to kill her. I didn't want to, not without kissing her first. Back to the matter at hand. Kill her? Or not kill her?

… Kill her.

Shut up. I already know what you want.

She'd come alone to the park and her elegant fingers bore no rings. And she could have given a false name to throw me off. Perhaps I should verify her identity before making any rash decisions. I might have to devise an elaborate and complicated plan to get close to her again. My blood heated for all the wrong reasons. I hadn't been with a woman since before. And then after, it had seemed irrelevant. Now the situation demanded attention as if my sanity depended on it. No wonder I'd been so restless lately. But could I seduce, just to kill her afterwards? Or would she expose me first?

I groaned and chased the thought away with monumental effort. Needing a strong distraction to obliterate her from my mind, I bounded down the stairs to the tavern. An inebriated patron had passed out near the door, slumped over, chin on his chest. Poor fellow. He'd get trampled if he stayed here much longer.

I crouched and shook his shoulder. "Hey. You need to move, friend."

Nothing but a wet snore in response. I sighed then hooked my arms under his and heaved him away from the door. His head fell back on the stone wall with a solid thunk. "Sorry, I didn't …" The words died in my throat. *Gods above.* "Rafe! Rafe, wake up." I slapped his cheek and his eyes flew open.

"Wha … wha …"

"Rafe, easy. It's me."

"Tar–"

I clapped my hand over his mouth. "Can you stand?" He nodded, and I helped him to his feet then guided him up the stairs to my room.

He blinked with bleary eyes. "You live … in the tavern?"

"Above the tavern, Rafe. Remember? Come on." We stumbled into the room together, barely staying upright. I dragged him to the bed and forced him down on top of it. He groaned while I pulled off his boots and unhooked his cloak. "I'm sure you feel terrible, and you probably will for a while. Try to sleep it off."

His eyes drifted closed. Better. But gods. What had he been doing down there? Trying to outdrink the whole town? His tolerance rivaled even the drunkest of drunks. He must have had twelve too many to end up in this state.

"You're an idiot, Rafe." I shook my head as I watched his chest rise and fall. "This doesn't make any sense." I slumped onto a chair and toed my boots off. He'd sleep, and then we'd talk. Or rather I'd talk, and he'd listen. He needed to go home. Immediately.

❦

A low groan pulled me from sleep, and I winced at the sharp pain in my neck, literal and metaphorical. Rafe sprawled on my bed, still half-drunk by the look of him. I kicked his foot, and he stirred then peeled his eyes open as if they'd been forged closed.

"Good morning," I drawled. "Sleep well?"

"Ungh."

"I see. A scintillating topic but I think we'll stick to a one-sided conversation for now, the one side being mine."

"Argnh."

"Thank you for your heartfelt agreement." I straightened in my chair and cleared my throat. "I am tolerant and reasonable. And patient to a fault. But gods man, you have tried my patience to no end with this foolishness. Coming here to drag me back home then following me, spying on me. I would be offended, but your heart is in the right place and you have the best of intentions." I drew a sharp breath. "But you need to leave. The sooner the better. I'll sell my sword to pay for it if I must but you're getting on a ship. Today."

He struggled into a seated position. "All right, Taryn. I'll go."

"You will? Truly?"

"Truly. I don't want to fight with you, and you clearly don't want to come home so …"

"So, you'll go?"

"Yes."

I smiled and clapped him on the shoulder. "Thank you, my good man. Now. Let's have some breakfast."

"Taryn, wait."

"*Gods*. What now?"

"I just need to know." He hung his head. "Did you kill Lord Harlesby?"

I barked a laugh. "Of course I did. Why do you think I came here?"

He raised his head, anguish written all over his face. "I suspected. And now … now I know."

I angled my head, trying to figure out what had upset him. "Surely you're not grieving for Lord Harlesby? I've heard nothing but terrible things about him. Pompous ass is the current favorite."

"No, Taryn. I'm grieving for you, for your soul."

"My soul is perfectly fine, thank you for asking. Now I'm done talking about this or anything other than food, and you leaving."

He nodded, finally sober, and climbed to his feet. I led him downstairs and parked him in the back of the tavern. He looked a little green, so I ordered coffee to start then eggs and bacon for myself and toast for him. We ate in measured silence while the morning rush eddied around us. I sipped my coffee, watching the scene unfold. The pattern never wavered, the same day after day. Reliable and comforting, providing order to an otherwise disorderly world. And then Amelia walked in and everything crashed down like a house of cards. *What is she doing here?*

Head swiveling, she scanned the room, clearly looking for someone. Her gaze found mine and she lifted her hand in a cheery wave before joining us. "Good morning," she chirped, setting my teeth on edge.

"What are you doing here?" I hissed. "I told you–"

"Who is your friend?" She flashed a grin at Rafe. He simply blinked, leaving the introductions to me.

"Amelia, this is Rafe. Rafe, Amelia."

"Pleased to meet you."

"Likewise." Rafe eyed her and then me with more than a little suspicion.

"May I sit?"

"Must you?" I sighed with dramatic emphasis but she didn't take the hint.

She perched on the chair to my left, fluffing her skirts. "What are you having for breakfast? It smells divine." She compared our plates then plucked a piece of bacon from mine. I scowled, which she seemed to find hilarious.

She beamed a bright smile, chasing the shadows from the room. "Oh, Taryn," she purred. "Do lighten up. It's too early to be in such a dark mood."

Her eyes sparkled with mischief while she chewed. I struggled to pull enough air into my lungs to stay conscious. Rafe seemed just as affected, opening then closing his mouth like a fish on dry land. Her gaze flicked between us, assessing, analyzing. My skin crawled with anxiety, and I pulled at my jacket collar.

"Something the matter?" she cooed, batting her eyelashes.

"Not at all. Why do you ask?"

"You're a little pale. And Rafe looks like he's going to faint any second."

I glanced at Rafe, who did indeed seem on the verge of swaying right out of his chair. I grabbed his arm to steady him. "What do you want, Amelia?"

"Just to chat."

"About?"

"Lord Harlesby."

"What about him? Has he risen from the dead?"

She leaned forward, eyes narrowed to slits. "You are going to pay for what you did, *your highness*. Just as soon as I can prove it."

I leaned forward, matching her glare. "Which you will never do. I did not kill him."

She sat back, wiped her glorious mouth on a napkin then stood. "We shall see." She turned with a twirl of her skirts and flounced out the door.

"Who …?" Rafe started.

"Quiet," I snapped, waving a hand. "Let me think."

I pondered all the ways to kill her. Slowly or quickly. With mercy or with copious amounts of pain. Each thought fueled the fire already blazing in my blood. Part of me wanted to call her bluff just to see where this would go, but the darkness insisted I end her now, before she did the same to me. Yet I couldn't for the life of me make this decision. Not on my own.

… Coward.

A second opinion might do some good. Perhaps Rafe would have an idea or two, once he no longer looked like death warmed over. "Rafe. Are you all right?"

"I … don't know. What's going on, Tar–"

"Not here," I barked. "Come on." I threw a few coins onto the table and hauled Rafe to his feet. We struggled up the stairs together, though I bore far more of the burden. I heaved him onto the bed and he slumped against the wall, his bulky frame nearly swallowing the mattress.

I raked a hand through my hair and paced. This Amelia situation had spiraled out of my control. Her behavior confounded me in ways nothing else ever had. Maddening, to say the least. Still, I admired her boldness if not her brashness and wanted to know all about her. Where she lived, what she did. Who she loved.

Rafe's pitiful groan snapped me to my senses. "She's the one from the park, isn't she?"

I sighed, already done with explaining myself to him. "Yes."

"How do you know her?"

"It's a long story. And I'm not sure I should know her."

"Why?"

"I have a feeling she's dangerous." He arched a brow. "Just trust me, Rafe. Please. I know what I'm doing."

He narrowed his eyes but wisely left it alone. I, on the other hand, couldn't. The sooner I uncovered her true intentions, the better.

~ Chapter Fifty-nine ~

Amelia aimed then hurled a dagger at the target, hitting it dead center. Right where she'd intended, of course. She smiled and retrieved it, turning to face her audience. "Any questions?" A dozen hands shot into the air and she chuckled. "Yes, Kendra?"

"What if you can't see your target? Should you still throw the dagger?"

"An interesting question. Anyone care to guess?" Silence. They all looked to her as the expert, and they should, yet she'd hoped at least one of them would take the initiative and speak up. She sighed. "No. I don't recommend it. You'll only lose your dagger. Best to wait until the target is closer so you can see exactly where to throw it. Or thrust it. Who else has a question? Don't be shy."

"I do," a deep male voice called from the back of the room. Every head swiveled to look as he stepped forward.

She stifled a groan. "Yes?"

"Where is the best place to thrust it? The dagger, I mean."

Her cheeks heated but she refused to give him the upper hand. "Several places come to mind. Would you like to demonstrate for the class?"

"I'd love to."

All eyes followed his lithe form as he sauntered through the group with predatory grace. He stood close but not too close then angled his head and smiled. Her pulse raced with alarming speed as if he could make her toes curl with a simple touch. She hated it. And him.

"Class." Her stern tone dragged their attention away from him. "Watch and learn."

She beckoned for him to join her on the sparring mat. He took off his jacket and rolled up his sleeves, revealing toned forearms. They each grabbed a practice dagger from the pile on the table. Feet planted underneath her, she glared a warning before she lunged. With a savage grin, he slithered out of her reach like a snake, faster than she'd thought a human could move. They circled each other while the class sat riveted.

She watched his feet, his thigh muscles flexing before he moved. He never reacted the same way twice, which threw her off. She couldn't determine his pattern or his tells. Brute force, then. She lunged again, with all her speed and strength. She'd anticipated he'd dodge back but instead he came at her straight on, grabbing her wrists as they crashed together. Her heart pounded and her chest heaved yet he seemed barely winded, smiling with maddening calm.

He applied just a bit more pressure to her wrist and she dropped the dagger. Disarmed. In less than five minutes. *Damn.* He let her go and stepped back then bowed to the class. After a heartbeat of stunned silence, they erupted into applause. She rolled her eyes and rubbed her wrist, wanting nothing more than to expose him right here. But she didn't have a death wish and kept her mouth shut. For now. "Class dismissed."

Smiling and talking like a flock of twittering birds, the students ambled out, some throwing admiring glances over their shoulders. She couldn't blame them, but he didn't need his ego stroked any more. The last student exited, and the door closed with an ominous click.

"So." He shrugged into his jacket. "This is what you do when you're not accusing innocent people."

"I teach these girls valuable self-defense skills. It's very important to me, and I take it seriously. If you have a problem with–"

"Of course not. I commend you, in fact."

She blinked. Had she misheard him? He flashed a wicked grin and butterflies swarmed in her stomach. "What do you want?"

"I thought it might be a good idea if we got to know each other. Then maybe we could come to an agreement."

"You think if we're friends I won't turn you in?"

"I'm hoping to be your friend, yes. But I simply want to keep my true identity a secret. There is no reason for you to turn me in, Amelia."

She considered his offer and the way her mouth had gone dry when he'd said her name. Other than pissing him off, she had no cause to reveal his identity, which she could live with. But something about him felt wrong. She always trusted her instincts. They'd saved her life countless times. But if she spent time with him, perhaps he'd slip and do or say something incriminating. More than worth the effort. And the risk. "Fine. Friends, then."

His grin broadened, and her heart leapt. Could she do this, keep him at arms' length and not let their relationship develop past platonic? She had to at least try. Hopefully she'd uncover his secrets in the process.

"Can we start with dinner? Tonight?"

"I ..."

He arched a brow. "Or would your husband mind too much?"

"I'm not married."

"Lover, then?"

Heat crept up her neck and she clenched her jaw. "No."

"Wonderful. Where can I call for you?"

As if she'd ever have him in her home. "I'll meet you at the tavern. Seven o'clock."

"Until then."

If she'd still held a dagger, his smile alone would have disarmed her. He breezed out the door as easily as he'd breezed in, leaving her breathless and wondering just what she'd gotten herself into.

❈

Amelia reviewed the facts as she knew them while preparing for dinner. Taryn Ellsbree. Crown Prince of Nogardia and heir to the throne. Captain in the king's army, decorated war hero. And murderer. All right, she didn't know for a fact he'd killed Lord Harlesby, but it felt true. She just couldn't prove it. Yet.

Her own list of titles and accomplishments numbered exactly zero. She frowned at her reflection, smoothing her hair and her skirts. Not nearly as glamorous as he likely preferred, but it would have to do; besides, they were just two friends having a friendly dinner. She rolled her eyes at her weak justification and stepped out into the night. She opted to walk, simply because she wanted him to wait. It had nothing to do with her shaking hands or racing pulse. At all.

He sat in the back, at the same table where she'd confronted him earlier. Her steps faltered as he stood and smiled, looking magnificent in a fitted black jacket and silver vest. His golden hair seemed to glow in the low light. She swallowed and almost turned around but then remembered her plan.

Shoulders back and chin high, she marched to the table. His smile dazzled, and her heart thumped. Gods, she needed to control herself. She could not allow these ridiculous reactions to his masculinity. She'd been with plenty of desirable men. Men just like him.

"Amelia." His silky voice sent a jolt of pleasure up her spine. "You look gorgeous."

"Thank you."

He held her chair out and she sat, glancing around at the other patrons. No one seemed to pay them any mind, however, and she relaxed a fraction, even daring a smile.

"Your smile is lovely."

"Flattery will get you nowhere."

"We'll see." His eyes sparkled like sapphires, and she became acutely aware of how little space separated them. Her body responded to every move he made as if she were somehow connected to him, like a puppet to its strings. Pulled, manipulated. She couldn't decide whether to like it or hate it.

Food appeared on the table, yet she didn't remember ordering. Of course he'd taken the liberty. Ordinarily, she would have balked at such blatant disregard for her right to choose, but somehow this seemed chivalrous, gallant. Gentlemanly. Not the behavior she expected from a cold-blooded killer. She would expect it from a prince, however.

They ate and talked, though she paid little attention. Her mind kept wandering, studying his mannerisms and facial cues, trying to translate his body language into anything other than sensual suggestions. By the end of dinner, she had a well-formed opinion of his character if not his conduct. The language lesson, however, left her aching in all sorts of uncomfortable places. She couldn't risk anything beyond friendship, but she also couldn't deny his raw appeal. He certainly knew how to charm a woman. Did he even realize the effect it had on her? Probably. Physical attraction aside, she didn't have to do anything about it. Unless she wanted to.

~ Chapter Sixty ~

I leaned back in my chair, smiling across the table at Amelia while she tried not to react, at least not in a positive way. She certainly had the whole scowling daggers thing down pat. Still, I smiled because I felt like it. And because it made her squirm.

I sipped my wine, though I'd had better, and studied her. She seemed beyond uncomfortable, much to my delight. I'd never had such fun pushing someone's buttons, including my sister. Amelia proved too tempting a target. And the idea, the slight chance of even the mere possibility of kissing her made my pulse race. She never said I couldn't kiss her.

She laid her fork down and licked her lips. I almost choked on my wine, dribbling red liquid down my chin. She laughed softly as I wiped my face. "Shall we go?"

"Go?"

"This place is about to get … rowdy."

"What's wrong with rowdy?"

I arched a brow. "I just assumed …"

She flashed a wicked grin. "Never assume anything about me."

"As you wish."

The revelers piled in, yet we stayed, grinning at each other while everyone around us got sloppier and sloppier. Then the band started to play. Bawdy lyrics rang through the room, louder as the night wore on. Amelia sang along more often than not.

The wine flowed, and she glowed, her grin widening by the minute. Apparently, she didn't drink often or to the point of inebriation. The poor girl couldn't hold her liquor. This wine paled in comparison to what I'd grown up with and hardly affected my senses. Clear-headed and clear-eyed, I watched her giggle and blush and slosh all over the table. "I think you've had enough, my dear. Let's get you home."

She pouted. "But I don't wanna go."

I stifled a groan. "I'm sure you don't but we should. It's late and you're very drunk."

She scoffed. "I am not drunk, sir."

"Yes, you are." I laughed under my breath. "Time to go." I lifted her up and steered her toward the door, bumping into every table along the way. We finally made it outside, where she promptly retched on the stone steps before passing out in my arms. I sighed heavily then hauled her up the stairs. Rafe shot to his feet as I barged in the door. "Help me."

He took her legs while I carried her top half. Together we laid her on the bed.

"What is she doing here?"

I blew out a breath and raked a hand through my hair. "Well, she's drunk."

"Obviously. But why is she *here*?"

"I don't know where she lives, only where she works. And we were just downstairs at the tavern. It seemed the best option."

"So now what?"

"We sleep on the floor, I suppose."

"Right. And in the morning, when she wakes up in your room with not only you but me?"

"I don't know, Rafe. Let's just go to sleep and deal with it then."

"Sir. Yes, sir."

I rolled my eyes and threw a pillow at his head. He caught it with a cocky grin. We lay down side by side, leeching each other's warmth and slept.

❧

"What. Happened."

I opened my eyes. Amelia's face hovered inches from mine, her dagger pressed to my throat. Rafe jerked upright and her other hand shot out with a second dagger pressed to his side. Where had she been hiding them?

"Someone better start talking. Now."

I swallowed then winced at the resulting sting. "Perhaps you could move the dagger." She growled a warning then lowered the blade. I cleared my throat and slowly sat up. "There's no need to worry. Nothing happened. You drank way too much, and I didn't know where else to take you."

"And what is he doing here?" Her other dagger still pressed against Rafe's side. He seemed to have stopped breathing. I blinked, and she angled it at the floor.

"He's staying with me while he's in town, which won't be much longer." I shot him a look and he released a shaky breath.

She glared at each of us in turn while we waited for her to decide our fates. "Fine." She sheathed her blades then straightened her skirts. "I'll be going now. Good day."

The door slammed closed and I cringed then glanced at Rafe, his glare almost as sharp as her daggers. I sighed. "I'm sorry, Rafe. Truly."

"Yes, well. Does she know who you are?"

"Unfortunately."

"And?"

"And what? I'm trying to get her to like me, so she won't expose me."

"What difference does it make if the people here know your name, your title?"

I crossed my arms in defiance. "A huge difference, actually. If for some reason anyone suspects me for Lord Harlesby's death, I can't be linked to Evanston. It's too dangerous."

He arched a brow. "Then why did you come here, Taryn? Why did you do it?"

I opened my mouth, but the flippant response died in my throat. Why had I come? I'd been so sure of myself, so confident in my chosen path. I never considered the reason behind my motivation. I couldn't blame revenge or justice this time. I'd simply needed to cover my tracks.

… Coward.

Shut. Up.

Rafe seemed to read each thought as it crossed my mind. His face softened. "Taryn. It's not too late. No one in Evanston knows what you did here. And your father will protect you, you know it. Just come with me. I swear–"

I shook my head, a stern expression on my face. "I can't go back, not after everything I've been through, everything I've done. At least here I'm free."

"What are you talking about? Free from what? You're not making any sense."

"I know you don't understand and you probably never will but you need to trust me. I need this, Rafe. I need to be here."

"No, you need to see a healer."

I shook my head. "I'm staying."

"Here? Like this?" He gestured at the cracked walls, threadbare carpet, and thin mattress.

"Please just go home and forget you ever found me." I hung my head, suddenly exhausted. Tired of arguing, of justifying myself. "Leave me alone."

"Taryn ..."

"Please," I croaked.

... *Now*.

He breathed a weary sigh then clomped to the door, pausing to look over his shoulder. With a solemn nod, he walked out. Exactly as I'd asked. So why did I feel betrayed?

~ Chapter Sixty-one ~

Free from Rafe's scornful judgement, I could get on with things. But I still didn't know what those things were. I'd come here with a purpose, a goal, which I'd achieved. Killing General Stark and King Rendon had felt right. Justified. At least at the time. We'd been at war with them, the enemy. Their deaths were perfectly reasonable.

Lord Harlesby, on the other hand, hadn't needed to die. Not really. I could've convinced him he'd mistaken Rafe for someone else. Or paid him for his silence. A simple solution to a simple problem, yet I'd blown the whole thing so far out of proportion it no longer resembled reality. I'd deluded myself into thinking only his murder would suffice. And then I'd ended his life, with brutal efficiency yet without a shred of remorse. Problem solved.

The guilt I'd thought a thing of the past came rushing in, shoving me toward the brink of despair. I teetered on the edge, one foot dangling over the precipice as I waited for the final blow. Perhaps Rafe had been right, and I needed a healer, or at least someone to talk to, someone who would understand. But no one here fit the bill. Only Grace had seen and accepted the darkness in my soul. And it had only grown more powerful since. I couldn't reveal it to someone else without losing myself in the process. Not when I'd already lost so much.

... Craven. Weakling. Quitter.

A soft knock jolted me out of my trance. Rafe? Part of me leapt for joy while the other scowled in consternation, a look which vanished the moment I opened the door. "What are you–"

Amelia brushed past me without a word then paced the tiny room like an agitated bird in a cage. I closed the door, watching as she mumbled to herself. "Amelia." She froze, her gaze snapping to me as if compelled to listen, a look I hadn't seen on her. It made my gut clench. "What's wrong? Has something happened?"

"Yes. No. I don't know."

I shoved my hands into my pockets. "Well, as long as we understand each other."

Her face remained a blank mask as she resumed her circular march. Clearly something had upset her. I just couldn't imagine what. Her dagger flashed as she absently twirled it. Had she come to kill me? Here, of all places? My own dagger laid across the room, where I'd left it in my haste to answer the door. *Idiot.* "Is there anything I can do?"

"Taryn Ellsbree. *Prince* Taryn."

I arched a brow. "Yes?"

"But you're using an alias."

"As you know. What is going on?"

"Why?"

"Sorry?"

"Why are you using an alias? Only guilty people, people with secrets use aliases."

"I ..."

"Wait. Don't tell me." She closed her eyes and sighed as if she'd come to a conclusion she didn't like. "I don't want to arrest you."

I narrowed my eyes, studying the way she prowled around me in her black pants and black jacket. No mask this time, though. "Who are you?"

"You know who I am."

I snorted. "No, I don't think I do." She leveled a gaze at me. I stared back with equal intensity. "Well? I'm waiting."

"Lady Amelia Ravencrest. At your service." She bowed with a flourish I found incredibly sexy.

"Your name is not who you are. Why all the cloak and dagger? There is much more to your story, yet you refuse to tell me."

She barked a laugh. "You should talk, your highness." She sneered with a contempt I found incredibly offensive.

Every instinct warned me to keep my mouth shut, yet I trusted her, even if I didn't trust myself. "Fine." I huffed a breath. "If I tell you mine, will you tell me yours?"

Her eyes widened, shining like silver. She sheathed her dagger with a jerk of her wrist. "You first." She sat on the mattress, legs folded underneath her as if I were a storyteller about to regale her with tales of wondrous heroism.

I frowned. "I'm … not sure where to begin."

"Should I ask questions? Would it be easier?"

Something about this reminded me of Grace, of her attempts to wrestle the truth out of me. Well, this time I intended to control the conversation, if not the situation. I swallowed past the uncertainty. "No. I'll just start at the beginning."

She grinned. "Once upon a time, there lived a young prince …"

I rolled my eyes. "All right. I don't need your help. But yes, once upon a time there lived a young prince. He had everything his heart desired right up until he didn't."

Her grin faded. "What do you mean?"

"Do you want to hear the story or not?"

"Of course, but–"

"Then shut your pretty mouth and let me tell it." Her cheeks flamed crimson, but she pressed her lips together. "Thank you. Now. Where did I leave off? Ah, yes. The prince and his heart's desire. Well, the prince joined his father's army, served as a captain and returned from war a hero. But at a great cost. He lost men in battle, men he cared for deeply and it stained his soul." Emotion tightened my throat, and I paused, the ache in my heart more acute than it had ever been.

"Taryn, you don't have to do this."

"No." I straightened my shoulders and my spine. "We had a deal." She nodded, and I continued. "He tried to come to terms with his grief and guilt but couldn't quite manage it, even with the help of a beautiful young girl, whom he thought he loved. Events then transpired which crippled the prince's ability to discern right from wrong, good from evil and he …"

… Stop.

"He …"

… Now.

Brow furrowed, I searched for the words, for a way to describe what had happened to me. But I couldn't. Instead, a gaping expanse of darkness yawned open in my head, blanketing every thought, every memory. I rubbed my temples against the building pressure. "What … is happening?"

Amelia jumped to her feet and rushed to my side, grabbing my arm. "Are you all right?"

I stared at her, wanting to divulge every secret but my mind refused to reveal the truth to anyone except me. Like a wolf protecting its kill. A shudder ran down my spine and darkness whispered its siren song, a lullaby to my soul.

… Freedom.

"Can we … just … sit?" I managed to say without choking to death on my words.

She guided me to the mattress then slowly helped me down onto it. My head felt three sizes too big. Pain almost blinded me, and I squeezed my eyes shut, but it only hurt worse.

She crouched beside me, concern etched on her beautiful face. "What can I do? Please, I want to help. Anything."

"Stay," I croaked. "Stay with me."

"Of course."

She crawled onto the bed and I laid my head in her lap. She combed her fingers through my hair, soothing away some of the agony pounding in my skull. "Tell me," I rasped as I closed my eyes. "Your story."

She shifted, settling in for the long haul. "All right, Taryn. I'll tell you." Her soft voice flowed like a purring rainstorm. "Once upon a time …"

~ Chapter Sixty-two ~

Taryn's golden hair felt like the purest silk in Amelia's fingers and she couldn't get enough. The motion seemed to relax him, so she kept stroking it while she told her story. His breathing slowed, and the tenseness seemed to drain out of his body as he drifted off to sleep. She didn't stop however, suddenly needing to tell him, to unburden herself after so many years of guarding her heart. They'd somehow formed a bond, and she trusted him to not hurt her, to keep her secrets safe.

Shadows lengthened as her voice grew hoarse, yet she continued until the sun had fully set and darkness filled the room. He slept with his head cradled in her lap, his face at peace. She traced his stubbled jawline with her fingertips, light as a feather. He stirred, murmured an incoherent string of words then settled. She eased his head from her lap and climbed to her feet. Leaving him pained her beyond logical thought but she needed to go. She had work to do, and her job did not allow for sentiment or emotion.

She hardened her heart and crept from the room, putting her feelings for Taryn back in their box and sealing the lid.

She'd evaluate and analyze what had happened between them later, after. Her focus now needed to remain as sharp as her daggers. She pulled on her mask and slipped between the shadows.

The full moon painted the cobblestones with milky light. Two men careened against each other as they stumbled from the tavern, blocking her way forward. They reeked of alcohol and regret yet smiled as she tried to go around them.

"Where to, sweet thing?" the tall one slurred, breathing putrid fumes in her face.

"Excuse me, sirs. I'm just on my way to meet my brother."

"Well, he's not here now, and we are," the short one drawled.

Saliva dribbled from the corner of his mouth, and she swallowed hard. She certainly didn't want a confrontation outside one of the most public places in the entire city. Perhaps she could entice them to follow her to the warehouse, a building she knew inside and out. She could easily lose them in its shadowy depths. Or kill them. She didn't much care either way.

"Indeed you are," she purred. "Why don't we go somewhere less conspicuous?" They swayed, blinking in confusion. "Private," she clarified. The tall one leered while the short one nodded. "This way, please."

She had to walk three times slower than her normal pace so the drunkards could keep up. She'd removed one of her daggers and held it under her cloak, just in case things got out of hand. She didn't doubt her skills or her resolve, but drunk men could be mean and unpredictable. A fact she knew from experience.

They reached the warehouse, and she ushered them inside. Moonlight shone through the high windows, casting the room in patches of shadow and light. She could see well enough and these two didn't need to see at all. The door closed behind them with a solid thud. "So." She pulled off her hood. "Now what?"

They gawked, finally noticing her mask, black clothing, fierce demeanor and savage grin. And the dagger she now held pointed at their crotches.

"We ..."

"Yes?"

"No."

"No?" She angled her head as she stalked toward them. "Don't hurt you? Don't kill you? I should, you know, for trying to take advantage of me. I can't say I'm not flattered, but you're not my type."

"What is your type, anyway?"

She spun around, almost losing her footing. "What are you doing here?" she hissed. "Go home."

"Not a chance," he crowed from his seat on a stack of crates. "I've never seen you in action. I can't wait for the show."

She rolled her eyes. "I'm not going to do anything. They're already scared enough as it is."

"It's true, miss," the tall one stammered. "We just want to go."

"Fine," she growled. "Get out before I change my mind." They practically tripped over each other in their haste to make it through the door in one piece. She sheathed her dagger then turned with her hands on her hips.

"What?" His voice radiated innocence and boyish charm.

"Nolan, something could've happened to you. How many times have I told you–"

"Too many to count." He hopped down with a cocky grin. "If you would just teach me the way you teach those girls ..."

"You are too young. And I promised Father I'd keep you safe while he's away." His lower lip trembled, and her resolve started to crumble. "Don't, Nolan. Please don't do this to me. I've had a rough day."

He took a deep breath then released it slowly. "All right. I'll stop. But you have to teach me at least the basics. What if I get accosted in the streets?"

She arched a brow. "Accosted?"

He winked and shoved his hands into his pockets. "It could happen."

"For gods' sake … Fine. I'll show you a few basics but nothing more. Understood?"

He tapped his hand to his chest in salute. "Milady."

"Shut up, little brother. Let's go home."

Nolan walked at a sedate pace next to her as they made their way home, even though she could feel him vibrating with excitement. For two years she'd refused to teach him anything other than simply running away despite his many requests otherwise. Their father's orders had been very specific, and she'd follow them, but holy gods the kid could sell it. A skill he'd learned from their mother, no doubt. Amelia could be persuasive when the need arose, but it usually involved threats of mild violence. Nolan simply opened his mouth, and people jumped to do his bidding. Sort of like Taryn's ability to compel her into doing and saying things she'd rather not.

She stifled a groan. Taryn. She still didn't know what to do with him or what to make of him. So far, she'd gotten only part of the truth whereas she'd divulged her entire life story. Granted he'd been asleep at the time and likely hadn't heard a single word but the fact she'd so easily opened up to him worried her. A lot more than she cared to admit.

~ Chapter Sixty-three ~

I opened my eyes, blinking in the semi-darkness. Amelia's intoxicating scent lingered, and I took a deep breath, inhaling through my nose. I hadn't meant to mislead her, but suspected she'd feel more inclined to share if she thought I'd fallen asleep. Her story had kept me riveted, and I wanted the sensation of her fingers trailing through my hair to never stop. Not to mention the way my head fit in her lap like it belonged there.

I sighed heavily. This had not been part of the plan. To care about her, think about her. Obsess over her. No, I certainly hadn't planned any of it. Yet I felt connected to her by a shared sense of tragedy, more acute after hearing her story. Such heartache and loss, so much like mine. How had she made it back from the other side of hell intact? By my estimation, she'd weathered the storm with admirable grace. Far better than I had. Perhaps if she knew all we had in common, she'd give up her ridiculous quest to prove my guilt and give in to becoming friends.

But could I trust her? Her story pulled at my heartstrings like fingers on a harp, but my entire future depended on her not finding out I'd killed Harlesby. And the only way to make sure she never did turned my stomach.

... *Liar.*

Back to my original plan, then. Friendship, at least enough to gain her trust, so I wouldn't have to kill her.

I found her easily enough and watched from the shadows as she threw a perfectly aimed dagger at the target, where it sank into the center with a dull thud. A young boy clapped in excitement from his perch atop the fence. Her cheeks flushed, but she grinned just the same.

"My turn!" he cried as he hopped down and raced over to her side.

She handed him a dagger, her face all business. "Do not throw this until I tell you. Understand?"

Eyes full of delight, he nodded with so much enthusiasm and youthful exuberance I almost laughed out loud. Had I ever been so young, so hopeful? My childhood seemed far away, a hundred years ago if not more.

She stood behind him, his head just under her chin. "Hold the handle like this. And your arm like this. The power comes from your shoulder, not your elbow. Look past the target then breathe out when you throw." He nodded in constant agreement as he mimicked her movements. "Now throw it."

The dagger flew and missed the mark, but not by much. Impressive for someone with little experience. No wonder she spent extra time with him. He seemed to need all the one on one help he could get. And she certainly knew how to teach. He smiled and wrapped his arms around her waist. She smoothed his hair then bent and kissed his forehead. "Try again, Nolan."

"Okay." He stepped back and started the process again, sticking his tongue out as he concentrated. The dagger flew, faster this time, and hit closer to the center. I had to give both her and her young student credit.

They chatted as they set-up the daggers for another round. I'd come here intent on spending time with her, but after watching the two of them, I didn't want to eavesdrop or interrupt. I turned to go then paused at the tone of her voice.

"What do you mean?"

"I mean, I don't mind you taking care of me while Father is gone but don't you want a family of your own?"

"Of course I do."

"Then why aren't you married? Theo's sister is two years younger than you, and she's already married. And James said his sister is going to have a baby in the spring, and Will also told me–"

"Enough," she barked. He snapped his mouth closed and hung his head. She sighed then lifted his chin. "I'm sorry, Nolan. I didn't mean to snap at you. You're the sweetest little brother a sister could ever hope for."

"Don't call me sweet, Lia. I'm not a baby."

She flashed a crooked grin. "If you insist."

"So?"

"So what?"

"Are you going to get married?"

She chuckled and tousled his hair. "Someday, perhaps."

"You really should, though." He started organizing the pile of daggers by blade size from shortest to longest. "What about the man from Evanston? The handsome one?"

She rolled her eyes. "Don't let him hear you say that. His ego is already bigger than you."

"But you like him?"

She opened her mouth but then seemed to reconsider. I smiled, imagining the thoughts running through her head. Hopefully similar to mine. My smile turned wicked.

"Yes, I do. But it's … complicated."

He snorted. "Everything with you is complicated, Lia."

"I know. You ready to go?"

"Yes. I'm starving. Can we eat at the tavern? Please?" My heart lurched as her face softened, a look I'd give just about anything to see.

"Sure. Why not?"

He grinned, and they left while I hid in the shadows, heart hammering. She'd mentioned her brother during her story, but I never thought he'd be younger. I groaned. This changed everything.

❈

I walked toward the tavern, dragging my feet. I couldn't risk running into Amelia and Nolan, but I also didn't want to spend more time alone in my pitiful, empty room. A sudden pang of homesickness washed over me, a yearning for the constant hustle and bustle of life at court. And my family. As annoying as I found Natalie's incessant meddling, she had my best interests at heart. My parents also meant well, but the thought of seeing disappointment on their faces filled me with guilt and regret. Still, I'd done the right thing, the best thing for my kingdom. Pride swelled through me then ebbed as anxiety chased it away. A dull ache bloomed at the base of my skull. I needed a drink.

I perched on a stool, a drink in my hand and my heart on my sleeve. I felt sorry for myself in a way I never had. It defied logic and reason and drowning it in alcohol seemed a wise course of action. I couldn't get carried away by self-doubt. I'd had enough to last a lifetime. I needed to steel my resolve and face the consequences here. Or crawl home to beg for leniency and forgiveness. I didn't know which I dreaded more.

My headache intensified the longer I stewed, yet I couldn't seem to drag myself upstairs. Five empty glasses clustered on the bar in front of me, which might have accounted for the lack of mobility. Or coherent thought.

"You okay?" The barkeep squinted at me with a baleful eye. "You look half-dead."

I managed a weak smile. "Thank you, sir. Exactly as I'd hoped."

He arched a brow then walked away to bother someone else. I didn't feel half-dead. I felt all dead, tired enough to lie down forever. I'd spent all my mental energy on refuting the lies in my head, battling myself in a war I'd never win. Defeated, dejected, destroyed beyond all hope of recovery. Tears blurred my vision, and I bit my lip.

"Hey."

I sucked in a breath and hastily wiped my damp eyes. "Amelia."

"Are you all right?"

"What do you care?" I growled then drained my glass. "And what do you want? I'm busy."

She placed her hand on my arm and I tensed. "I only want to help."

I barked a laugh. "Help with what, exactly? You … You …"

"You," she repeated, taking over the conversation, "are drunk. Let me at least help you upstairs."

"And into bed?" I drawled, leering. "Please say you're taking me to bed."

"I'm taking you to bed." I grinned as she threw my arm over her shoulders. "Nolan," she called. "Come on."

Nolan scampered to her side, eyeing me warily. I tried to smile but only managed to bare my teeth. We stumbled up the stairs and into my room. I took two steps inside then retched in the sink. Gods above. Why did I keep doing this to myself? I slumped to the floor.

"Is he sick, Lia?" Nolan whispered.

"Not really. He'll be fine after he sleeps it off. Get me a wet rag, would you?" She knelt beside me, brows drawn together in concern. She shook her head then helped me up. "Time for bed."

I nodded, which made the room spin. She set me on the mattress like a sack of grain then pulled off my boots. Nolan handed her the rag. She wiped my forehead and neck with gentle pressure. I grabbed her wrist before she could pull away. "Why are you doing this?" I croaked.

"Get some rest, Taryn. I'll be back in the morning."

"But–"

"Sh." She placed a cool finger on my lips. "Sleep." She stood and gazed down at me then turned to Nolan. "Let's go home."

Home. The word echoed in my skull long after she'd shut the door behind her.

~ Chapter Sixty-four ~

I woke with a splitting headache and a roiling stomach. The room had ceased spinning, but my mind whirled. What happened? I squeezed my eyes shut as I slowly sat up. Never in my life had I felt so miserable. And lonely. I needed to fix whatever had broken inside me. I just didn't know how, at least not without returning home.

There had to be another way to get past whatever mental block had formed in my mind. Each day, reality slipped further and further from my grip as grief and guilt eroded my sanity. The time had come to swallow my pride and hold myself accountable for my actions. Starting with Rafe.

I lurched from bed, stumbling about my tiny room as I pulled on my boots. If I could find him, I'd convince him to help me. He'd practically demanded I let him anyway. Surely the offer still stood.

I shielded my eyes against the glaring sun as I searched for any sign of Rafe. Puzzlement became frustration, which turned into panicked worry. I'd told him to go, but had he left Verlandia altogether? What if I couldn't find him?

What if I never found a way out of the darkness?

My breath hitched, and my pace quickened into a run, up and down street after street. I jogged to a stop at the dock, sides heaving as I gasped for air. If Rafe had left, the harbormaster would have record of it. I swallowed hard and headed for his office.

"Good morning."

The harbormaster glanced up from the pile of papers on his massive desk then held up a finger. I sat in the only chair while he muttered under his breath. After a mind-numbing eternity, he stood and stretched, arching his back while his buttons strained in protest.

"Where you headed, son?"

"Nowhere, sir." The irony slammed into me, yet I forced a smile onto my face. "I'm hoping you can help me find a friend. He might have sailed earlier today."

He nodded and scratched his stubbled chin. "Sure enough. I have today's logs right here. Name?"

"Rafe Morgan."

He ran a blunt fingertip down several columns of names then shook his head. "Not here, I'm afraid. Destination?"

"Evanston."

"The west bound ship sails at dusk. Evening tide. You should try the inn. Most passengers hole up there while they wait to board."

"Thank you sir." Genuine gratitude washed through me. I hadn't thought to look there.

Anxious hope churned in my stomach as I stepped into the inn. The plush carpet muffled my bootsteps, and I swiveled my head, surprised by the ornate furnishings. Could Rafe afford to stay here?

The innkeeper smiled as if new customers brightened her day. "Good afternoon, sir. How may I help you?"

I hated to disappoint her, but I had to find Rafe. "I'm looking for someone. He might be a guest of yours. Rafe Morgan."

Her cheeks flushed. "Oh, yes. He stayed here last night. I believe he's in the game room now. Just through those doors."

I smiled my thanks then followed where she had pointed down a short hallway and into the game room. Smoke curled in lazy spirals along the rafters, making my eyes water and my lungs constrict. I blinked back tears and scanned the room. Men from all walks of life crowded the tables, heads bent over cards or dice. I cruised among them, checking faces and clothing. I'd almost given up but then heard a gruff voice from the back of the room.

"Thank you, gents. I'm done here." A chair scraped against the floor and Rafe stood, gathering his winnings.

I took a tentative step forward, not sure how he'd receive me. We hadn't parted on good terms the last time we spoke. An epic understatement. "Rafe."

His head snapped up, eyes going wide as he recognized me. "Tar–" He cleared his throat as he strode toward me. "What are you doing here?"

"Is there somewhere we could speak? In private?"

"Yes, of course. This way."

I trailed behind him, barely keeping up as we ascended a flight of stairs. He stopped on the landing, and I crashed into his back. "What is it?"

He whirled around, almost knocking me down a step or two. Like I deserved. "What do you want?"

"I ..." His jaw tightened, and my heart sank. I'd hurt him deeply with my selfishness. "Rafe, please. Let me explain."

"Fine." He turned on his heel and led me down the corridor and into a well-appointed room with a pretty view of the harbor. He tossed his jacket on the bed next to his packed bag. "Drink?"

"Yes, thank you." I sat on the couch, wondering how he could afford such lavish accommodations. Then again, my father probably funded this mission. He handed me a glass then sat as far away from me as possible. I needed his help, a fact he seemed to ignore as he stared at me. I'd have to tell him everything about my time here, every event since my boots had hit the dock. "I'm sorry, Rafe. Truly. Please understand I never meant to hurt you. I only want …"

"What, Taryn? What do you want?"

"I want to feel better. I want to feel like myself again. I hate what I've become, yet I can't seem to control it, to fix it, or even understand it. Can you …" I swallowed hard. "Can you help me?" I held my breath as I waited for his judgement.

"Taryn." His quiet voice rumbled in the stillness. "I still don't know what to say other than come home. Please."

I shook my head soberly. "I'll do anything else but it's not going to happen. Ever. So just stop thinking about it, talking about it, asking me about it. Right now, I just need to know if you're still willing to help me."

Rafe arched a brow. "You do not want my honesty. Trust me."

"But–"

He held up a hand. "It sounds like you have the situation, as you called it, well under control. You don't need me for anything." He hung his head as if this whole mess were somehow his fault.

"Rafe … I don't …"

"Taryn." His anguished look ripped a hole in my heart. "I want to help you more than anything but I can't."

I raked a hand through my hair, the prince of awkward moments. Rafe had been like a brother to me, someone I truly cared for. My stomach dropped at the thought of losing him, yet I couldn't cross the giant chasm yawning open between us. Not if he didn't meet me halfway, which didn't seem likely given the resignation in his tone. I had no choice but to rally my spirits and plaster a grin onto my face. The only way out is through.

"Let's get you to a ship, then. You can sail with the evening tide if we hurry."

Rafe stared at me, nothing but sadness in his eyes. "Lead the way."

We walked to the harbor, the sound of our scraping bootheels filling my head. I needed to say something. Wanted to bridge the gap with a desperation bordering on obsession. But nothing I could say seemed right or fitting or even remotely close to how I felt. If only my time with Grace had cured me of my ridiculous inability to share my feelings. Apparently not.

Rafe, on the other hand, seemed more than comfortable sharing his. He stopped as we approached the dock. "I don't want to leave you here, like this."

I arched a brow. "Like what?"

"Alone. Scared." He stared at the glimmering horizon. "Reckless."

"I am none of those things, Rafe, I assure you." I flashed a cocky grin, but he shook his head.

"You can deny it all you want but you cannot hide forever. Not from those who love you." He took a deep breath. "Promise me you'll be careful."

"Of course." I waved away his concerns, pretending his words hadn't torn a hole in my heart.

Rafe grabbed my shoulders. "Swear it."

I blinked at the worry in his voice. As if I wouldn't honor a promise. Then again, I hadn't kept my word about a lot of things lately. "I swear it."

He nodded once then turned on his heel and strode toward the harbormaster's office. I watched him go, torn between calling him back and chasing him down. I had no intention of returning home, yet the thought of being alone made my chest ache. And I could no longer trust myself to discern right from wrong, good from evil. A startling realization to say the least. It scared the hell out of me.

I took a step to follow him, and Amelia called my name. I spun around to find her hurrying toward me, a determined look on her face. She didn't break stride as she grabbed my hand and towed me along the wharf. I stumbled behind her and glanced over my shoulder in time to see Rafe's bulky frame disappear onto a ship. I swallowed hard then dragged her to a stop. "What are you doing?" I demanded, glaring a warning at her. "You can't just–"

"I need to talk to you. Now."

"Fine." I stood my ground and crossed my arms. "Talk."

"Not here, you idiot. In private." I arched a brow and she blew out an exasperated breath as if I were one of her unruly students. "It's important. Trust me, Taryn. Please."

"All right, but can we walk like normal people? I'm in no mood for physical exertion." Violence flashed in her eyes, and I wanted to laugh but the look on her face warned me against it. Instead I tucked her hand into the crook of my elbow. "Where to?"

She peered up and down the wharf. Business had ceased at sunset and we stood alone. The only two people not rushing home. "The warehouse."

Most of the crates had been removed. Now the place sat empty, eerie and quiet except for rodents scurrying in the rafters. Shadows curled around me as we stared at each other. My patience, already at an all-time low, had just run out. "What. Is. It."

She wrung her hands, a nervous tic I'd never seen, and started to pace. Dust swirled at her feet and I sneezed. "I've been looking for you all day."

"Why?"

"Lord Harlesby brought one of King Rendon's servants back with him. The magistrate interviewed her after his murder but she'd been too shaken to remember much. Apparently her memory has cleared. She told the magistrate she recognized Rafe. Said he was in Regnevar with Harlesby."

Impossible. "So?"

"Rafe disappeared the night of King Rendon's murder." She approached where I stood, slowly closing the distance as if she thought I'd bolt. But I had no reason to run and stood my ground. My pulse raced, yet I remained calm. She held my hands and looked me directly in the eye. "Did Rafe kill the king?"

I gaped at her even as fear jolted through me. "What?"

"You heard me, Taryn. Just tell me what happened. Please."

"There is nothing to tell."

"I know Rafe is your friend, and I understand your need to protect him but–"

"Rafe. Is. Innocent," I growled.

"Of killing the king, perhaps. But what about Harlesby? The servant said–"

"I don't care what the servant said. I'm shocked and more than a little insulted, frankly. I can't believe you'd take a servant's word over mine."

"Don't change the subject," she snapped. "Fine. Let's say Rafe is innocent. But then who killed Harlesby? You?"

I briefly closed my eyes, hoping she wouldn't hear the panic in my voice. "No."

She stifled a frustrated growl and resumed her pacing, mumbling under her breath every few seconds. I shoved my shaking hands into my pockets and tracked her movements, admiring her lethal grace despite the circumstances.

My mind whirled with worst case scenarios. I fought the urge to rake a hand through my hair, cursing myself for not putting Rafe on a ship sooner. Yet I could still protect him. But I couldn't stay here while she fit the pieces together.

"Amelia." She hadn't heard or didn't care. "Amelia." She stopped, and her head whipped around, hope burning in her eyes. I hated to destroy it but I could offer only more lies. "I have to go."

"What? Where? Taryn, wait …"

"I'm sorry. I … I have to." I hurried out the door then ran through the empty streets wishing I could outrun the truth. I bolted up the stairs and into my room, leaning my forehead against the closed door. I let out a shaky breath. Thank the gods Rafe had already sailed. Soon he'd be home where he belonged, under my father's protection. Safe. And free. But for how long? I couldn't guarantee his safety now any more than I could before.

… Unless.

Unless I turned myself in, admitted my crimes. And then I'd swing for them. Savage fear clawed at my heart, widening the already gaping hole. I didn't want to die, yet what choice did I have? I cared for Rafe and would give my life for his in an instant.

I closed my eyes, wishing the answer would simply fall into my lap. This servant girl could shatter everything I'd built, layered with painstaking effort, sealed with blood and lies and death.

… Unless.

No. Unthinkable. Though it would solve everything, wrap it in a nice tidy bow. A simple, final solution. Rafe would never worry again about my mistakes causing him harm. But the thought of taking another innocent life soured my stomach, even if it guaranteed Rafe's security. I growled in frustration, cursing my indecisiveness. Pacing in angry circles, I stewed and seethed, weighing my options until I thought my head would burst apart.

A tremor wracked my spine as pain exploded at the base of my skull. I clutched my head in agony and collapsed onto the bed. My vision faded in and out. The air tasted like ash and destruction, a promise of eternal rest. Shadows writhed as they thickened, feasting on the last of my morality with savage delight.

I abandoned my soul and embraced the darkness.

~ Chapter Sixty-five ~

Amelia thrashed in her bed, trying and failing to find a comfortable position. Her head swam with thoughts of Taryn.

The forlorn, lost look on his face when his mask had slipped had nearly broken her heart. She'd almost gone after him to catch him before he did something reckless, like leave town. Though why she wanted him to stay remained a mystery. She had to get him out of her life before *she* did something reckless, like fall in love with him. Physical attraction she could handle. Anything more would end only in disaster. But something about him compelled her to care. He'd known pain. Agony. Soul-wrenching sorrow. And he used arrogance as a shield to protect his heart, just as she did with hers.

If he stayed, she'd have to deal with what she now accepted as the truth about his involvement in Lord Harlesby's death. Her suspicions had only strengthened since she first glimpsed him strolling down the street in the dead of night, dressed all in black. And though he hadn't confessed, she'd recognized the look in his eyes. Guilt.

Yet she couldn't act on her suspicions alone. She needed proof. Hard evidence. But if she had it, would she accuse him outright? Could she with her feelings for him such a complicated mess?

She turned over onto her side and jerked the blanket to her chin. She'd run out of options and out of time. Lord Harlesby's family had waited long enough and needed closure almost as badly as she did. They'd paid her to bring his killer to justice, not let him get away with murder. Yet she'd given him the benefit of the doubt. More than once.

With a frustrated sigh, she got up and changed into her work clothes. He'd had several opportunities to come clean. And he hadn't. She'd get the truth out of him now. Or die trying.

Darkness pooled in alleys and doorways as she prowled toward the tavern. She loved this time of night, so late everyone had gone home to their beds, to sleep and dream. She held the city in the palm of her hand and wandered the streets, more at home here than anywhere else. Taryn might be asleep as well, but she didn't care. If she had to wake him, so be it. He could sleep in prison.

A scraping sound from a nearby rooftop caught her ear and she stopped, head angled to listen. Another scrape had her scaling the wall. She crouched at the top, one hand on her dagger, but nothing moved in the shadows. Bright moonlight left only a few places to hide. She climbed all the way up then turned in a slow circle. The other rooftops were just as empty, just as quiet. But she'd heard something. Somewhere. Her head whipped around.

Taryn stood a few paces behind her, his eyes full of wicked promise. "Well, well," he drawled, moving closer. "What brings you here this time of night? Spying on the citizens?"

She stood her ground even as butterflies took flight in her stomach. "Looking for you, actually."

He swept his arms outward and bowed with a flourish. "You've found me. Now what?"

"We need to talk."

"Must we? I have far better things to do."

She glared. "Liar."

"Perhaps." He shrugged as if their conversation weren't a matter of life or death.

"Why are you out so late?"

"Why are you?" He shoved his hands into his pockets and rocked back on his heels, teeth gleaming as he grinned.

"Look." Her patience had worn paper-thin. "This is your last chance to tell me the truth."

His jaw tightened as his grin turned feral. He stalked closer, forcing her to take a step back. "Or what?" The menace in his voice sent panic racing up her spine.

She swallowed hard. "I ..."

"You."

"Taryn ..."

"Amelia." A dark chuckle rumbled from his chest. "You have no idea, do you?"

"About what?"

"How utterly charming you are. How beautiful and alluring. And you smell amazing." He leaned forward, and she stilled, every sense on alert. He trailed his nose up her neck and inhaled.

She tried not to react, but her core tightened as his breath warmed her skin. "Taryn."

"Hm?" He nuzzled the spot just under her ear. She gasped, falling into him, her traitorous body ignoring the warning fizz in her blood. His teeth grazed along her jaw and she sighed, closing her eyes. She hadn't felt this good in a very long time. A voice in the back of her head reminded her why she'd come. She silenced it with an angry groan. She couldn't imagine anything more important than this feeling. She didn't want it to stop. Ever.

Steel whispered, and her eyes flew open. The tip of his dagger rested against her throat. She moved to grab her own weapon, but he pressed the blade into her skin. The coppery scent of blood wafted in the air as warmth trickled down her neck.

"Don't," he growled in her ear. "Or I'll have to hurt you and I really don't want to."

"Taryn …"

"I'm done playing this game, Amelia. It's been fun and could've been even better, but you ruined it with all your questions and suspicions and manipulation."

"I never manipulated you. I only–"

"Save it," he snapped. "Right now, I have to take care of something. And you're not going to stop me. In fact, you will do exactly as I say or your sweet little brother won't live to see the sunrise."

White hot fury lanced through her, but she simply nodded, taking his threat seriously. She believed without doubt he'd lost control, had turned into a monster, a vicious animal snarling like a rabid wolf. One she knew how to destroy.

"You will stay here on this rooftop until first light. Then go home and forget you ever met me or Rafe. Understood?"

She nodded again, wincing as the blade nicked her skin. He stepped away and she sucked in a breath with a scowl. He grinned, his soulless eyes devoid of humanity. With a devilish wink, he escaped into the night.

She did as he'd ordered and stood on the rooftop, shaking with ice cold dread. Not for Nolan's safety but for Taryn's soul. His self-destructive behavior could only mean one thing. He'd surrendered to the darkness, had given up the fight. Her heart confirmed what her head already knew. And she had to stop him. Before she lost him forever.

~ Chapter Sixty-six ~

I readied myself for the task ahead. One last loose end to tie up. Then freedom. Escape from all the pain and regret, everything weighing on my soul. Nothing left to feel. No more reason to hurt. *Numb.*

A running start landed me safely on the next rooftop as I danced across them. Lord Harlesby's estate loomed just one more over. My heart thudded in my chest as I landed, adrenalized by the night. I paused to catch my breath with the moon smiling encouragement from the midnight sky.

Hoofbeats clattering on cobblestones drew my attention to the street below. Perhaps Harlesby's solicitor here to settle his affairs. Or his family returned from another futile search for his killer. I stifled a laugh in my gloved palm. *Fools.*

The carriage passed through the gates and then turned a corner. I crouched in the shadows, watching as a young couple stepped down. They walked inside, and I blew out an exasperated breath at the delay. Now I'd have to wait until they fell asleep. *Unless.*

I chuckled with wry humor then sat against the chimney, twirling my dagger between my bent knees. The blade winked with each turn in a hypnotic rhythm. Back and forth, over and over until my eyes grew heavy and my breaths slowed.

❈

I jerked awake. How had I fallen asleep? And what had woken me? The sound of approaching footsteps, apparently. I rolled my eyes at whoever had the gaul to sneak up on me. I climbed to my feet, scanning the area for the uninvited guest. A dark figure stalked toward me, features hidden beneath a hooded cloak.

I stepped from my hiding place. "Close enough. Take off your hood." The hood fell back, and I grumbled a curse. "What the hell are you doing here? Didn't you hear me before?"

She shook her head. "I don't believe you, Taryn. You'd never hurt him."

"How do you know what I'd do? You think I killed Harlesby, don't you?"

"I know you did but I also know you had valid reasons for doing it. And hurting Nolan would serve no purpose. You're not cruel."

So very wrong. I growled and closed the distance between us, stopping mere inches from where she stood. She stared at me, deep into my darkened soul. Her eyes shone in the moonlight, mesmerizing, as if luring me away from the darkness. I shook my head against a sudden jolt of pain. "Just … leave me alone."

"No. I can't let you do this." Her gaze flicked toward the estate. "It isn't you."

"Oh, but it is," I snarled in her face. "More than you know."

Her chest heaved as she drew in a sharp breath. "But I do know."

And then she kissed me. I tried to pull away, but she grabbed the back of my neck and deepened the kiss. Desire arced through me even as my mind fought against the urge to kill her right here. A growl rumbled in my chest as I pinned her against the chimney. My hands seemed to move on their own, roaming over her body, feeling her heat even through her clothing. She buried her fingers in my hair and pressed her hips toward mine. *Evil temptress.*

She bit my lip and I tasted blood. *Wicked seductress.* A hunger like I'd never felt roared to life inside me. Before I could satisfy it, a sharp pain sliced through me, burning with the heat of a thousand suns. I jolted, leaning back, gripping my side. Warmth seeped through my fingers. I hissed at the sting. "Amelia …? What …" *No.*

"I'm sorry, Taryn. This is the only way."

She reached for me and relief flooded my system, quickly replaced by panic as the world slipped away underneath me. Air whistled in my ears, the only warning before the ground rushed up to greet me with a brutal smack to the face. Darkness devoured me, body and soul, heart and mind. *Forever.*

❈

Voices hummed around me, fluttering like fairy wings as I drifted through nothingness. No pain or misery or guilt. Or life. Death had come to free me at last. A gift of everlasting serenity. Finally I could rest in peace.

❈

Light bloomed around me, teasing my eyelids as I surfaced from the soothing blackness of eternal sleep. I blinked then blinked again, and my vision focused.

"He's awake!"

"Sh, Nolan." Amelia sat at my side, peering into my face with undisguised hostility.

I shifted but couldn't move past the rope binding my wrists. "What …" I tried to say but only managed a strangled croak. Hazy images blurred in random memories, yet I couldn't recall what had happened. Or why she'd tied me to this bed. She handed me a glass of water and I took a tentative sip.

"How do you feel?"

I swallowed hard, throat clicking with the effort. "Dead."

Nolan snorted a laugh but quieted at the scornful look she shot him over her shoulder. "Do you remember anything?"

I shook my head, wincing at the dull ache behind my temples. I paused, trying to piece together recent events. My mind had betrayed me again, stealing precious minutes, hours, perhaps even days from my life. I briefly closed my eyes and stifled a groan. Too much, too soon.

"Here." She held a small vial to my mouth. "Drink this. It will help with the pain."

"I don't feel any pain."

"You will if you don't drink this."

Her tone convinced me, and I drank, almost choking on the foul brew. I sank back onto the pillows. Nolan watched me, a curious tilt to his head as if I were a strange creature he wanted to study. "What?"

Amelia glanced behind her then at me. "I've never invited a man here before." Not an explanation. Of anything.

"I'm honored."

"Don't be," she snapped. "You weren't invited, as you might have guessed."

"Are you going to turn me in?"

"Don't think I haven't thought about it. But it's really up to you."

"What do you mean?"

"I'm willing to let you stay here and recover but on one condition."

"Which is?"

"As soon as you're well enough to travel, you leave Verlandia altogether and return home. To your family."

My heart lurched but I held myself together. "Why?"

"You'll be better off with people who love you."

I swallowed past the sudden tightness in my throat. "Do I have any other options?"

"Not if you want to stay out of prison. And alive."

"Well. I suppose it's settled, then. But can you at least tell me what happened? I don't understand any of this."

"Perhaps later. For now, get some rest. I have work to do." She stood, looking down her nose at me. "Time for your lessons, Nolan."

"But–"

"No arguments."

He hung his head then followed her to the door where he paused to turn back. "Good luck."

I had a feeling I'd need it. I blew out a long breath, fighting to stay awake so I could figure out what the hell had happened. But she'd given me something far too powerful and I surrendered to oblivion.

~ Chapter Sixty-seven ~

I drifted in and out of consciousness for three long days while the pain receded. A dull ache replaced it, and I finally stayed awake long enough to remember running home after Amelia told me about the servant girl recognizing Rafe. I'd agonized over a decision but what? Then I'd gotten another headache but my memory didn't extend any further. Next thing I knew, I'd woken here. Without thought or reason.

I glanced around the room, presumably Amelia's if the lace curtains and heirloom vanity were any indication. But why here and not prison? She'd spared me even though she claimed to know what I'd done. But how?

The door slowly opened, and Nolan poked his head in, eyes wide as I smiled. "Hello."

"I ..."

"It's all right. You can come in, if you'd like."

He glanced over his shoulder then slipped into the room. "Amelia told me I couldn't visit you."

"But?"

"But I'm not a very good listener." He grinned like an imp.

I chuckled under my breath, and he came closer, curiosity outweighing caution. "What's your name?"

"Nolan Matthew Ravencrest."

"Quite a name."

"Who are you?"

"Your sister didn't tell you?"

He shook his head. "She didn't tell me anything about you, but I think you're the man from Evanston. She said you were handsome."

I barked a laugh and pain burned in my side. I drew a shaky breath. "What would you like to know?"

His eyes lit up as if he'd just discovered buried treasure. "Everything!"

"Have a seat." He jumped on the bed, jostling my leg. I clenched my jaw to keep from passing out while he settled beside me. "My name is Taryn Alexander Garrick Ellsbree."

"Wow. Even more names than I have. Are you truly from Evanston, all the way across the sea?"

I nodded. "I'm actually the prince of Nogardia. And Regnevar, I suppose."

He sucked in a breath. "Does Amelia know?"

"She does."

"What are you doing in Verlandia? I've never heard of a prince visiting here before. Is it a secret mission? Are you here to conquer us?"

Clearly he enjoyed adventure and intrigue, as any boy his age would. I hated to disappoint him, but I couldn't tell him when I hadn't even confided in Amelia. And his tender heart needed shielding from my dark deeds. "I'm just visiting."

His face fell. "Oh."

"But I do like Verlandia. Especially here. Is this your house?"

"Our family has lived here for generations. My great grandfather built it. Do you live in a castle?"

"Of course."

"With the king and queen?"

"And the princess."

"There's a princess, too? Can you take me there? I've never seen a princess before. She's beautiful, isn't she?"

"What do you think?"

He stared out the window, a faraway look on his face. "She's probably the most beautiful girl in the world."

"Don't tell her that."

His gaze snapped back to me. "I want to go with you when you return."

"I'm sure you do, but I doubt your parents would allow it."

"Father isn't here, and Mother died a long time ago. Amelia is in charge, but I can convince her."

I arched a brow. "It's not very nice, Nolan, to manipulate your sister. She cares about you and wants to keep you safe."

He scoffed. "I can take care of myself. Besides, I'm old enough. Please?"

I shook my head. "I'm sorry, but I can't. And I don't even know when I'm leaving." Surely, Amelia wanted to be rid of me sooner rather than later. My continued presence here would only become a burdensome hinderance, and she had done enough already.

He shot a knowing look at my leg. "You were very hurt when she brought you here. I thought you were going to die."

I rolled my eyes. Just like a child to exaggerate. "Yet here I am. Do you know what happened? Amelia still won't tell me."

He glanced at the door. "You fell," he whispered. "Off a roof."

Surely, I would remember such a thing, yet my mind remained blank as if it had been erased or someone else had experienced it. The pain I knew all too well, but memories of the events leading up to my current state eluded me. I blew out a frustrated breath. "Anything else?"

"No, though you were also bleeding. There." He pointed to my left side, where the pain had burned earlier.

I lifted my shirt, revealing a bandage the size of my palm. I peeled it away, hissing at the sting, and frowned. Something wickedly sharp had sliced into me. Another stolen memory. I slumped against the pillows, suddenly exhausted. "Nolan? Would you mind if I rested now? Only for a bit."

"Can I come back later?"

"It would be a pleasure."

He flashed a bright smile then hopped off the bed. I lifted my hand in a wave as he breezed out the door. Though his visit had drained my energy, it had renewed my spirits. Just talking with another human being, one who didn't want to kill me or imprison me, did wonders for my bruised heart. I didn't know the extent or severity of my other internal injuries. Healing them at all seemed an impossible task. Such a pleasant thought. With a weary sigh, I closed my eyes and begged the nightmares to stay away.

~ Chapter Sixty-eight ~

Amelia hurled another dagger at the target. It hit with savage force and sank to the hilt, buried deep in the wood. Her anger at Taryn almost outweighed the blame she placed on herself for her carelessness. She'd let her feelings for him blind her to the truth. Now she had him in custody, though in her room. Her *bed*. She'd fantasized about this very situation but never these circumstances.

She hadn't known for sure if he'd intended to kill the servant girl but had decided not to risk it and done the only thing she thought would stop him. Thank the gods it worked. And even though he'd barely survived the fall, she didn't regret pushing him off the roof. Or stabbing him.

Logic dictated she turn him in and let the magistrate sort out the rest. She'd done her part, had earned her pay, but still. She didn't know whether she wanted such a final, permanent resolution. But she did want to be wrong about him, to believe his claim of innocence.

She smothered a scream of frustration as she wrestled the dagger free then scrubbed a hand over her face. Things had gotten so complicated so quickly it made her head spin. Ever since Taryn Ellsbree swaggered into her life, it had been filled with nothing but chaos and confusion. Yet despite everything he'd put her through, she loved him. A problem of epic proportions. Gods, she wanted to hate him. More than anything.

She sighed and put the daggers away then trudged inside with a heavy heart, hoping her father wouldn't return any time soon. He'd have a thousand questions and she would have to lie to him, which she'd never done.

"Nolan!" The front door closed behind her, echoing in the empty hall. "Nolan?"

He usually came running the second she walked in. Panic whispered but she refused to listen. Cautious yet confident, she strode through the house, down corridors, peeking into every room she passed. No sign of him. She paused at the stairwell. Perhaps he'd gone outside, though he knew better than to break such an important rule.

"Nolan!" Still no response. She ascended the stairs, hand resting on her dagger, and hurried to her room. Voices floated into the hallway and she stopped to listen.

"And then what happened?" The wonder in Nolan's voice brought a smile to her face.

"They lived happily ever after, of course." Taryn laughed and her heart sighed.

"Oh. How boring. Isn't there a story with knights and dragons and heroes? I like those best."

"Of course but there is more to life than danger and adventure. You need a little happily ever after to balance it all out. Do you understand?"

"I guess so."

Amelia stifled a laugh. At his age, Nolan wanted nothing to do with romance. She'd stopped telling those stories years ago.

"I do have one story about a brave young hero. No dragons, though. Would you like to hear it?"

"Yes!"

"Once upon a time, there lived a handsome young prince."

Her smile faltered. She had heard this story before, at least the beginning. Pulse humming, she listened, hoping Taryn would finish it this time. She ached to know what had happened to him. She'd always suspected his pain mirrored her own and wanted nothing more than to ease it. She knew too well what it felt like. Innocent or guilty, no one deserved to suffer the way she had.

Taryn continued through the story, pausing every so often but eventually made it all the way to the end. A brief silence descended, and she held her breath.

"What happened to the prince next?" Nolan's whisper barely reached her, even in the quiet.

"I don't know. The story isn't finished yet."

She blinked at his raw honesty, so different from his usual cocky arrogance. He seemed vulnerable and lost. She knocked softly then opened the door. Their heads turned toward her as she entered.

Nolan beamed a smile. "Amelia! You're back." He jumped up from his seat on the bed and rushed over to wrap his arms around her waist.

"Whoa. What brought this on?" She stroked his hair. "Are you all right?"

"I missed you." Her heart lurched. "Taryn just told me a story about a hero prince. Do you want to hear it?"

She glanced at Taryn's pale face and shook her head. "Taryn and I have other things to talk about. Why don't you get cleaned up for dinner?"

"Okay." He bounded out the door, leaving her alone with whichever version of Taryn now resided in his body. She'd seen several over the past few weeks and approached him with cautious steps.

"I'm not going to hurt you, Amelia."

"I know." She sat in the armchair and studied his drawn features. "You look like hell."

He forced a smile. "I feel even worse."

"Pain?"

He nodded, and she handed him another cup of blackthorn tea, but he waved it away. "No. Not yet. I … want to apologize before I fall asleep again."

She arched a brow. "Go on, then."

He swallowed, his throat bobbing. "I'm so very sorry, Amelia. I don't have an excuse for whatever I did, whatever I said. But I am sorry nonetheless. I've been through a lot recently and it has taken its toll on my mental stability. I … honestly don't remember anything. I must have lost control but I don't know how. Or why."

"I do." She studied her hands, the floor. Anything but his face.

"You do?"

She nodded. "I heard what you said to Nolan. The story about the hero prince is your story, isn't it?"

He blanched, practically disappearing against the white sheets. "Yes."

She raised her head, daring to meet his steady gaze. "Do you know the legend of the shadow wolf?" He shook his head and she went on. "The shadow wolf lives in each of us. It is made of darkness and violence and evil. It feeds off our negative emotions and is always fighting for dominance. When the shadow wolf is strong, we do things, say things to hurt others and ourselves."

He swallowed. "What makes it strong?"

"Sadness. Despair. Pain." She paused, searching his face for hints of understanding. "When these feelings become too intense, too overwhelming, we retreat into ourselves, trying to get as far away from them as possible. Then the shadow wolf pounces, drawing us in, whispering promises of peace and relief. But it is a liar. It only wants to control you. The more heartache you feel, the stronger it becomes until it takes over."

His chin dropped to his chest, and her heart cracked. But she still had hope. She'd seen firsthand the damage caused by the shadow wolf but also knew how to tame it. She could show him. Help him. Heal him.

"Taryn." She took his hand. "Do you understand what I'm saying? Does this make any sense to you at all?"

He raised his head, unshed tears in his eyes. "Is it possible …" He cleared his throat and tightened his grip on her hand. "If the shadow wolf feeds off us, is it possible to starve it? Kill it?"

She nodded. "And I can teach you how. But you need to let me in. To trust me. I have to know everything."

He bit his lip, and a tear slipped down his cheek. "I don't think I can."

She moved from the chair to the bed and took his other hand. She'd done terrible things while under the shadow wolf's control and couldn't hold him accountable for his actions. She wanted to help him the way her family had helped her. She'd see him healthy and whole. And hers. "*We* can."

He briefly closed his eyes. "All right. I'll try. For you."

Love blossomed in her heart and she smiled. He'd suffered far more than she ever had yet he wanted to try. And she wouldn't let anyone or anything stop them. No one here would ever know what he'd done. Justice be damned. His self-punishment had gone on long enough.

He'd survived the shadow wolf. Now they just had to conquer it.

~ Chapter Sixty-nine ~

I dreamt of wolves. Their eager jaws snapped as they chased me through the forest in the dead of night. I managed to outrun them then woke shaking with dread.

The nightmares never ceased and likely never would, despite Amelia's confidence. Darkness had merged with my soul, and no amount of effort could ever cleave the two. Yet as painful as the process might be, I would try. For her. A soft knock interrupted my morbid thoughts. "Come in."

Amelia walked in bearing a breakfast tray. Her critical gaze swept over me as she set it across my lap. "How are you feeling today?"

"Better."

"Well enough for your first lesson?"

I arched a brow. "As ready as I'll ever be."

"Good. Now eat. I need to make sure Nolan isn't getting into trouble. I'll be back soon."

It sounded more like a threat than a promise, but I nodded. My uncle would have admired the way she asserted authority and demanded compliance. She'd make a fine captain.

I took a bite of porridge. It reminded me of breakfast at the garrison. My throat tightened at the thought of my men. What had they been told about my sudden disappearance? Did they think I'd abandoned them? Nothing could be further from the truth. I came here out of respect for them and everything they'd fought so hard to protect. Our freedom. Our kingdom. Much good it had done me.

I sighed and shifted under the heavy blanket. Eventually I'd return home. But then what? Resume my duties? Return to my previous life, my previous self as if nothing had ever happened? Three people no longer breathed because of my actions, my decisions, yet I'd managed to live with myself, somehow justifying their deaths as noble acts of valor and not the heinous crimes they were.

Gods above.

I shoved the tray onto the table and threw back the blanket. I could no longer sit idle, avoiding the consequences. My family, my friends, if I still had either, deserved far better than what I'd given them. They had suffered in my absence, a wrong I intended to right. Just as soon as I could get out of this gods' forsaken bed.

"Taryn, what are you doing?" Amelia hurried into the room. She caught me under my arm and eased me back onto the bed.

"I'm sorry. I ..."

"What is it, Taryn? Are you in pain? Or is it something else?"

Her gaze pierced my soul, uncovering all the secrets I'd so valiantly tried to hide. "I'm fine. Can we just ... get started?"

She hesitated, and I held my breath. "Of course." She sat on the foot of the bed, legs tucked underneath her.

"So. Where do we begin?"

"Breathing."

"Come again?"

"Breathing, Taryn. It's the most important step. This is how it's done."

Her tone rang with assurance but I stared, which she took as an invitation to continue. "Just do as I say." I opened my mouth to argue but she held up a hand. "Don't take offense, your highness. But you do need to follow my instructions."

"All right."

"Take a deep breath and hold it for three seconds. Then exhale slowly while you count your heartbeats. Wait at least six seconds before breathing again. Try it."

I took a deep breath per her instructions, letting it out while I counted my heartbeats in my head. She nodded. "Good. Practice for an hour in the morning and another before bed."

"And then?"

She blinked. "Then we'll see."

I remained skeptical. "So, all I do is practice breathing? Remind me how this will help."

She rolled her eyes. "You are the worst student in the history of the world. Why can't you just do what I say?"

"Because you're the worst teacher in the history of the world. And I'm not used to taking orders."

She laughed and some of my reluctance eased. "Trust me, Taryn."

"I do trust you." I shifted in my seat, itching to move more than an inch at a time. "I'm just eager to get past it all."

"I know, and I understand but you can't expect immediate results, not with something like this."

"Can you at least tell me what's next?"

She arched a brow. "I don't think you're ready quite yet."

I crossed my arms like a child denied dessert. "Why not?"

"It's the worst part, Taryn. The telling."

I cringed as if she'd struck me, my optimism plummeting. I'd have to come clean sooner or later, as she'd explained, yet I wished I could avoid it. My heart twisted every time I imagined the way she'd look at me afterwards. We'd begun to enjoy each other's company and my confession would surely ruin whatever friendship we'd built. "Who have you told about your experience?"

Her throat bobbed, and she lowered her head. "Father and Nolan know about the accident but not about … after."

"I see. Well, you can add me to your list."

Her head snapped up. "What?"

"I heard what you said that night. I only pretended to be asleep."

Her eyes widened as she sucked in a breath. "But …"

"I'm sorry, truly." I shrugged. "It seemed like a good idea."

"So, you've known, all this time, yet you never said anything. Why?"

"You've been hurt just as badly as I have. I didn't want to add to your burden. I never wanted to cause you pain, Amelia. I swear it."

She exhaled slowly, a perfect demonstration of the breathing technique then slid her gaze to me. I forced a smile and tried to stop my palms from sweating. I'd hurt her, more than once. I could blame the shadow wolf all I wanted, but I had to take responsibility for my actions if I ever hoped to earn her trust. And be worthy of her forgiveness.

"Well." She stood, clearly abandoning our conversation. "We're done for today. Try to get some rest."

"Amelia, wait." I struggled to stand but my leg buckled. "I …"

She'd reached the door but turned back, a strange look on her face. "Yes?"

I raked a hand through my hair. "Can we just … start over?"

"I think it's best if we continue from here as we are. This is … difficult for me. Please."

"Of course. I understand."

With a curt nod, she walked out the door. I sat in the resulting silence and brooded, contemplating my new reality. My physical injuries were healing well and while my mental health left a lot to be desired, at least I had a path to follow. I only hoped I didn't stumble on my way to recovery.

~ Chapter Seventy ~

Days turned into weeks as Amelia continued to talk me through the arduous process of battling my inner darkness. Each lesson left me drained but also emotionally stronger, as if a light had bloomed in my soul to chase away the shadows. At least during the day. They slunk into my dreams at night, yet I woke with newfound confidence and a fierce determination to fight even harder. Being here surrounded by beauty and comfort helped more than I could say.

"You look rested." Amelia's smile broadened as I hobbled into the library for our daily chat.

"I feel rested, better than I have in a while, actually. I wonder why?" I cracked a wry smile, and she laughed. Her laughter bubbled to the surface often these days, and my heart soared to hear it. I still sensed her hesitation when it came to our relationship, but I didn't test those boundaries. I forced myself to wait, despite the obvious tension in the air whenever we were in the same room, which happened as often as I could orchestrate it.

"How are you otherwise? Your leg seems better."

I grimaced as I lowered myself onto the couch. "The pain comes and goes, and I can't really bear any weight on it. But I haven't needed the blackthorn tea in over a week."

She grinned, clearly pleased with her ministrations on my behalf. I had to agree, though I still couldn't fathom why she'd taken pity on me in the first place. I'd behaved incorrigibly, a regret I'd never get over. Yet here we were, comfortably ensconced in her home while she sacrificed hours of her life to treat my injuries, both physical and emotional.

"I'm glad to hear it. Anything else you'd care to talk about?"

"I'm ready. To tell you."

She shifted in her seat. "All right."

"But first, I want you to know I'll understand if you arrest me or take me to the magistrate or whatever it is you need to do for your own peace of mind. I deserve whatever punishment I get, whether it's here or in Evanston."

She nodded. I took a deep breath then told her everything. I didn't hold back. Everything I'd done. Every thought, every emotion poured out of me. My walls came crumbling down as I laid my shattered soul at her feet. She listened in silence, her face a blank mask of indifference.

I finished with a heavy sigh then slumped against the couch cushions. The adrenaline ebbed as she studied me, each second an infinity. She kept her thoughts well-hidden and I almost screamed in frustration while I waited.

She eased to her feet and panic pumped through my limbs, making my hands shake. I reached for her, but she simply stood there, eyeing me with caution. She stepped closer, stopping right in front of me. "Thank you."

I stared at her wooden features, her rigid posture. "What …"

She didn't say another word and disappeared out the door without a backwards glance. Not quite the reaction I'd expected. Outrage or betrayal or disgust. Something other than the emotionless tone of her voice as she'd thanked me. I couldn't blame her for bolting. I'd hardly been able to stomach my own reflection. No doubt she couldn't stand the sight of me, either.

She left me to my own devices after our awkward encounter. I tried to engage her at dinner, but she ignored my attempts at conversation, scowling at me like I'd tried to steal the silver. Nolan, to his credit, asked a million questions and laughed at my silly jokes. Amelia's gaze remained vacant as she stared at the wall, the table. Anywhere but at my face.

Her compassion dwindled, though I felt a little better when she made sure my favorite chair stayed close to the fire. Yet the awkwardness had reached an all-time high and I needed to clear the air, needed to know if she hated me or if she simply didn't care at all anymore.

I mostly wanted to thank her. I just didn't know how without sounding like an idiot. Her unlimited generosity had saved me in so many ways. I'd been a shell of a man, held together by stubborn will and arrogant pride. She'd seen past all of it and had rebuilt me piece by jagged piece, forging my shattered soul back together. I would gladly spend my remaining days repaying her. If she'd only let me.

I found her in the library curled up on the couch with a book propped open in her lap.

She glanced at me as I entered but didn't smile. "Is something wrong?"

"Does something have to be wrong for me to talk to you?"

She blinked then hung her head as she slowly closed the book. "No."

My gut clenched. This conversation would be the death of me or at least the end of our friendship. I steeled myself against the rising panic. "Do you hate me?"

"Of course not." A quick, knee-jerk response.

"Are you sure? Because it seems like you do. Ever since I told you … I can't stand it, Amelia. Please just tell me the truth. I can take it."

She studied me as if she doubted I could take a paper cut let alone the pain her words would inflict, yet I kept my chin up, prepared for the worst.

"Did you love the girl in Evanston?"

I blinked, not sure I'd heard her correctly. "I thought so at first. But I don't think I did. Not really. Why do you ask?"

"It's a strange thing to love someone, to want to be with them all the time and protect them from everything no matter the cost."

"Where is this coming from? Did you meet someone?" My stomach dropped.

She turned toward me, firelight framing her like a halo. "I'm in love with you, Taryn."

My mouth must have fallen open because I snapped it shut. I stared, hoping she hadn't meant it as an elaborate joke to humiliate me after all I'd done. Her gaze reflected nothing but sincerity as she sat on the edge of her seat. Waiting for a response, yet I had no idea what to say. My feelings for her were complicated to say the least.

The silence stretched and the thought of asking her to come home with me crossed my mind. Could I? Should I? Then again, I had no clue what my future held. Somehow the uncertainty only made me bolder. An unquenchable desire for her suddenly blazed in my blood. "Come with me." Probably not the three words she'd hoped to hear but I had to start somewhere.

She blinked. "I can't." Her answer sounded rehearsed as if she'd prepared for the question.

Though I'd expected it, her answer stung. "I understand." All too well. I didn't deserve her.

She faced me with a strained smile. "Well, then. At least I know where I stand."

"Amelia, wait …"

"It's all right, Taryn. I just wanted you to know."

She stood and strode from the room before I could even think of what to say, let alone say it.

~ Chapter Seventy-one ~

Spring hastened toward summer with daily rainstorms. The grounds around the estate became a soggy mess so I spent my time indoors. Amelia insisted I needed solitude, not distractions and left me to struggle through my issues alone. Just as well. I had serious work to do repairing all the havoc the shadow wolf had wreaked. It took every ounce of my mental energy.

I needed a break and limped outside then over to where Nolan stood with Amelia, a pile of daggers at their feet. He threw one, sinking it dead center. With a triumphant grin, he trotted over to retrieve it.

"He's gotten so much better."

"I know." Her smile lit up her face. "He's almost as good as I am."

I smiled back. "Impossible."

"How's the leg today?"

"Aching but healing well. I still can't put all my weight on it but it's improving."

"You broke it in two places, so it might be a while before you're fully recovered." She angled her head. "How about the rest of you?"

I shrugged. "The cut in my side is just a scar now."

She shook her head. "I didn't mean–"

"I know." I grinned and shoved my hands into my pockets. "I'm … progressing. Nowhere near where I'd like to be but I'm getting there."

"It takes time." Her face softend. "Patience, your highness."

I snorted. "I have time but I'm running out of patience. And I've overstayed my welcome."

"You can't go!" Nolan whined, handing the daggers back to Amelia. "Please stay."

I smiled and placed a hand on his shoulder. "I'm afraid I can't." His face fell, but he nodded soberly then trudged back into the house. I would miss him. Despite my reluctance to return home, I couldn't stay here any longer. And I'd given my word.

After a quiet dinner and a rousing game of chess, Nolan went to bed while Amelia and I sat in the library on opposite sides of the couch. She gazed at the fire, presumably lost in thought. I swirled the amber liquid around the glass in my hand, wondering how on earth to say goodbye to her. She'd become an essential piece of my puzzle and without her, the picture would never be complete. Life would go on but with far less joy and a lot more loneliness.

"Amelia?"

"Yes?"

"Since I'm leaving tomorrow, will you tell me what happened? What I did?"

"Taryn …"

I set my glass on the table and turned my body toward hers. "I know you think I'm weak. And you're right. But I need to know. Please."

She studied my face, my injured leg. My battered heart. "Does it matter? It's in the past. And you've come so far." She bit her lip. "I don't want to hurt you."

"You won't."

Indecision flitted across her face. "All right. But first, I need you to know I don't blame you. At all. It wasn't your fault."

My pulse roared in my ears. *Gods, what had I done?* Suddenly I didn't want to know. But I needed to. "Go on."

"You gave in. To the shadow wolf. It had you in its claws, under its spell." She shook her head. "You were going to kill Lord Harlesby's servant. I stopped you."

Her voice broke and I swallowed hard. "You pushed me off the roof, didn't you?"

She nodded. "And stabbed you." She leaned forward and grabbed my hand. "I'm so sorry Taryn but I couldn't lose you too. Not after … everything."

I suspected she'd left out vital information but I didn't press her for more. "Thank you."

She wiped a tear from her cheek. "What?"

I squeezed her hand then ran my thumb over her wrist. "You saved me. From myself. No one's ever done that for me before." I flashed a crooked smile.

She breathed a laugh. "You're welcome, then."

"Anything else?"

"Such as?"

"I don't know. It feels … unfinished. Did something happen between us?" *Please say yes.*

"No."

I nodded and she pulled her hand from mine. "I'm going to bed."

"Amelia, wait." I stopped her at the door. "Will I ever see you again?"

"I don't know. But I'd like to."

"Even after all I've done?" I dared to ask.

Her shoulder lifted in a small shrug. "I love you, Taryn. And I always will."

She disappeared out the door, leaving me gaping after her. Her heartfelt declarations didn't make our parting any easier, yet just hearing the words from her mouth thrilled me. If she loved me despite my wicked past, then I stood a chance at redemption.

Hope burned like a blazing star in the darkness, lighting my way home.

~ Epilogue ~

"Stop squirming," I teased. "I can't do this if you're squirming." I straightened Rafe's shirt collar again then smoothed the front of his jacket. "There. Perfect."

"Are you sure? I feel ridiculous."

I rolled my eyes. "My tailor is the best in Evanston, if not the kingdom, and I paid him double to make sure you looked spectacular. And you do." I grabbed his shoulders and spun him around so he could see for himself. His expression changed from skepticism to wonder, and I grinned. "Told you."

His grin matched mine as he turned to face me. "Thank you, Taryn. Truly."

I slapped him on the back. "The least I could do. Now let's get you married."

I led Rafe to the front of the chapel where over a hundred people had gathered to bear witness. I couldn't have been happier to see my two best friends get married. I stood beside Rafe, biting my cheek to hide a smirk while he pulled at his collar. "Stop fidgeting. You're acting like a child."

He dropped his hand and swallowed hard. "Taryn … What if she …"

"Relax. She'll be here." His smile wobbled as he reached for his collar. Again. I grabbed his arm. "Stop."

He nodded and faced forward just as the music announced Grace's arrival. I peered down the aisle, but a cloud of white obscured my view. Everyone stood as she started the slow procession toward happily ever after, her father beaming. They stopped, and Grace turned so her father could kiss her cheek before she walked up the steps to stand with Rafe. I'd never seen two people more in love, more perfect for each other. I wiped a stray tear from my cheek and the ceremony began.

❈

The great hall reverberated with joyous laughter. I sat on the sidelines, watching Rafe and Grace dance. Their bodies never broke contact and they only had eyes for each other. I sighed wistfully then drained my glass.

There were plenty of eligible young ladies here tonight, but my thoughts kept straying to Amelia, as they'd done almost every minute since my return home. I'd written to her a few times, letting her know I'd arrived safely and continued to progress toward recovery. She still hadn't replied. The rejection had initially knocked the breath out of me, but then I realized I had no right to expect anything more from her. She'd declared her love and like an idiot, I hadn't reciprocated, even though I did love her. With every fiber of my being.

"Your highness?" a young boy asked at my elbow.

"Yes?"

"Will you come with me?"

I arched a brow. "And who are you?"

He shrugged and grabbed my hand. "Come with me, please."

Intrigued, I followed him from the hall, down a long corridor and out into the garden. Summer bloomed everywhere, a heady scent cascading over me. I glanced around but no one roamed through the blossoms. Why had he led me here, of all places? I crouched at his level. "Are you lost? Do you need my help with–"

"He brought you to see me."

My breath hitched and the little boy flashed a gap-toothed grin then scurried back inside. I straightened and turned to find Amelia standing mere feet away as if my thoughts had conjured her. My collar suddenly felt too tight, and I cleared my throat with a bow. "Lady Ravencrest. Welcome to Evanston."

"Your highness." She dipped into a demure curtsy then peered up at me through lowered lashes.

I shoved my hands into my pockets before I did something stupid, like grab her and never let go. "What are you doing here?"

"I heard about this party ..."

"And thought you'd crash it?"

She shrugged. "I've been dying to wear this dress. A party seemed like the perfect excuse."

I swallowed hard at the thought of her not wearing the dress. "Where is Nolan?"

"Home, with Father. After he returned, I realized I needed a vacation.",

"I'm pleased you chose to visit our fair city."

"No, Taryn." She shook her head, closing the distance between us. "I chose you."

Her eyes glittered with wicked promise and my pulse tripped. Here she stood, a dream come true, her warmth the sweetest embrace. She rested her palm on my cheek, and I briefly closed my eyes, savoring the sensation of being touched. By her. "Amelia, I don't know what to say."

"You don't have to say anything. Just kiss me."

I lowered my head as she raised hers, and our lips met, sending sparks coursing in my blood. She threaded her clever fingers through my hair, and I groaned. I grabbed her waist and crushed her to my chest. Need and want and desire collided around me.

She laughed against my mouth then slowly pulled away. "Well, now. I hadn't expected such a heartfelt welcome. Are you this hospitable with all your guests?"

I chuckled. "Never."

"I'm the only one?"

I nodded. "The only one."

"So, you love me?"

"With everything I am."

Her smile outshone the stars with a light so bright it severed the shadows from my heart and dissolved the darkness in my soul. Forever.

#